Nobody had warned her.

Not even her mother, who had sneakily arranged this whole thing.

No one had warned her how sexy a man tending to his children could be, or how much she would envy a crabby two-year-old his father's comforting voice, a broad chest to lean against, the tender stroke of a strong masculine hand against a cheek.

Nor had anyone warned her how easily kids—some kids—could steal your heart. Or if they had, she hadn't listened. More than once that evening, in spite of relentless squabbling and messiness and loudness and pickiness, they'd caught her off guard, made her laugh out loud. Nudged to life something deep inside her, something she really hadn't thought was there. Had been afraid to admit to, at any rate.

None of which altered the fact that she was still gonna kill her mother.

Dear Reader,

Once again, Silhouette Intimate Moments brings you an irresistible lineup of books, perfect for curling up with on a winter's day. Start with Sharon Sala's *A Place To Call Home,* featuring a tough city cop who gets away to the Wyoming high country looking for some peace and quiet. Instead he finds a woman in mortal danger and realizes he has to help her—because, without her, his heart will never be whole.

For all you TALL, DARK AND DANGEROUS fans, Suzanne Brockmann is back with *Identity: Unknown.* Navy SEAL Mitchell Shaw has no memory of who—or what—he is when he shows up at the Lazy 8 Ranch. And ranch manager Becca Keyes can't help him answer those questions, though she certainly raises another: How can he have a future without her in it? Judith Duncan is back with *Marriage of Agreement,* a green-card marriage story filled with wonderful characters and all the genuine emotion any romance reader could want. In *His Last Best Hope,* veteran author Susan Sizemore tells a suspenseful tale in which nothing is quite what it seems but everything turns out just the way you want. With her very first book, New Zealander Fiona Brand caught readers' attention. *Heart of Midnight* brings back Gray Lombard and reunites him with the only woman strong enough to be his partner for life. Finally, welcome Yours Truly author Karen Templeton to the line. *Anything for His Children* is an opposites-attract story featuring three irresistible kids who manage to teach both the hero and the heroine something about the nature of love.

Enjoy every one of these terrific novels, and then come back next month for six more of the best and most exciting romances around.

Yours,

Leslie J. Wainger
Executive Senior Editor

Please address questions and book requests to:
Silhouette Reader Service
U.S.: 3010 Walden Ave., P.O. Box 1325, Buffalo, NY 14269
Canadian: P.O. Box 609, Fort Erie, Ont. L2A 5X3

ANYTHING FOR HIS CHILDREN

KAREN TEMPLETON

Silhouette®
INTIMATE™MOMENTS®

Published by Silhouette Books

America's Publisher of Contemporary Romance

SILHOUETTE BOOKS

ISBN 0-373-07978-8

ANYTHING FOR HIS CHILDREN

Copyright © 1999 by Karen Templeton Berger

Visit us at www.romance.net

Printed in U.S.A.

Books by Karen Templeton

Silhouette Intimate Moments

Anything for His Children #978

Silhouette Yours Truly

*Wedding Daze
*Wedding Belle
*Wedding? Impossible!

*Weddings, Inc.

KAREN TEMPLETON's

extensive background in the theater and the arts, combined with a lifelong affinity for love stories, led naturally and inevitably to her writing romances. Growing up in Baltimore, she studied art, ballet and drama, and wanted nothing more than to someday strut her stuff in a Broadway show. However, although she was accepted into North Carolina School of the Arts as a drama major, halfway through she switched to costume design, in which she received her B.F.A. degree longer ago than she cares to admit.

A twelve-year stint living in New York City provided a wide variety of work experiences, including employment in the bridal department buyer's offices of both Saks Fifth Avenue and Henri Bendel. New York also provided her with her husband, Jack, and the first two of her five sons.

Between sons two and three, the family moved to New Mexico, where Karen established a thriving in-home mail-order crafts business that she gave up almost the instant the family bought their first computer and she discovered the magic of erasing mistakes without White-Out. Now writing romances full-time, she says she's finally found an outlet for all that theatrical training—she gets to write, produce, design, cast and play all the parts!

This book is dedicated to my five sons, who provide me with so much rich material for my books, and to my husband, Jack, who provided me with those sons…and who, for twenty years, has continued to prove that happily-ever-after isn't just in fairy tales.

This book is also dedicated to all the dads in the world who answer a child's cries in the middle of the night, who know all the Teletubbies' names, and which child will gag if the orange juice isn't strained, and who can *cheerfully* sing Barney's theme song…those remarkable, wonderful men who nurture as well as protect.

Keep the faith, guys.

Chapter 1

"Good heavens, Elizabeth! What happened to you?"

"*Hell* happened, Mother." Handicapped by one heelless shoe, Elizabeth hobbled past the reception desk, batting her wind-churned hair out of her face. "Right here in idyllic, sleepy Spruce Lake, Michigan." She ditched her jacket and purse at her desk, then backed up to the wheezing air conditioner in the tiny real estate office she shared with her mother, plucking at the silk blouse shrink-wrapped to her skin. The cold breeze made her shiver, then sneeze. And sneeze again. Her nose scrunched up in readiness for round three, she frantically flapped her hand at the tissue box on her desk.

Her mother—Debbie-Reynolds-flawless in a pale rose sheath—handed her daughter a tissue, ash-blond brows drawn into a neat little frown. "So I repeat—what happened?"

"The electricity went—ah-*choo!*—" Elizabeth blew her nose, sniffed, let her brain cells settle back into place "—out, so my alarm didn't go off, so I couldn't get breakfast, all my good panty hose had runs in them..." She snatched a second tissue from her mother's expertly manicured hand, got it to her nose just in time for the next sneeze to fizzle. "*Then,*" she continued despite her maddeningly tingling nose, "the air-conditioning died in the Lexus, which meant I had to leave the windows down...'' she gestured lamely at her hair; her mother's lips formed an O of understanding ''—and last, but God knows not least, I caught my heel in that damn crack in the sidewalk right in front of the door.''

She sniffed again, shoved her glasses back up onto the bridge of her nose, and caught the flickers of concern in her mother's golden eyes. ''It's okay,'' she said, slipping off the dead shoes. ''I promise to clean myself up before I meet my public.''

''No, it's not that.'' Maureen sighed. ''Charlene had her baby last night.''

''Oh, terrific.'' Elizabeth's bottom desk drawer squawked as she yanked it open, lobbed the shoes inside. ''No receptionist. Just what we need. For crying out loud—she wasn't due to start her maternity leave for another week!'' The phone rang. She lunged across her desk to answer it, banging her hip. Hot, aggravated tears bit at her eyes.

''Millennium Realty, Elizabeth Lo—'' Click. *Rrrr...* ''Same to you, buster!''

Maureen Louden calmly pried the receiver from her daughter's clasp and hung up the phone. ''As I'm sure even you are aware, dear, babies come when they're ready. Not when you are.''

''More's the pity,'' Elizabeth mumbled, rummaging in her purse for a comb. She stomped into the rest room in her stockinged feet, leaving the door open as she efficiently combed and retucked two feet of hair back into what had been a fairly decent French twist a half hour ago.

''This is hardly a life-and-death situation,'' wafted in from the reception area. ''And the agency said we'd have someone by tomorrow morning.''

''Yeah, well, that doesn't do us much good today, does it?'' Elizabeth padded back into the office. ''Did I leave that pair of black pumps here?''

''In the closet, I think. Elizabeth?''

She'd dropped down on her knees and was now pawing through shoes, umbrellas, and assorted Target and Kmart bags littering the closet floor, stuffed with the ghosts from shopping trips past. ''What?'' was her muffled reply.

"Cope, dear."

Muttering, she crept farther into the closet, feeling for her shoes—

"Oh, yuck! Who the *hell* left the vacuum bag open?"

"Wasn't me."

Whoa. Granted, sound was a mite distorted with her mother's raincoat draped over her head, but unless she was way off, "me" was a man.

Elizabeth backed out of the closet, slowly, realizing dignity was a pipe dream in this position, then heaved herself to her feet, sneezing again as she held the dusty pumps away from her light-gray skirt. Cautiously, she made her way to the front, peering around the Plexiglas wall that separated the reception area from the offices.

Hmm. No one.

Before she could even frown, the phone rang again. She spun around, wedging the phone between her jaw and shoulder as she took another tissue to the dusty shoes, then let them drop onto the floor.

"Mother!" she yelled, shimmying into the shoes. "Line one for you—oh, hell!" Line two rang, swiftly followed by line three. As she put the second call on hold in order to answer the third, a trio of thoughts zipped through her head. One, thank God they only had three lines. Two, the crotch of her panty hose had slipped six inches below hers and was driving her nuts. And three, a man with dark glasses and wide shoulders—which she noticed before it was too late not to— was backing through the front door clutching a beat-up box overflowing with heaven-knew-what in one arm and the sorriest excuse for a plant she'd ever seen in the other.

She rapidly wrote down line two's and three's phone numbers, then went out front, briskly crossing past the tree hugger to the reception desk to flip on the answering machine.

"Busy morning, huh?" she heard behind her.

Elizabeth turned, fighting the urge to tug at her panty hose. "You might say that. And you are…?"

"Wondering if I'm in the right place." The man hitched the box farther up on his hip, wiggling his nose like a rabbit in order to keep his sunglasses from slipping. Then a smile appeared. A *charming* smile.

She frowned.

The smile turned into a chuckle, a warm, mellow sound that set her insides to rumbling. Or maybe that was because she'd skipped breakfast. "Is everyone else around here this hospitable?" he asked.

A smile twitched at her lips. She squelched it. "You're in luck. When the medication wears off I tend to get nasty."

That got a second chuckle, followed by a little grunt as he set down the box and the alien plant. One hand removed his Ray·Bans, the other extended in her direction. "Guy Sanford," he said, turning up the wattage on the smile. When she shook her head, uncomprehending, he added, "The new agent? You must be Miss Louden...."

Blue eyes smiled into hers. Mel-Gibson-blue. Cloudless-autumn-sky-blue.

The-bedroom-is-right-this-way-blue.

*Oooh*migod.

"Miss Louden? Is something wrong?"

She hadn't taken his hand, she realized. So she did. Quickly.

"Oh. Yes. Mother told me about you." She immediately tucked her hands behind her against the receptionist's desk. "From Chicago, right?"

"Not originally. I was born and raised in Ann Arbor. Family's still there."

By this time, she'd gotten past the eyes far enough to notice the wavy dark brown hair tucked into a ponytail, the pansy-purple shirt underneath a hunter-green jacket, and a football-pennant-size tie decorated with—no, her eyes were not deceiving her—dozens of itty-bitty Tweetys and Sylvesters. And an earring. Understated, discreet, probably eighteen karat gold. But definitely a piece of jewelry stuck in a male ear.

Oh, well, then. Eyes? What eyes?

"Guy?"

Her mother floated back out front, hand outstretched, beaming when Guy returned her mother's welcoming smile in that certain way certain men have that make them look like little boys. Except that *this* guy was far too sexy to look like a little boy, which was why Elizabeth's stomach was knotted and her brain aflame and she realized she really, *really* had to talk to her mother about this man as soon as possible.

Sooner.

"We're extremely fortunate to have Guy join us," Maureen announced, looping her arm through her daughter's. "Top producer in our Chicago branch. Sold more properties than any other agent in northern Illinois two years running."

Reality alert.

"You don't say." Elizabeth was competitive, but that did not mean she liked competition. Especially competition with boudoir-blue eyes and the taste of a visually impaired gypsy. She crossed her arms and met his gaze head-on, ignoring the trembling in the pit of her stomach. "Why'd you leave?"

"Needed a change." He shrugged. "Got tired of the city."

There was more to the story, she was sure. Not that she was interested.

"Would you like some coffee?" her mother asked, handing him a cup without waiting for his answer.

"Uh, yes, I guess so." He took the cup, sneaking a wink at Elizabeth as he brought it to his lips.

The blush went all the way to her toes.

Her mother was chattering about…stuff, while Guy simply stood there and nodded or gave an occasional "Really?" or drank his coffee. He didn't look at Elizabeth. Didn't have to.

There were plenty of things she should be doing. Like answering the phone. Checking her schedule. Breathing. Instead, all she could do was stare.

She shut her eyes, willing her heart to cut out the damn hippity-hopping, already. *Honestly, Elizabeth. He's just a man. What's the big hairy deal?*

A man who was about to horn in on her territory. A man who, from what she could tell with his coat on, looked pretty solid, like maybe he ran or something. Not overly tall, maybe about six feet. Which still made him a head taller than she…

"Elizabeth?"

Blinking, she turned and ran right smack into her mother's "we have company, dear—please *try*" expression. "Would you mind helping Guy get settled in while I return some calls?"

"Oh…" Her gaze shifted to Mr. Charm, just finishing off his coffee, those impossible eyes twinkling—*twinkling!*—at her over the rim of his cup. "Sure."

She needed this man in her life like she needed fleas.

As the phone rang again, Elizabeth desperately searched for something else to look at. The four-foot-tall plant seemed as likely a candidate as any, its spindly fronds or bracts or whatever they were waving at her in the air conditioner's breeze, like a kid wanting someone to come play with it. "What does it eat?"

The answering machine picked up the call. "Fish emulsion," Guy said, leaning one hip against the edge of the desk. Nice, trim hips. The thighs, from what she could tell, were nothing to sling hash at, either. "And the occasional small child."

Her eyes shot back up to his in time to catch the grin. She allowed a smile, a small one, forcing herself to focus on the earring instead of the eyes. "I, uh, see." She moved toward the back of the office. "Here. You can put it by the win—"

"Not *it*," he whispered. "Alastair."

Once again, the phone rang; once again, the answering machine clicked, whirred, clicked, went silent.

"Alastair."

"Mm-hm."

An earring, no discernible taste, and he named plants. Uh-huh. "Well…you can put *Alastair* right over—" she gestured toward the picture window behind the desks "—there."

"Miss Louden?"

"Yes?" she said, pivoting back.

Guy was staring at the answering machine, one hand hooked on his hip, the other rubbing his chin. "There are fourteen messages here." He looked up at her with a tilted smile that annoyed the life out of her. "Think we should start answering the phone?"

Maureen Louden hadn't been kidding about the office's size: the space probably measured no more than thirty feet square. The understated decor was in excellent shape though, in unobtrusive shades of beige, charcoal and peach, the artwork on the walls an assortment of restful watercolor landscapes. Pale peach shades covered a pair of large picture windows in front, suffusing the room in softly glowing light. A pleasant office, peace-inducing, stress-reducing.

Right.

Guy smiled to himself as he lugged the plant through a wide opening in the translucent Plexiglas partition which divided the reception area from the back offices. He figured the left side of this area was his, judging from the empty desk and blank bulletin board hanging slightly askew on the wall above the desk. But the right side, Elizabeth's side, reeked of obsessive-compulsiveness, with faint overtones of a reserved, but otherwise very pleasant, perfume. He eased the plant down in front of the window as his new colleague's officious voice wheedled in his ears.

"The bathroom is through that door over there," she was saying, even though he had his back to her and couldn't possible see where "over there" was. "And there's the closet where you can put...well, whatever." Oh, yeah. He remembered where the closet was. As well as the pretty little rump that had served—quite well—as his first view of the prickly Elizabeth Louden.

"And that's your desk. Make yourself at home." Somehow, her tone didn't quite match the hospitality of her words. "I've got to get some work done. The receptionist's out, so we have to pinch hit until the agency sends over a temp. I suggest we answer the phone in turns until then."

"Sounds fair to me." Guy shucked off his suit coat, hung it over the back of his desk chair and sat down at the computer. "The receptionist sick?"

"Worse. She had a baby."

He filched a glance at Elizabeth's profile as she sat at

her desk, riffling through a stack of papers she'd just taken out of her attaché case. Odd duck, this one. During his phone interview, Elizabeth's mother had told him more about her daughter than he'd told Mrs. Louden about himself, which he somehow figured would irk said daughter no end if she knew. Twenty-eight, MBA by twenty-two, brilliant, successful, independent. Top seller in a Detroit agency for six years until her return to "help out" a little more than a year ago. There had been a pause, then, in the conversation, which had caught Guy's attention. As thrilled as her mother obviously was to have her only child—yes, she'd told him that, too—home again, she was clearly worried about her. She hadn't been specific about that, either, but he got the gist. God knows, he'd been the victim of his mother's well-I-suppose-it's-your-life-dear voice enough to easily recognize it in Maureen's.

He listened to Elizabeth make a phone call, noting undertones of warmth in an otherwise—what?—*cautious* voice, he decided. Although he thought he heard her start to chuckle, once or twice, she swallowed the sound as if it wasn't proper somehow. Guy liked to laugh. Guy *loved* to laugh. Give him reruns of *Jack Benny* or *The Honeymooners* or *The Red Skelton Show* and you had to scrape him off the floor afterward. He couldn't imagine anyone not wanting to laugh. And yet, Elizabeth Louden sure seemed to go out of her way to hold it in.

Why? And what was with the schoolmarm routine? Was she one of those types who thought she couldn't be effective or taken seriously in the business world if she allowed her natural femininity free rein? As if she could control her womanhood.

As if no one would notice her clear skin, that hair the color of winter sunshine, pulled back into a meticulous French twist corralled behind tiny ears decorated with pearl studs. Not to mention that softly pointed chin cantilevered out over a long white neck now unfortunately strangled by a huge frowzy bow. The sweet little nose that probably spent a great deal of time out of joint, almost too small to hold up such big amber-framed glasses. A mouth that reminded him of one of Ashli's dolls, perfectly shaped, barely tinged with color, the bottom lip slightly fuller than the top lip.

A very kissable mouth, he decided. Then smiled, wondering how much practice it had ever had doing just that…

He cleared his throat. "Uh…what's the program that gets me into the local Multiple Listing Service?" he asked.

With a sigh that spoke volumes, Elizabeth swiveled out of her chair and crossed the five feet to his desk, poked at a few keys to bring up the property listings program. Guy was so distracted by her fragrance that he forgot to watch what she did. He started to ask if she'd mind showing him again, but she was already back at her desk.

Hmm. If he'd allowed himself to be thrown by every redolent female who'd crossed his path he'd never have achieved squat. He glanced at the lovely Elizabeth with her pursed lips and haughty nose and wondered what the hell was going on. With him, with her, with everything. After all, he'd just met her. Nor was she exactly overflowing with geniality. In fact, he was pretty sure he detected resentment along with the perfume. Elizabeth Louden plainly did not want him around.

No matter, he reminded himself as he turned his attention back to the monitor. A romantic involvement was the last thing he needed in his life, too. So he'd just mind his own business, and get back to the task of making some money, and forget about cute noses and pouty lips and wondering how someone might go about cracking Miss Elizabeth Louden's facade. Might have succeeded, too, had it not been for the elderly couple who picked that moment to come into the office.

"Mr. and Mrs. Gunderson!" Elizabeth swept from behind her desk with outspread arms and an enormous smile. Guy's heart *boinged* into his throat. "How *are* you?"

Seems Elizabeth had just helped them sell the old family home and then personally seen them settled into a new condo. They clearly adored her, and Elizabeth not only smiled and laughed, but actually joked with the couple. At one point, Mrs. Gunderson leaned into the back office and said to Guy, "We just love this little girl to death. Did so much more than just sell our house for us. Why, you know what she did?'' only to have her husband cut her off with, ''Now, Thelma, I'm sure the man's got more important things to tend to.'' He then ushered his wife back toward the door, and amid many hugs and kisses and ''Now you take cares,'' the couple went on their way.

Wow.

By the time Elizabeth returned to her desk, however, the warm, ebullient young woman he'd just witnessed had already been banished to wherever this she-devil kept her. He wanted to shout, ''Come back! Come back!'' But the phone rang.

She smiled, far too sweetly. ''Be my guest.''

Still nonplussed, Guy fumbled for the receiver, realizing as he did that his desk was devoid of writing implements. ''Millennium Realty, Guy Sanford speaking. How may I help you?'' He twisted one arm around, fishing in his jacket pockets for a pen. No luck.

''I need to sell my house, Sanford,'' came the gruff, nasal reply. ''You an agent?''

Guy gestured for Elizabeth to hand him something to write with, swallowing a wince when a Bic smacked into his palm.

''Yes, sir, I sure am.''

''Good. You know the Hancock house, up on Spruce Lake Road?''

''The Hancock house.'' He met Elizabeth's questioning green eyes with a shrug, hoping she'd give him a clue. ''Of course. Lovely house. And...you want to list it?''

A clue was not what she was giving him. What she was giving him were narrowed eyes, compressed lips and rapid, rabid breathing. A slow, satisfied grin slid across his mouth. Somebody else must have wanted this listing *real* bad.

''Of course, Mr....''

''Hancock. What else?''

''Yes, of course. Mr. Hancock. When would you like me to come out?''

''Ten-thirty. You know how to get here?''

Guy glanced at his watch, wondering if twenty minutes was enough time to find a house he had no idea how to get to. "No problem, Mr. Hancock. That address again?" He scribbled it down. "Good. I'll see you then."

He believed the scientific term for what Elizabeth was doing was *seething*. In fact, he could swear those were faint wisps of smoke curling out of those cute little ears.

He couldn't resist. "Your client, Miss Louden?" he said with a cool smile.

"I've been buttering up that old buzzard for three months, hoping to get my hands on his house. Then you waltz in, answer the phone, and badda boom, badda bing, the listing lands in your lap."

"I'm sorry. But I repeat—was he your client? Had he signed with you?"

"N-no, but…"

"Then perhaps you should just concentrate on finding someone to *buy* the house." Guy stood, slipped his jacket back on, then headed for the door. "I should think you'd be enough of a professional to congratulate me on getting my first listing so quickly."

Her mouth sagged open; she popped up and charged him like a poodle after the postman. "Professional!" she squeaked. "You might have at least asked if I knew anything about this before yanking it out from under me!"

Guy peered down into her face, then slowly pushed her glasses back up her nose with the tip of his index finger. Although he'd been the object of his four older brothers' merciless torment while growing up, he'd never had a tormentee of his very own. And such a cute one, too.

"Had Mr. Hancock asked for you specifically," he said, resisting the urge to grin at her stupefied expression, "I would have handed the call over to you without a word. As he didn't, I see nothing wrong with what I did." His finger found its way to the apex of her chin, tilting it up, her skin so soft he could hardly feel it. "And don't tell me you wouldn't have done the same thing. Your mother told me you won *awards,* for God's sake, for your sales in Detroit. You're ruthless, Miss Louden. You know it. I know it. And now you know I am, too. So—" he forced himself to lower his hand "—let the games begin."

Then, with a wink, he sauntered out of the office.

*   *   *

Elizabeth vented her fury on her panty hose.

Ducking behind her desk, she kicked off her pumps, hiked up her skirt and wiggled out of them with such force she tore them in three places. Muttering curses that would have made a Brooklynite blush, she tied them into no less than a half-dozen knots, each knot accompanied by an emphatic grunt, then slammed them with a loud "Oooh!" into the wastebasket by her desk. The pitiful little *whump* they made in the metal can was spectacularly unfulfilling.

She had just managed to get her skirt resettled and her shoes back on when her mother appeared.

"Now what? You look ready to spit nails—"

"I told you we didn't need anyone else, that the two of us could easily handle whatever came in, but you *had* to place that ad." She paced in front of the desks, prattling like a crazed person. "And *this* was the best you could do? Did you even *look* at the man before you hired him?"

There was no answer.

Elizabeth let out a loud groan, then sat back against the desk. "Let me guess—no one else answered the ad."

Maureen gave a short, impatient huff. "Most Realtors go to the city. Not away from it." She crossed to Guy's desk and idly straightened out his phone. "Besides. I think he's...charming."

"And your next eye doctor appointment is when?"

Maureen ran one finger along the top of the computer monitor, wiping away nonexistent dust. "I admit, his clothes are a little colorful, maybe—"

Elizabeth snorted.

"Now, dear, it's not that bad."

"Uh, yeah, it is. Besides, we just don't need him, Mother. Or...or anybody. The office is just too small. I think...you should just tell him we've...changed our minds."

"I can't do that. He's moved here specifically for this position." Then her mother speared her with a look meant to quash any further discussion. "Let's just give the boy a chance, shall we?"

"*Chance?*" Elizabeth squealed, suddenly remembering.

"Hah! That *boy* hardly needs me or anyone else to give him a chance! You wanna know what your long-haired Chicago hotshot did? He stole the Hancock house from me!"

That actually seemed to make a dent. "Oh, honey..." Her mother leaned on the desk beside her, gave her a one-armed hug. "But I thought you had that one in the bag?"

Elizabeth expelled a huge, frustrated sigh. "So did I. But when Guy answered the phone, the rotten worm didn't even ask for me. An agent's an agent, far as George Hancock's concerned." She shoved her glasses back up her nose as she met her mother's gaze. "That house is worth a fortune. And I already have a buyer interested. If I could list it, too..." She sighed again, watching her dream fade. "The double commission would have been enough to put me over the top for the down payment on the Lakeside house without having to go into my investments."

The tiny crease between her mother's brows alerted Elizabeth to what was coming, but she was helpless to avoid it. "Honey," Maureen began in the deliberately controlled tone of voice mothers use when they have to be mothers, "that house has, what? Twelve rooms? And it's completely run-down. It'd take a fortune to fix it up. And another fortune to maintain it. The annual heating bill alone could feed a small country for several years. Besides...you don't even know if you're going to stay in Spruce Lake. This was supposed to be a temporary arrangement, remember?"

"I know, I know..." Elizabeth looked out over the office, avoiding the concern in her mother's eyes. The plan had been for her to come back for six months or so, to fill in for a retired agent. Except then another agent had left as well...and six months had already turned into a year, with no indication Elizabeth was going anywhere, anytime too soon...or why she wasn't. Six years ago, she couldn't wait to move away, get to the city. Now, though... Well, she just didn't know what she wanted, what she was supposed to do. Detroit held no appeal, but she didn't really want to stay here.

And then there was this house—this bring-on-the-six-kids-and-a-swing-set house—which kept pulling her to it like a puppy in a pet shop window. A whole lot of sense, this did not make.

"I just want it," she said. "That's all. But, in any case—" she pulled herself away from the desk and circled behind it, collapsing into her desk chair "—since Sybil Bennett told me she thought she had another buyer anyway, I suppose that's that."

Her mother suddenly noticed the plant, though how she missed it until now was beyond Elizabeth. But then, a lot about Maureen Louden was beyond Elizabeth. Like the way she'd list all her objections to something Elizabeth wanted to do, then turn right around and encourage to do the very thing she'd just said was foolish and illogical, or dangerous, or pointless, or whatever.

Like now. As Maureen cautiously approached the specimen, she said, "Now, dear, don't be such a pessimist. You're a very determined young woman. I'm sure, if you want that house so badly, you'll figure out a way to get it. So get your bid in. A good, high one. You said yourself the house was undervalued. And it wouldn't kill you to tap into some of your capital, you know."

"You know I can't do that, Mother."

Maureen glanced back at her. "*Won't* do it, you mean. Honey, you're only twenty-eight. You've got a few years left until retirement. Live."

Elizabeth had no comment. They'd never seen eye to eye about her investments. While Maureen said she understood—and admired—Elizabeth's desire for financial security, the word *obsessive* had also come up a time or two.

Today, she really wasn't in the mood.

Maureen took the hint, gracefully changing the subject. She traced one Misty Mauve fingernail over a spiky frond, setting the whole plant aquiver, then said, "It's too bad about the Hancock house. Really. But if the seller didn't ask for you, Guy had every right to pursue the listing. At least the commission will stay with the office."

Elizabeth harrumphed in grudging agreement, grateful that one confrontation had been avoided at least, and let her chin sink into the palm of her hand. "If the doofus ever finds the place to begin with."

"What was that?"

She peered at her mother through her glasses, her smugness rapidly dissipating. "I...um...didn't tell Guy how to get...to...the house...."

"Elizabeth! You mean you'd let the office commission on a sale that size go down the tubes because you're miffed that *you* didn't get it? For heaven's sake, if Hancock thinks Guy stood him up, he'll list with Sybil!"

And heaven knew, a plague of frogs would be acceptable over that. Not only for her mother's ego, but because neither of them wanted to listen to the redhead's gloating for the next ten years. "I guess I didn't think about that."

"I guess you didn't. Did he give you his cell phone number?" She shook her head. "Then I suggest you get yourself out there, pronto, make excuses for Guy, whatever you have to do, until he shows up. And when he does arrive, you be sure to hightail your little fanny out of there. You hear me?"

There were times when Elizabeth really, really hated being a good daughter. With a weighty sigh, she dislodged herself from behind her desk, slipped into her clammy jacket, and fetched her handbag from the closet. Then she hesitated, glowering at the plant. At *Alastair*.

"Elizabeth Marie!"

"I'm going, I'm going." She raised her chin and headed for the door. "But he owes me for this," she called over her shoulder as she left.

And so do you, Mother, she thought, gasping for oxygen inside her sweltering car. So do you.

Chapter 2

As she neared the Hancock house, it occurred to her she had no idea what Guy's car looked like, so she'd just have to ring the doorbell and ask if he was there, wouldn't she? Then wouldn't it look a little strange if she said, "Oh, good. Just checking," and left?

Actually, it was a pretty good bet the silver Volvo wagon with the Illinois plates was his, but, oh well.

She pulled up behind the Volvo and got out, took a futile swipe at her once-again wild hair, unpeeled her blouse from her damp back. Muttering, she leaned back into the car and retrieved her jacket, purse and a folder of forms, then slipped on the jacket before heading toward the house, trying to keep her heels from sinking into the thick layer of gravel in the circular driveway.

Some "house." Three stories, six bedrooms, five baths, and an indoor pool, thank you very much. With its solid stone walls, the English manor house dripped with ivy, pretension, and Gothic undercurrents. Damn thing even had its own private lake.

She climbed the granite steps and rang the bell, jumping

when the massive oak door opened before her finger was off the button. Sumptuously cool air flowed out from behind a balding man with ramrod-straight posture. *Butler,* would be her guess.

"Oh, hello." She bestowed a charming-but-sincere smile at the bored-looking visage in front of her. A breeze blew a hunk of hair into her mouth; she snatched at it, trying not to sputter. "I'm Elizabeth Louden, Mr. Sanford's associate. I was supposed to meet him here, but I got held up in a meeting." She smiled again. Hairlessly, this time.

"Of course, Miss Louden," the man said with a slight bow. "Right this way."

She tried to keep her ogling discreet as he led her through a two-story marble-floored entryway with a matching curved staircase leading, no doubt, to heaven, and into a cigar-smoke choked, wood-paneled library complete with burgundy leather furniture and a cherrywood mantel and life-size portraits of not-very-attractive rich people staring at her from every wall.

"Who is this?" grated the lizardlike little man from the other side of the room, bedecked in a toupee obviously stolen from one of the Duracell people.

"Miss Elizabeth Louden, sir," intoned the hooded-eyed butler. "She's with Mr. Sanford."

At Guy's raised eyebrows, Elizabeth said on a rush of air, "I'm so sorry I wasn't here on time. Here are those contract forms you need."

"Thank you...so much, Miss Louden." There was almost a question mark at the end of the sentence. "And...you've already met Mr. Hancock?"

Her hair was a shambles and she was sweating like a pig in an aerobics class, but she could flash those dazzling smiles with the best of 'em. "Why, yes. *Several* times. Weren't you at the Galways' barbecue last week?"

The old man squinted at her, then flicked his tongue from one side of his mouth to the other before resettling his ever present cigar on overlarge lips. "Yes, I think I do remember you...."

How could you not remember me, you plastic-headed old coot?

"...so, sweetheart—you work for this guy?"

"Oh—no, sir," Guy interjected, briefly intercepting Elizabeth's wrist. "Miss Louden is a colleague. We work out of the same office."

"I see." Then he glared at Elizabeth. "Well, sit down, girl. No need to stand there gawking, for God's sake. Whittier!" he bellowed, even though the butler stood no more than six feet away. "Bring Miss...whatever-her-name-is some tea or coffee or something."

Whittier turned to her. "Would iced tea be suitable, Miss Louden?"

"Yes..." A smile flitted over her lips as she settled into a leather wing chair in the still, cool room. "Iced tea would be fine, thank you."

So here she sat, feeling like a fifth wheel, while the two men discussed marketing strategies as if she weren't even in the room. Of course, she only had herself to blame for that. No one had told her to crash the party. Still, it needled.

The tea duly appeared, which she nearly spilled when Guy said, "Perhaps, Miss Louden, you could you give Mr. Hancock a ballpark figure of the house's worth, since I've just moved back into the area and haven't had a chance to check out any recent sales figures?" He zinged her with a brilliant smile that heralded from the same school of rump-kissing from which she'd graduated *summa cum laude,* then turned his attention to the old man. "You do understand, of course, that this is just a preliminary figure? Until we get the appraisal, I suggest we hold off on setting a selling price."

"Yeah, yeah, I understand," the old man said, jabbing the cigar in Guy's direction, already focused on Elizabeth, "So? How much?"

She met his slit-eyed gaze. "I'd say somewhere in the neighborhood of three-quarters of a million dollars."

His eyebrows shot so far up on his forehead the toupee slid. "No bull?"

"No bull. Sir."

Hancock shook his head slowly. "I built this place in forty-eight for fifty thou. Now you say it's worth..." He bowed slightly at the waist and squinted at her. "*How* much did you say?"

"Seven hundred fifty thousand."

"Unbelievable."

"That's just a ballpark figure, sir," Guy reminded him.

"Hell, anywhere near that ballpark is just fine with me." Hancock spread his heavy lips into what Elizabeth assumed was a smile. "If you can sell this place for that much, you're worth every damn penny of your commission." He took a long pull on the cigar, which Elizabeth noticed had been unlit for some time. "So...where do I sign?"

"Let's go over to this table," Guy suggested, not quite touching the old man's elbow as they crossed over a well-worn Turkish carpet. Then he looked at Elizabeth and smiled. A real smile. And handed her the contract. "Miss Louden will go over the contract with you, answer any other questions you might have." The blue eyes found their way to hers again, and her heart did this little tap-dancing number. "I assure you, you're in excellent hands."

"Yeah, yeah, I'm sure you're right," Hancock muttered distractedly, now trying to light the dead stogie.

"Now, folks, if you'll excuse me," Guy said, picking up his briefcase and heading toward the door. "I'm afraid I have another appointment." Baffled, Elizabeth looked down at the contract.

He'd already printed in her name as the listing agent.

Guy spent the rest of the morning hanging up all the framed pieces of paper that legitimized his presence in the office. His license to practice in Michigan, obtained just a week before his move. His degrees, a B.S. from the University of Michigan and MBA from University of Chicago, earned at night after he'd started working. His awards and achievement certificates and citations for outstanding sales and all the stuff he put up to knock the socks off of whoever happened to notice them. Like—maybe?—Elizabeth.

Air whooshed from his lungs. He might be aggressive, but he wasn't devious. The Hancock house was Elizabeth's by rights, whether the old man seemed to think so or not. Besides, if there was a choice, Guy usually preferred being the good guy in the situation.

A good guy with bills up the wazoo and no income in the foreseeable future who just let go of a potentially huge commission because it was the right thing to do, even though he doubted Miss Elizabeth would even thank him.

But he wanted her to thank him.

He wanted her to smile at him. Like she had at the Gundersons.

He wanted to know how she felt about large dogs and old movies and jazz and the space program and whether Puerto Rico should become the next state.

And children, he thought, setting up the latest Olan Mills portrait on his desk. Specifically a precocious eight-year-old blonde who could probably run the country better than those yokels in Washington if she could stay up past nine o'clock, a four-year-old who still wet the bed most nights but was almost reading already, and a toddler who gave the best hugs and sloppy kisses in the world.

And why did he care what Elizabeth Louden felt about *anything?* The last thing he needed was a woman in his life. Especially this woman. Weren't three kids enough? Three kids would send any sane woman screaming in the opposite direction. Hell—their own *mother* had gone screaming in the opposite direction.

Guy leaned back in his desk chair, his palm bracing his chin, and stared at those three little faces at the moment stuck in some institutional day care until he could make other arrangements, whatever they might be. Faces who depended on him and no one else for everything. Faces he knew, without a doubt, he'd kill for. Then, for reasons he wasn't even sure he fully understood, he removed those little faces from their place of honor next to the phone and slipped them into the middle right-hand drawer of his desk.

By noon, Guy's head was hopelessly jumbled but at least

his side of the office was ready for business. He now had a full complement of pens and pencils and paper clips and a stapler and at least twenty copies of every form necessary to his profession. His Dr. Who mug sat on the little rolling table with the coffeemaker, rubbing up against Elizabeth's plain white porcelain cup with the understated gold handle. He'd set a big stack of scrap paper by the phone for doodling. He'd blitzed with the computer until he knew how to access all the programs. He'd answered the phone a dozen times and made three appointments. Now it was lunchtime, and he was starving, but he wasn't going to leave until Elizabeth came back. Which she did about a quarter past the hour.

"Oh," she said, her brow slightly creased as she slipped off her jacket and hung it on the coatrack by her desk. "I thought you had an appointment."

He pretended to be taking notes on something from the computer. "Only to get my desk set up." Then he allowed his gaze to drift up to her face. His fingers itched to touch those strands of pale gold that refused to stay confined, to tuck them behind her ear, to stroke her cheek and wipe away the hint of a crease on either side of her mouth. Wasn't this woman ever happy?

She set her handbag on her desk, staring at it and worrying the handle. "Why did you give me that listing?"

He waited until she faced him, then caught those sweet, confused green eyes in his and wouldn't let go. Couldn't let go, he realized with a jolt. "Because it was already yours."

The frown grew more pronounced. "But you said…"

"I know what I said. I changed my mind. *And*—" he held up one warning finger before she could protest "—if I were you, I wouldn't mention it again, okay?"

After a long moment, she echoed, "Okay," and with a nod, he turned back to the work on his desk. So. He was right. She hadn't said—

"Thank you."

He hadn't heard her come up behind him. Her hand, so soft and light he could barely feel it, was resting on his shoulder. He looked up into her face and thought maybe her eyes were a little shinier than normal. Then again, that was probably just the window's glare on her glasses.

"You're welcome, Miss Louden," he said, then couldn' resist adding, "But from now on, the bone goes to whoever digs it up first." He felt the slight pressure change as she removed her hand, then removed herself to her desk.

"Fair enough, Mr. Sanford," she said without looking a him, then picked up the phone to return her messages. The rosebud mouth looked as set as stone, until he noticed that i curved upward, just the tiniest bit, at the corners.

"These are nice," her mother said, fingering the blue checked place mats on Elizabeth's dining table, then offhand edly added, "And wasn't that sweet of Guy to give the Han cock house back to you?"

They were only halfway through the salad. Elizabeth had hoped, however pointlessly, that they'd at least make it t dessert before his name came up.

"Not really, no," she lied. She could feel her mother's to paz eyes on the side of her face. "It was nothing more than he should have done."

"Which doesn't necessarily mean he would have done it.' Maureen popped a piece of tomato into her mouth. "He's lovely young man, isn't he?" When Elizabeth pretended no to hear, her mother added, "And did I tell you he was one o the top producers in our Chicago office—?"

"Yes, Mother. Several times." Elizabeth jabbed at her let tuce, nearly spattering honey-Dijon dressing on her sill T-shirt. "Which still doesn't mean he'll be any good for us you know. He's used to dealing with big-city real estate, no small-town stuff. Takes a completely different mind-set."

Maureen blew out a tiny sigh and met her daughter's gaze "Would you listen to yourself? I don't recall your havin much trouble adjusting to selling the 'small-town stuff,' as yo put it, and I don't imagine a young man of Guy Sanford' reputation will, either. And I needed to fill Amanda's vacanc anyway."

"No, you didn't," Elizabeth interrupted, not caring that sh

was being needlessly argumentative. "Business was slow last year, which was why Amanda left to begin with."

"And did *you* have a bad year, dear?"

She went silent, toying with her fork. "No," she finally admitted.

"Well, then. In fact, you pulled in more business than Amanda and I combined for the past two years. Of course, Amanda wasn't very aggressive—"

"Was lazy, you mean," Elizabeth mumbled with a full mouth.

"Whatever." Maureen dismissed her daughter's comment with a wave of her hand. "Honey, the point is, you ferreted out the business, you went after it and you got it. And there's more coming, what with all this new development in the area. Besides, if you're leaving soon…"

"More wine?" Elizabeth held the bottle poised over her mother's glass.

"Oh, no, no. Not for me," her mother said, her hand shooting over the top. The diversionary tactic apparently worked. "Did you know I got three calls today alone from people wanting us to handle entire communities?" Maureen leaned over, the glint of a promised prize gleaming in her eyes. "Entire communities, Elizabeth! Not just single houses. Shadywoods Estates alone will have more than two hundred units."

"Which makes me ill to think about," Elizabeth said with a scowl as she sank back against her chair. "I don't know which bothers me more—that someone wants to build two hundred homes on that lovely old farm site, or that someone actually thinks there are two hundred families willing to move out to Nowhere, Michigan."

"Elizabeth."

She met her mother's tight-lipped expression. "What?"

"You can't stop what's happening. So you might as well make some money off it. Right?"

Arguing was pointless. Besides, at one time, the whole state had been undeveloped. The old homes in town that she loved so much hadn't existed, either, a hundred years ago. So what right did she have to be so high-minded now?

She snapped to and realized the salads were done, so she got up, cleared the salad dishes and carried them into the blue-and-white kitchen. By the time she'd returned to the table with the fettucine, her mother was ready to resume their conversation about Guy. She couldn't stop that, either.

"Did you see the way his eyes crinkle up at the corners when he smiles?" Maureen asked, then forked in a bite of pasta.

"No," Elizabeth lied.

A dreamy smile settled on pink-frosted lips. "Ah, to be thirty again."

Elizabeth just *harrumphed.*

"Oh, come on. Admit it. He's *cute.*"

"Mother. He has a ponytail."

"And an earring. Yes, dear, I noticed." Maureen delicately wiped her mouth with the corner of the linen napkin. "I also noticed those eyes. Did you ever see eyes like that on a man?" She settled her chin in her hand and stared at the candle flame, her eyes slitted. "I wonder what he looks like naked."

Elizabeth nearly dropped her fork. "Mother!"

Maureen laughed. "I'm not dead yet, honey. Or blind."

"I know, Mother, but…" She knew she was blushing. Furiously. Suddenly, the perfectly maintained climate control system in the condo wasn't working worth a damn.

Maureen touched her daughter's wrist. "You weren't brought by the stork, you know." She leaned over, her honey-blond coif gleaming in the overhead light. "Maybe your father was my only lover, but I daresay my experience in matters of the bedroom was more than adequate. And let me tell you, what your father and I shared was something I'll cherish the rest of my life."

The silence that followed was filled with unspoken regrets that were never discussed, although, at times, Elizabeth almost wished they would be. She knew her mother didn't really blame her for a decision made years before. But she heard the breath of bitterness in the words "my only lover," even if her mother didn't. On top of everything else, the last thing Elizabeth needed to deal with was sixteen-year-old guilt.

But Maureen had continued. "There's no substitute for love, honey. The complete, no-holds-barred love between a man and a woman." A devilish smile softly creped the skin around her eyes, making her look wise and pretty and alive all at the same time. "And I emphasize the word *complete*." Then she sighed. "Don't let habit make you blind to opportunities."

But was it habit that kept Elizabeth from making any real connection with a man? Or something deeper? What was it that had made her only too eager to accept her mother's invitation to help out, giving her the perfect excuse to leave Detroit…and Rod Braden's increasingly persistent attention?

The same Rod Braden who hadn't yet given up, it would seem, if his dinner invitation for Friday was any indication.

She shuddered away the questions, poking at a noodle. "What *are* you suggesting, Mother? That I go pick a guy up in a bar somewhere?"

Maureen hooted with laughter. "Oh, right! You'd probably wipe off the bar stool first before you slid up onto it." Sobering, she shook her head. "Of course that's not what I mean. I'm just saying keep your eyes—and your heart—open. I wouldn't want you to miss out on the kind of happiness I had, and frankly, the way you're going, I'm afraid that's exactly what's going to happen."

Like Elizabeth couldn't figure out where this conversation was headed.

"Why don't we invite him to dinner on Friday?" Maureen said, not looking at Elizabeth, who knew better than to ask "Who?"

"I have plans," she immediately answered, taking a gulp of wine, making a spur-of-the-moment decision she wasn't sure she was going to regret any less than accepting her mother's invitation, which she *knew* she'd regret. "Rod invited me to come into Detroit to have dinner with him." Which, up until this very moment, she'd intended to decline. She gave her mother a sweet smile. "Remember Rod?"

"Of course I remember Rod, dear." Maureen raised her eyebrows as if to say "I wasn't sure *you* did." What she did

say was, "It's been quite a while since you mentioned him."
Her mother stood up, tugged her silk short-sleeved sweater
down around her hips, and began to clear the dinner plates.
"Didn't think you two were still seeing each other."

"Yes. We are. Still seeing each other. Which we're doing
on Friday night."

"Saturday night, then?" her mother called from the kitchen.

Geez, Louise...

"Sorry," Elizabeth called back, picking up the glasses.
"I'm spending the rest of the weekend with Nancy." One of
the few regrets Elizabeth had had about leaving Detroit was
leaving behind her former colleague-turned-best-friend. "She
called earlier this evening. Threatened me with bodily harm if
I didn't come see her soon." Elizabeth joined her mother in
the kitchen, whipping a pastry box out of the refrigerator and
flinging back the top. "Cheesecake, Mother?"

"Ooh, yes, that looks wonderful." Maureen snatched the
box out of Elizabeth's hands, plunked it on the counter.
"Well, good." A pair of cranberry-glass dessert dishes clattered to the counter; her mother cut them each a generous
chunk of cheesecake, licked one finger. "Maybe she'll knock
some sense into your head while you're there. Especially about
Rod."

Rats. She hadn't thought of that.

Sleeping through this weekend suddenly seemed like an excellent idea.

Chapter 3

Arguing the whole way as they clanged up the outside metal stairs leading to the second-floor apartment, Ashli and Jake tripped over each other in their zeal to see who'd get to the door first. Guy followed at a careful distance, a bag of groceries on one hip, a smelly, shrieking two-year-old on the other. Ignoring his older two was the safest policy at the moment, he decided.

"Get out of my way, turtle-brain." Ashli followed this directive by shoving her four-year-old brother aside with her bony hip. "I got here first."

"*I* did!" rasped the little boy, shoving back, amazingly throwing his twice-as-tall sister off balance. Which made her madder than a wet cat.

"Dad-*dy!* Tell him to get out of my way!"

"Tell her to get out of *my* way!"

"Excuse me, but you both can just get out of my way," Guy said wearily, reaching the top of the stairs. He unlocked the door and they all tumbled over each other into the apartment. Guy winced at the musty, rancid smell that still permeated the place, even after days of airing and a case of Lysol.

A large electrified-furred dog of dubious parentage slinked over to them, his tail wagging his body, his sheepish expression screaming, "Guilty dog here!"

Guy didn't want to know.

"Ashli, take Einstein out before he piddles all over the place." Guy let the baby loose, heaved the groceries up onto the counter that served to divide the "living room" from the "kitchen," then grabbed the dog's collar and leash off a hook next to the door and snapped it around the beast's neck.

"C'n I go, too?" squeaked Jake.

"Please." Guy steered them all out the door, which he left open so he could keep an ear out. A breath and a half later, they all clamored back up. Damn.

"Did he go?"

The two older kids raced to the TV and plopped down onto olive-green shag carpeting that predated hula hoops, immediately sucked into a rerun of *The Simpsons* Guy was sure they'd seen at least a half-dozen times.

"Gallons," Ashli called over her shoulder.

He looked at the dog, who seemed to be happy enough, then glanced around the apartment. A real prize, this.

What would Elizabeth Louden's reaction be to the place, with her designer suit and silk blouse and expensively soaped skin? She'd probably hoist that pert little nose in the air and declare, "See? Men *haven't* evolved."

At the moment, he'd probably agree with her.

Wasn't as if he'd planned it this way, he thought as he grabbed the chattering baby and trudged to the tiny bedroom all three kids shared. He quickly changed the little boy, barely able to think about dinner, let alone about finding a house where they could all sit in one room without inhaling dog hair.

Actually, he had seen one property he really liked, just a few blocks away. But he doubted he could swing the down payment, not at the price the owner was asking. Not to mention the mortgage—he tossed the baby into the air and kissed his tummy—which was a shame, because Ashli had immediately fallen in love with the old Queen Anne.

So it was either lower his sights, or risk slow death from

asphyxiation and overexposure to Avocado and Harvest Gold. Or pray his house in St. Charles sold quickly, which, considering current market conditions, seemed unlikely. This apartment had been an act of desperation, the only thing immediately available that would allow three kids and Godzilla-mutt here. Knowing it was temporary helped a little, but it didn't make the situation any more pleasant.

A brief but vociferous argument flared in the other room. Commercial break, he figured, waiting out the fracas until the theme song from *Home Improvement* started and peace was restored.

Guy set a much sweeter-smelling toddler on the floor and returned to the kitchen, which is where he discovered the source of the dog's guilty slink. Making little whuffing noises and determined to kiss and make up, Einstein plastered himself against Guy's shoulder as he cleaned up the spilled garbage.

"Get out of my face, you miserable beast." Guy halfheartedly shoved the dog away so he wouldn't track in the orange juice concentrate before he could wipe it up, then looked up to see a snakelike tongue repeatedly licking the air three inches in front of Guy's face. Maybe after a nap, he'd laugh. Right now, he didn't have the oomph.

"C'n we go to the park after dinner?" piped a gravelly soft voice right behind him as he stood up, making him jump. How *did* they sneak up like that?

He turned to face a pair of imploring brown eyes. "I don't know, squirt. I'm really pooped."

"*Please,* Daddy?"

Jake only whined when he was tired and irritable. But so did Guy, who snapped, "I *said,* we'll see," before he caught himself.

After all, he was the grown-up. *The* grown-up. He let out an enormous sigh, then squatted down eye level with the child. "I just walked in, same as you. Give me a minute to unscramble my brain, okay?"

God, he was beginning to sound like his mother. However, *he* handed the little boy a bag of pretzels and sent him back to the electronic baby-sitter, knowing the crumbs would be lost forever in the hideous carpet. Man. Here he'd thought he was pretty understanding and sensitive and all that stuff, helping out with the kids and cleaning a bathroom now and then, making the bed every morning and pancakes every Saturday. You know—the new improved liberated male? *Ha!* As contrite as Einstein, Guy had given his mother a *very* nice present that first Mother's Day after he'd become a single father.

Okay…food. Guy methodically opened cupboards, closed them again, tried to push nagging self-pity out of his brain, then repeated the procedure with the refrigerator, sidestepping the eighty-pound Brillo pad planted in the middle of the worn linoleum floor. He grimaced. Guess it was spaghetti again.

He put on a big pot of water, then opened a jar of Ragu and dumped it out into a saucepan. He hated spaghetti. If he never had to look at another plate of pasta the rest of his life, he'd die a contented man. But it was the one thing he knew the kids would eat no matter what, unless they were sick, and it had the added advantage of hitting three of the four major food groups in one fell swoop.

He stood watching the steam rise from the simmering water as if watching an oracle, a handful of dried pasta clutched in his hand. If nothing else, no one could accuse him of not being honest with himself. The past year and a half had been hell.

Thank you, Dianne.

He dumped the spaghetti into the water, stirred it, turned to get the milk out of the fridge, pouring it into the plastic Tupperware cups he and his brothers used to use. From the living room, another shrill dispute snagged his attention.

"Ashli—" he warned, and was rewarded with a pair of angry blue eyes.

"Jake started it, Daddy," she began. "He's such a dork-face—"

"Ashli Nicole! No more!"

With a scowl that could freeze the sun, she turned back to the TV, scooting cross-legged away from her brother, and rammed her chin into the palms of her hands.

He hated raising his voice at her, but her perpetual bad mood was beginning to get to him. Had gotten to him, months ago. He knew she'd been devastated when her mother had left, but why she felt the need to take out her pain and frustration on her little brother was beyond him. Kids fought—as the youngest of five brothers, *that* he knew—but she really seemed to dislike Jake at times. And that, he couldn't tolerate.

"Okay, guys. Dinnertime." He settled Micah into his high chair as the other two wiggled into their chrome-and-vinyl chairs with much floor scraping and giggling and one cup of milk, per usual, spilling. Guy silently cleaned up the mess, then sank into his chair, exhausted, and just watched his children eat.

He'd thought at first that staying in a familiar environment was the best thing to do. After one shock, Ashli couldn't have stood relocation as well. Or so the experts said. But as time wore on, and the child's sullen mood didn't seem to improve, Guy decided to explore other options. Obviously, what he had been doing—drifting aimlessly in the status quo—wasn't working. Trouble was, he'd had no idea what to do.

Then, three weeks ago, his mother told him about an ad she'd noticed in the Ann Arbor paper for an opening in a Realty office in Spruce Lake, just twenty miles away. Wondering why he didn't immediately say thanks but that's okay, Mom, he'd put the kids to bed, shoved a vintage Ella Fitzgerald cassette into the player, then stood in the middle of his nearly empty living room. Just stood there, thinking, in a house he'd been able to hang on to only by selling most of the stuff in it. Finally, after what might have been ten minutes or two hours, it dawned on him that a lot more was missing than furniture.

Chicago wasn't his home, and it never had been. He'd only settled there because that's where Dianne's family lived. Since there'd been no Dianne for some time, why was he still there?

He'd called Maureen Louden the following morning, and she'd hired him sight unseen. He'd been tempted to wonder what he'd gotten himself into, but before he could chicken out he told her he'd be there a week from the following Monday and would she mind lining up a few apartments that might take a dog and three kids until he could find someplace permanent? And get him the name of a day care center, too?

She'd apologized, at least five times, that this was the best she could do on such short notice. *At this price,* she diplomatically refrained from adding.

Micah squealed, interrupting his thoughts.

Guy sighed and wiped a splotch of spaghetti sauce off the baby's pink face, looked at his own bowl, pushed it away. He'd make a sandwich later.

"You guys done?"

They both nodded, Jake noisily finishing off his milk. "Daddy?" he asked through a milk mustache. "Can we? Can we go feed the ducks?"

Guy caught Ashli's groan and held up one hand to squelch any comment about stupid ducks, stupid ponds, or stupid younger brothers. She liked feeding the ducks as much as Jake did, and he was having none of her contrariness this evening. So he nodded, even though he was so tired he wasn't even sure he could feel his feet anymore. "Sure," he said, and was rewarded with a grin that had a remarkably salubrious effect on his nerve endings. "There're some old bread heels in the Roman Meal bag. Go get 'em."

Amid Jake's chatter and Micah's high-pitched mantra of "Baby go gucks? Baby go gucks?" he heard Ashli ask, trying to keep anything resembling enthusiasm out of her soft voice, "Can we go by the house, too?"

He knew which house she meant. "Sure, baby," he said, planting a kiss on top of her head. "Why not?"

As they all scrambled down the stairs, each kid trying to yell louder than the others, Guy vaguely wondered if Elizabeth Louden also liked feeding ducks and strolling around lakes on warm summer evenings.

Elizabeth shook the last of the crumbs from the Pepperidge Farm Honeyberry Wheat bag into the water, inadvertently dusting the few mallards still circling and *whank-whanking* at her from the lake's edge. One pecked idly at the floating bits before deciding it wasn't worth the effort, then glided across the lake to join its comrades already settled down for the evening on the little marshy island jutting up a hundred feet away. Actually, the man-made water hole at the entrance to her apartment development was more of an oversized pond than a lake, but it was water, and it did have ducks. And now, as the sun began to set, both it and the sky, as well as the maples and pines and lazy willows along the path, were kissed with streaks of fiery tangerine.

She neatly folded the bag into a small square, tucked it into her shorts pocket, and started back home. Her mother had left a half hour before, to catch an old movie on cable that Elizabeth had no desire to see. She took with her a serving each of fettucine and cheesecake; she left behind more muddled thoughts for Elizabeth to sort out.

A sudden, cooler breeze wicked the sheen of perspiration off Elizabeth's neck and collarbone, making her shiver. She already regretted her Friday night plans. She really would have to decide something about Rod. Soon. She'd moved away, yes, but...

But what?

Somehow, she didn't think her mother meant Rod when she warned Elizabeth against missing opportunities. Rather, there was something missing *about* this opportunity. Like...sparks.

Sparks?

No, wait, back up a minute. Sparks meant losing control. Complications. Besides, Elizabeth wouldn't know a spark if it singed her eyebrows.

In any case, sparks or anything close wasn't going to happen with Rod, rich and handsome and intelligent though he might be. When she'd talked to Nancy, telling her she'd be there late Friday after her date, her old friend had honed right in on her ambivalence.

"So just break it off, already," she'd said. "For God's sake, Elizabeth—you don't even like his *kids*."

Oh, yeah. Rod's kids. Now *there* was a pair of charming creatures. But their father... Well, he was something else again. "Hey. Whatever happened to 'on a scale from one to ten, the man is like a fifteen, already.'"

"That was months ago. Since he's obviously not ringing your chimes—though God knows why—it's time to move on, *bubelah*. So, why haven't you?"

She couldn't tell Nancy the truth, couldn't bring herself to admit what a selfish, conniving, manipulative, wicked woman she was, to confess that the only reason she hadn't ditched Rod before this—a man she barely let kiss her good-night, let alone share her bed—was because he'd said he was interested in the Hancock mansion. Then again, Nancy—who was no slouch herself in the nail-the-sale department—would have probably understood.

Slowly, Elizabeth climbed back up the stairs to her apartment and let herself in, tossing her keys on the spindly legged marble-topped table by the front door. Had it come to this? Dating a man she was never going to love, whose children raised the hair on the back of her neck, just to sell a house?

Scary.

Well. Home again, home again, jiggety jig, to that comforting mixture of lingering coffee, eucalyptus and an intriguing blend of the trio of perfumes she alternately wore. The muffled chime of the Seth Thomas clock on the buffet punctuated the dishwasher's soft whirr; the air inside was cool, and still, and at this time of day radiated a soft, powdery luminescence she could practically feel.

So perfect. So peaceful. So...empty.

She turned on the lamp next to the sofa and sank into its corner, then riffled through a stack of paperbacks on the end table—a couple of novels, a new book on investments, a bestseller on human relationships which Nancy insisted was "fabulous." What had seemed fascinating two days ago held no allure now, and she stared at each one in turn, wondering why she'd bought it to begin with.

She replaced the stack on the table, got up, walked into her bedroom for no good reason, immediately returned to the living room. Nothing on TV except reruns, too late to go into the village to rent a video... Frowning, Elizabeth stood with her hands on her hips and huffed loudly...then grinned, grabbed her car keys, and left.

The house was barely five minutes away, in an older part of town. Centering the neighborhood was a lake—a *real* lake, not a pond, though still small enough to see all the way around. On the far shore, bungalows huddled at the water's edge; but cupping a full three-quarters of the shoreline on this side, the dwellings having been set back far enough, was a generously wooded park, perfect for picnics and letting dogs run free and just plain hanging out. Some of the houses were a little run-down, and a fair number of them had been converted from single-family dwellings into apartments. But by and large, it was a pleasant neighborhood, with tidy lawns and lush gardens. And folks over there were genuinely friendly, unlike her condo neighbors who never said "boo" to her unless it was to gripe about their latest maintenance fee increase.

Elizabeth pulled up alongside the large corner lot, some three or four blocks back from the park, and cut the ignition, smiling at what she couldn't help feel was an old friend. There she stood, timeworn but still grand. A conglomeration of unmatched gables and turrets, porches with broken gingerbread, a missing step in the back. Tangled, overgrown wisteria and honeysuckle still fought to bloom over hip-high weeds, while along the back stone wall, masses of heavy, ruby-red roses taxed the capacity of an uninhibited twenty-foot rambler that by rights should have died years ago. The Poole-Strong sign was still there, but there was no Sold placard on top of it. Yet.

She got out of the car and approached the house, nearly to the front porch steps when she heard the voices. A man's, vaguely familiar, and childrens'. Two or three, she couldn't tell. A family out for a walk, she figured, and sprinted up the creaky stairs.

She peered through the big bay window into the living room. Or parlor, more likely. Actually, she'd long since committed the room to memory. The crown molding around the ceiling, the old parquet floors desperately needing loving attention, the marble fireplace still miraculously intact. She knew just where her crystal collection would go—

"Daddy, what's that lady doing?"

The resulting silence as good as tapped her on the shoulder

to get her attention. She turned, mild curiosity exploding into instant shock. There stood Guy, in cutoffs and a Chicago Bears T-shirt, looking as though he'd just been goosed. And *with* Guy were children. Three of them. The girl had his eyes, the middle boy his dark curly hair. The baby…oh, Lord—he had a *baby?*

A thousand thoughts crashed into each other in her head. Had she missed something? Why had she assumed he wasn't married?

Why did it bother her that he was?

And why, she thought, becoming more confused by the second, hadn't he informed her mother of his marital status, because obviously if he had, her mother wouldn't have just wasted most of a perfectly good evening trying to ram Guy Sanford down her daughter's throat? If not other parts of her anatomy?

"Well," she said, smoothing her hand down the side of her shorts.

"Yes." Guy smiled, but the attempt reminded Elizabeth of a match that didn't quite ignite. "Do you come here often?" he joked, weakly.

She made her legs move and descended the steps, stuffing her hands in her pockets when she reached the sidewalk. "Actually, I do. I…" She shook her head, hoping her laugh didn't sound as hollow as it felt. "Well, it's not a secret or anything. I've had my eye on this house ever since I moved back, a year ago." She glanced back over her shoulder at it. "I don't know why. She's pretty sorry, I guess." Then she looked back into a pair of troubled eyes, and matched the expression with a frown of her own. "But…I'm afraid I've fallen in love."

"I can see why," Guy said after a moment, then seemed to take a very deep breath indeed, simultaneously nuzzling the baby's honey-blond curls with his lips. "Why haven't you made an offer for it?"

"Well, for one thing, I haven't been in the position, financially, to manage it." She shrugged, as if it didn't really matter. "Besides, she's really far too much for me to take on by myself."

"But if you're in love..." His eyes locked with hers; her face grew warm.

"I've never been one to let my heart rule my head, Mr. Sanford."

"Never?"

"Never."

For a long moment, they just watched each other as if waiting to see which one would blink first. Elizabeth was damned if it was going to be she. If Guy had been smiling, she would've said he was flirting with her, which would not have amused her, seeing as he was married.

But he wasn't smiling, which meant he wasn't flirting, which meant she wasn't sure *what* he was doing.

"Daddy?" Guy jerked to attention, turning to the little girl, whose pale brows spoke of a wariness that put Elizabeth on guard. "Do you know her?"

"I'm sorry," he said as a general apology. "Yes, honey, this is Miss Louden, one of the ladies I work with. These are my children, Ashli, Jake, and this rascal—" he tickled the baby's tummy, who let out a delighted squeal "—is Micah."

Ashli, who appeared to be around eight or nine, eyed Elizabeth as if she were an item she might consider purchasing. No smile, no discernible expression on the smooth, delicate features, the eyes nothing more than camera lenses, taking it all in. "Daddy was right," she said after a moment's contemplation—and with just the slightest upward curve of her lips. "You *are* pretty."

"Ashli!"

Elizabeth fought a smile. "Why, thank you, Ashli," she said, then turned to Guy, meeting the embarrassed eyes, even more blue set in a red face, and asked with cool deliberateness, "Why didn't your wife join you on your walk? It's such a beautiful night."

A froggy little-boy voice immediately volunteered, "Mama doesn't live with us anymore."

"Mama got mad at us," Ashli added matter-of-factly. "So she left."

"Now, we've been over this, honey," Guy said with a

shaky laugh as he palmed his daughter's dark-blond head and drew her close to his hip. "Mama's leaving had nothing to do with you guys—"

"Then why hasn't she ever called or written or *anything?*" the little girl asked with that exhausted frustration that comes from having asked a question many times before but never getting a good enough answer, and Elizabeth realized she'd just gotten into the middle of something she had no business being in the middle of and didn't *want* to be in the middle of and why on *earth* had she gone back out this evening?

Then it hit her. "Your wife walked out on you?"

"Uh, yeah," he said, offering another one of those half-hearted, completely inappropriate smiles because he obviously didn't know what else to do.

"You mean, she just said 'See ya' and left you with three kids to raise?"

"Pretty much."

Elizabeth was speechless. Mainly because what she wanted to say she didn't dare in front of the children. "How long…?" she finally managed.

"Year ago February."

Eighteen months! She looked at Micah, who couldn't be more than two—the woman had left an *infant?*

"I'm…sorry," Guy said, hitching the baby farther up on his hip. "This has nothing to do with you."

Before she knew what she was doing, Elizabeth put her hand on top of Guy's. "No," she said softly, feeling an alien sensation in the pit of her stomach. "*I'm* sorry."

And she was. In more ways than she could even begin to sort out at that moment. She removed her hand, shoving it into her pocket again.

"Daddy, I need to pee," Jake suddenly announced, tugging on his father's shirt and hopping up and down with a near-panicked expression on his face.

"Guess you need to be going," Elizabeth said. Then smiled. "Or at least, Jake does."

Guy tried to meet her smile, and Elizabeth thought her heart would break. Considering how hard it had been on her mother to raise her on her own, she couldn't imagine what Guy must be going through with *three*.

"Yeah, it would appear so. Gotta get these scamps in bed, anyway. Well. See you tomorrow, Miss Louden."

"Yes, Mr. Sanford. Tomorrow, then."

Then, before either of them could sound any less intelligent than they already had, she turned and went back to her car.

Kids. He has kids.

A breeze flicked at the hems of Elizabeth's shortie pajamas as she sat cross-legged on a wrought-iron patio chair on her balcony, elbows on knees, chin in hands, staring at the taunting shadows snaking across the back lawn.

So? What does that have to do with me?

From inside the apartment, she heard the Seth Thomas politely chime 2:00 a.m.; she shot up out of the chair, banging her palms down on the top of the balcony railing.

A hundred times, more, she'd gone over it. She just met the man. He wasn't her type, whatever that was. She didn't get involved with co-workers. She didn't get involved with *anyone*. Especially when the *anyone* had kids. Just ask Rod, the most recent victim of Elizabeth's noninvolvement policy.

With a groan, she pressed her palms against the sides of her head, shaking it slowly from side to side. She didn't like or know how to act around or what to do with kids, she didn't get off on men who wore ponytails or earrings or strange ties or had blue eyes that shorted out her brain whenever she looked at them. She didn't trust men who stole listings out from under her, then gave them back for no apparent reason, other than, maybe, they were decent human beings.

And she especially didn't like or trust or want to have anything to do with men who were all of these things, and had kids, and who kept her awake all night in spite of the fact that they were all of these things. And had kids. Even though these seemed like sweet children. And she felt awful for them that their mother had walked out.

Just about as badly as she felt for the father.

No! She paced the small balcony, back and forth, back and forth. *No, no, no, no...*

It was too ludicrous to even consider. Children were noisy and messy and loud and demanded constant attention. Children took a bit more care than periodic dusting. Of all the things she was good at, playing mom wasn't one of them. Just look at her horrendous attempt at being a camp counselor when she was sixteen. By the end of the summer, all the girls in her cabin went to the camp director and begged her to never hire Elizabeth again. And baby-sitting? She'd tried it once, when she was about thirteen, so inept at taking care of the Rodgers's three-year-old twins she actually refused to let them pay her. Since they'd had to redo the brand-new wallpaper in the dining room after Joey gooped nail polish all over it, which happened while Elizabeth was desperately trying to even out Cassandra's hair after she'd lopped off one of her ponytails with the kitchen scissors... Well, she just hadn't had the heart. She'd never forgiven her mother for not immediately moving them to a new town, either. So there was no way she was going to believe that, just because she wasn't sure she could feel the ground underneath her feet whenever she looked into Guy's eyes, that she was actually...*attracted* to him. That she felt...sparks. Fate wouldn't be that mean.

She dropped back into the chair.

Would it?

Near-hysterical laughter bubbled up in her throat.

Okay, so maybe she was a little burned out, maybe she needed some new direction in her life. Maybe she was still in Spruce Lake because the idea of going back to Detroit and the fast lane smacked far too much of been-there-done-that-itis for her comfort. Fine. She'd accept that. She didn't like it, but she'd deal with it. But a husband and children had never been on her agenda, because...

Because...?

Because she'd been absent the day they doled out maternal instinct.

The clock chimed the quarter hour. Elizabeth grabbed a

throw pillow off the chair next to her, stuffed her face into it and screamed for thirty seconds.

When she came up for air, she'd made two decisions. The first was to avoid Guy Sanford as much as possible. Especially his eyes. And that blasted smile. The second, which seemed to come out of nowhere, was to finally make an offer on the Lakeside house.

So she'd have to go into her investments. Big deal. Her mother was right. What was she going to do with her stash…take it with her? She not only wanted that house, she *needed* it. And she needed it *now,* not at some hypothetical point in her future when everything was All Sorted Out. She needed a project. Something that would require something of herself, her *real* self, to make it work.

Relief washed over her like a warm bath. The Lakeside house could be her new goal, her new reason to wake up every morning. And it would surely keep her busy enough to quash thoughts about men with ponytails and three children for at least ten, maybe twenty years down the road.

Damn. Talk about things being screwed *up.*

Guy sat at the top of the stairs to the apartment, scratching the dog's mangy head and wondering what was wrong with him. Guy, not the dog. He'd just met the woman and for sure she wasn't his type and he had these three kids and why on *earth* couldn't he get her out of his mind?

That look in her eyes—damn, again. Sheer undiluted, right-up-there-where-God-and-everyone-could-see-it horror. Unless he was way off track, Elizabeth Louden was not the cookie-baking, costume-sewing, Earth Mother type.

Either.

He'd been down that road once already. What good would it do to even think about someone else who wasn't wild about kids? *His* kids, at least?

But damn it *all,* there was something in the woman's eyes that had hooked him the moment he'd met her this morning. And those eyes had swept him way beyond the prim outfits and the obsessively controlled hair and the smart mouth, someplace he had a feeling Elizabeth didn't even know existed. Someplace he wanted to be. And, in spite of how foolish or stupid or crazy it was, he wanted to take Elizabeth to that place in her eyes, to show her that life was more than sales figures and designer clothes and always getting in the last word.

But Guy liked to think, at this point in his life, he was beyond deliberately doing things that were foolish or stupid or crazy. So, somewhere around two in the morning, sitting outside the ugliest apartment west of Detroit, he made two decisions.

First off, he was going to ignore whatever it was he thought he saw in Elizabeth Louden's eyes.

Secondly, tomorrow morning, seeing as Elizabeth had as good as sworn she was not going to bid on that old Queen Anne, Guy was going to make an offer for it himself. If he could bring the price down, he could swing it. After all, that sorry old pile of boards had been the first thing to make his daughter's eyes sparkle in almost eighteen months. And to rid his daughter of her demons, he'd arm wrestle the Devil himself.

Chapter 4

Elizabeth stood beside her car, in the middle of blissful nowhere—soon to be known as Shadywoods Estates—shielding her eyes from the morning sun. To the east and south stretched meadows heavy with midsummer flowers, yielding to expansive views of rolling hills; to the north and west marched the woods, as they had for probably centuries. How could a fancy-shmancy housing development possibly be better than this? She lifted her gaze to catch a pair of turkey buzzards lazily swirling on eddies high above her head, her own thoughts swirling much the same way.

It had already been a full morning. Sybil Bennett had gleefully accepted her bid on the house, promising to present it to the owner the instant he returned from vacation next week; and her mother—even more gleeful—had called, snagging Elizabeth on her way out the door, to tell her that Millennium had gotten the contract for Shadywoods.

Elizabeth had tried to be happy for her. She had. But now, taking careful sips of coffee from a foam cup as she surveyed what would be sacrificed for her mother's success, she realized exactly how difficult that was going to be.

She recapped the cup, yawning so deeply her eyes watered. Not even caffeine was helping this morning. To her intense dismay, what little sleep she'd managed to get the night before had been repeatedly interrupted by what would have been erotic dreams about Guy, were it not for the dozens of children that kept cropping up out of nowhere, screeching and caterwauling and clawing at them for attention. Each time, Elizabeth would wake up with a jolt, her head pounding, declaring anew she would not, could not, let this man get as much as one iota of a foothold on her heart.

A footfall crunching the gravel to her right made her jump. She pivoted to find herself face-to-face with the person who was, all too literally, the man of her dreams. And, tagging behind him, children. Not dozens, at least. Just three.

Small consolation.

Guy had taken hold of her arm when she flinched. "Sorry," he said, offering her a slanted grin underneath the sunglasses. She noticed he was one of those men whose face hinted of beard even when just shaved. "I thought you'd hear us."

His voice was like her father's—not particularly deep, maybe, but mellow, comforting. She looked up into that smile, and realized his hand was still on her arm. She wondered why she didn't care, why she didn't move. Why she suddenly couldn't remember a damn thing about ponytails and agendas and control. At that teensy-tinsy spec of a moment, she didn't even care about the kids.

Something was very wrong.

She smiled back, nervously. "I did hear you. Just too late."

"Daddy?" called his daughter from twenty feet away. "Who's that?"

"It's Miss Louden," he offered over his shoulder as he removed his hand, then the sunglasses, keeping his gaze locked with Elizabeth's. Then he turned to Ashli. "Remember meeting her last night?"

The child nodded, giving Elizabeth what she guessed was a daylight reassessment. Then: "Can I take the boys into that meadow?"

"*May* I?" Guy corrected, then said, "Just Jake. Micah's shorter than the grass. You'll lose him."

Ashli nodded again, then grabbed her brother's hand and dragged him into the field. Within seconds, they'd plowed through to the middle of it, chasing bees and butterflies and giggling so hard they almost threw themselves off balance.

"Would you look at that?" she heard Guy murmur. When she glanced at him, she saw a cross between amazement and relief play across his features.

"What?"

He jerked, as if he'd forgotten she could hear him. "Oh, nothing, really. Ashli just hasn't wanted to play much with Jake lately, that's all."

Elizabeth had the feeling there was more, but Guy wasn't saying.

"So—" she leaned back into her car to place the tepid coffee on the dashboard "—why are you here?"

But before Guy could answer, the baby had pranced over to him. "Up! Up!" he pleaded, his arms raised. Guy scooped Micah up into his arms, whereupon the child cried "Hug!", threw his arms around Guy's neck, then planted a noisy, sloppy kiss on his father's mouth, only to promptly squeal to get down again. With a laugh, Guy let the toddler go, watching the tiny boy as he dropped to his hands and knees to study an ant.

"What did you ask me? Oh, yes," he said before Elizabeth could repeat the question. "Your mother called me at home, just before we left, told me she'd gotten the contract. So I decided to check out the site before the meeting with the developer and land planner." He nodded toward the children. "Used it as an excuse not to plunk them in day care so early, too."

As if on cue, another round of sparkling giggles floated up from the field. Guy chuckled as Jake jumped up after a butterfly and fell flat on his face, vanishing into a clump of snowy Queen Anne's lace. "You okay?" he yelled, his answer a grinning, nodding head popping up over the flowers. Guy then turned to her, and she thought she'd like to disappear into his smile. Fear, so distant as to be nameless, lapped at her subconscious with a single word:

Don't.

She quickly looked away.

"So…why are *you* here?" he asked.

She closed her eyes, thought. Then said, "Visiting my past, you might say."

"Saying goodbye?"

She scanned the view, let out a whoosh of air. "Lord, I hope not."

He slipped both hands into the pockets of a pair of pleated khakis, then walked a few feet away, his blue chambray shirt—nearly the color of his eyes, she realized—rippling across his broad back in the breeze.

"What's this piece of land mean to you?" he asked over his shoulder.

It was a small thing, but she could tell he understood how she felt, even before she explained. Pleasure and terror tangled around her heart.

She stayed where she was, lifting her voice so he could hear her. "I used to come out here for picnics and outings, when I was a kid. There were times—" she caught herself, then let go "—I felt free here. Happy." She shrugged. "My childhood is out there, in those meadows. The good part of my childhood."

She caught Guy grinning at her. "Well, now, Miss Louden— I wouldn't have pegged you as the sentimental type."

What was it about this man that made her want to smile right back? And go hide under a bed at the same time? "Neither would I, come to think of it."

His smile broadened, softened. Rattled her. Her eyes darted to the old apple orchard not far from where they stood, the trees already heavy with the summer's fruit. "A rite of passage or two even took place in that orchard."

Guy's raised eyebrows brought an immediate blush.

"My first kiss," she hastily filled in. "That's all."

He was quiet for a moment, studying her. "That's a lot," he finally said, to which she had no reply. Then he rubbed one finger underneath his lower lip as he returned to her car, leaned against it. His aftershave, newly applied, sent her nerve endings into a tizwaz. Why on earth had she mentioned *kisses,* of all things? "We stand to make a lot of money on this," he said.

"I know."

He shifted, focusing on her face. "Isn't that at least some consolation?"

"Not much, no."

"Why?"

She thought. Said, "Because it burns me up that someone can just come in and destroy all this, and that I'm helpless to do anything to stop it."

He nodded, then looked back out over the meadow, at his children, now far enough away they could barely be heard. Acting on an instinct she didn't know she had, Elizabeth looked around for the baby, who was now lying on his tummy in the middle of the road, jabbering and poking at a line of ants. "I know what you mean," he said. "We can both hope, then, they don't screw this up."

She looked up at the side of his face, at the hard line of his darkened jaw so at odds with the ponytail. The worry lines were more pronounced this morning; selfishly, she wondered if his night had been sleepless, as well. Even more selfishly, she found herself aching to touch him. Knotting her hands together in front of her, she said, "So...we're actually in agreement about something?"

His laugh was as soft as a caress. "Appears so."

Two things occurred to Elizabeth in the silence that followed. One was that her heart reacted like a Geiger counter to plutonium the closer she stood to Guy; and two, that she did not find the sensation to be wholly unpleasant.

She hauled in a rattling, almost panicked breath and pushed out in its place, "Mother said you knew this developer?"

She could feel those eyes, drinking her in, studying her. Her hands went clammy, and it wasn't just from the humidity. "He's okay. I don't know the architect, though. And that's where the problem could come in. If the guy doesn't have a clue how to balance it all." He took a deep breath. "People need this as much as they do roofs over their heads. Maybe more."

Elizabeth crossed her arms and shook her head, snickering softly. Guy turned to her, a half smile pulling at his lips.

"What's so funny?"

"What was that you said about your being ruthless? That's the word you used, wasn't it?"

"Ah. I believe that was the word I used to describe *you*."

"Yes, you did," she agreed. "But then you said, and I quote, 'and now you know I am, too.'" She couldn't help the laugh. "What a fake! You're about as ruthless as..." She waved her hand helplessly, searching for a word—any word—to finish her simile. "As a squirrel," was the best she could manage.

"Hey—you ever see those little devils in the fall, when it's gathering time? They'll grab the nuts right off each other."

Elizabeth had never seen a man turn that shade of red before. When she realized why, she burst out laughing.

"I'm...so sorry," he began, but she waved away his objection.

"No, no..." She paused to catch her breath. When had she last laughed this hard? "No, that was very good." Then she started giggling all over again.

Guy rubbed the back of his neck, underneath the ponytail. "I first thought maybe you wouldn't get it. Then I was petrified you would."

The words rising on sporadic bubbles of leftover laughter, Elizabeth managed, "For heaven's sake, I'm not a prude."

His glance took in her hair, her outfit. "Coulda fooled me."

That effectively stanched the laugher. "And what's that supposed to mean?"

"Look at what you're wearing," he said softly, almost as if he were puzzled. "The way you fix your hair. If that doesn't say 'prude,' I don't know what does."

Since her choice of attire had often been calculated to keep men—to keep complications—at a distance, his comment didn't particularly bother her. Besides, there was nothing wrong with her outfit, a simple navy-blue shirtwaist dress and a string of pearls. She hadn't had the energy to do the French braid, so had just pulled her hair back into a basic chignon at the nape of her neck. Glamorous, it wasn't. But this morning, she was just aiming for *done*.

So, if she wasn't bothered, why did she feel the need to explain herself?

"How I dress," she said, "is not necessarily who I am inside."

He squinted at her, his head inclined to one shoulder. "Really."

She didn't understand. "Yes. Really."

"So...appearances have nothing to do with who we really are?"

"Well, no, I didn't say that, exactly...."

"Then what did you say? Exactly?"

By rights, she should have been irked with him. After all, he was deliberately goading her. Instead, she decided to think about what he was asking her instead of just reacting. For a change.

"I...hadn't really thought about it," she finally admitted. "I guess...that we can't choose who we are, but we can choose how we present ourselves to the world?" She wrinkled her nose, like a student who's been called on unexpectedly and hopes she got the answer right.

Guy just continued to stare at her. Little by little, she was finding his gaze reassuring rather than unsettling. Which made her even more unsettled. After a long moment, he nodded. "So, perhaps, we would both do well to remember that what we see is not necessarily what's really there."

Now she understood.

She knew she was blushing and there wasn't a blessed thing she could do about it. Trying to appear casual, she took a few steps down the road, her hands loosely clasped behind her back.

"I'm right, aren't I?" Guy asked, not following her. "My hair, the earring, the clothes. They all put you off, didn't they?"

She whirled around, suddenly angry with him for figuring her out so damn easily, for tricking her into confronting something she didn't want to think about. "If you know they're so off-putting, why do you insist on wearing them?"

He took a step closer to her. "Because *I'm* comfortable in

them. Because fancy suits and hundred-dollar shirts aren't *me*. Because maybe I'm a middle-class schmoe who's learned how to make a buck, but that doesn't mean I feel that gives me the right to pretend to be someone I'm not. Besides, no matter what I wear, somebody's sure to not like it. So I might as well be true to myself.'' He hesitated. ''Just like you are.''

''Prudish, you mean.''

He tilted his head at her. ''Actually, the Donna Reed look suits you, now that I think about it.''

Not sure what to say next, Elizabeth again trekked down the unpaved road, her heels not taking kindly to the unstable surface. Guy saw her timorous footsteps and chuckled again.

''Look, right there. Do you even own a pair of sneakers?''

''Of course, I own a pair of sneakers, you twit,'' she said, fighting not to lose her balance. ''But I don't generally wear them to work, and I hardly knew I'd be tromping around on a dirt road today.''

''Point taken,'' he admitted. ''And by the way, I happen to think Donna Reed was a knockout.'' Before she could react to this, he said, ''I tried to get you at home after your mother called me. You were already gone.''

To make the bid on the Lakeside house, she realized. ''Personal business,'' she carefully replied, then met his gaze, smiling. ''And none of yours.'' He studied her for a moment, a brief nod his only comment.

Guy picked up the baby again and they walked on for a moment, occasionally dodging a bee making its way across the road from one wildflower orgy to the other. Elizabeth saw Ashli, a little closer again, bounce up from where she'd been hiding in the long grass, then canopy her eyes with her hands to get her bearings. When she saw her father, she called out to him and waved madly until Guy returned her salutation.

''Where's Jake?'' he called back.

Ashli made a jabbing motion toward a spot a few feet to her right. ''Keep an eye on him,'' Guy reminded her, which brought the little girl's hands up on her hips and an exaggerated head shake.

''I take it she thinks you're being overprotective?''

"What she thinks is, that I'm interfering. Between being a girl and being the oldest, not to mention…" He hesitated, then continued. "Not to mention her conviction that the role of mother was accorded to her when her own mother walked out, she watches over her little brothers like a cross between Mother Theresa and Rambo. At least, when she's not jumping down their throats."

Elizabeth dodged another bee, then said, "They're good kids, aren't they?"

That got a pair of raised eyebrows and a crooked grin. "They're mine," he said, letting the squirming toddler have his freedom again. "I'd think they were great no matter what. But they're kids." He batted at a clump of overripe wildflowers at the edge of the road, dusting both of them with a cloud of seeds. "Which means they're messy and they fight with each other in these awful, nerve-shattering, piercing little voices and they have far more energy than any normal adult should have to endure."

She wasn't sure if he was trying to protect her—or issuing her a challenge. She wasn't sure of much, at the moment.

Picking fluffy seeds off the front of her dress, she asked quietly, "But *you* would never leave them, would you?"

Another wondering look. "Never." They'd come to the edge of one of the meadows, bordered by a rotting fence. Guy cautiously leaned against it, the splitting timber creaking under his weight. "Which reminds me of our earlier discussion."

Elizabeth demurred leaning against the unstable wood. "Which discussion was that?" she asked, impatiently pushing back a strand of hair that was tickling her left eyebrow.

"About my being ruthless."

She started snickering again.

"Oh, geez, forget the damn squirrels, will you?" he said, coloring slightly even as he echoed her laughter. "What I was going to say, before I choked on my foot, was that having these little people all to myself somehow changed my priorities. At first, I thought the best way I could be a daddy was to lug home the biggest kill, and any way I could bag that kill was okay. As long as it was legal, anyway. And I did some pretty impressive bagging, I must say. Got me a nice cave to put it all in and everything. Then, suddenly, I had to be Daddy *and* Mommy, and it began to dawn on me that there was a whole lot more to all this than even I realized. But it's taken me nearly a year and a half to figure out what, exactly, *all this* was." He stopped.

"And have you?" Elizabeth encouraged.

"I think maybe," he said, not looking at her. "Shoot, I don't know if this even makes sense to anyone but me...."

"Try me," she said with a smile. "I'll let you know."

He laughed. "I'm sure you will. Okay—" He twisted around, his expression intent. "What does every human being want? Security, right? Safety. Contentment. And I thought I had it—money in the bank, the nice house, the family, the whole nine yards. Suddenly, all I had was the kids. And, not so suddenly, it occurred to me that security comes from doing what feels...*right,* not necessarily what makes the most sense."

He nodded toward the field. "So I came back to someplace where my kids can see land instead of buildings, where their view of the sky won't be interrupted by anything but trees and birds. My old life-style had outlived its usefulness, but it took me a long time to realize the world wasn't going to fall in on itself if I tried something different." The light breeze teased his hair when he looked at her again. "So does it? Make sense?"

His words had bumped into a mental bruise she hadn't known she had. A particularly tender one, too, judging from how much the impact hurt. "Yes," she said, her eyes burning. "It does."

He lifted one hand to her face, but she abruptly turned. "Elizabeth—?"

"I just got some dust in my eye," she said, cursing herself for using the sorriest excuse in the book. "I'm fine."

"You sure—?"

"*Yes.*" She pressed a finger to her eyelid for a moment, then sniffed. "There. All gone." She turned to him. "You were saying?"

A beetled brow told her he still didn't believe her, but he at last looked away. Crossing his arms, he leaned more heavily on the fence, squinting into the morning sunshine which warmed his hair to a coppery bronze. "Anyway, since I came back here for land that looked like this... Well, I just hope this developer feels the same way." He slanted a slightly apologetic glance in her direction. "Don't get me wrong. I'm delighted this project landed in the agency's lap. Money may not be everything, but poverty holds no appeal, either. As long as one thing isn't sacrificed for the other..."

He turned to her, pulling her into those impossibly blue eyes with an intensity both urgent and unmistakable. "I just want the best for my kids. And little by little, I'm learning to trust that I might not be able to predict exactly what that's going to entail."

Inexperienced or not, Elizabeth wasn't a fool. She needed to stop this craziness before it went any further. She'd known this man for less than a day, and already he was shattering her composure, her resolve, her prided ability to be logical, practical, wise. But all she knew was even his casual touch was enough to electrify her all the way to her toes. One could even say the sensation was a lot like...sparks. But the children...

Their existence took precedence over sparks.

They *were* nice children, as far as children went. Beautiful children with sweet faces, Ashli's haunted, too old, too hurt. She ached for those kids, for what they'd lost. And Guy was absolutely right. Of course they deserved the best.

But Elizabeth wasn't it. She was as sure of that as she was that their father was one very special guy, and how, if things were different...

If she was different...

But they weren't and she wasn't and there was no point dwelling on things that weren't going to happen. That she wasn't going to *let* happen.

"I need to get to the office," she said, turning back toward her car. "Mother will be wondering where I am."

He'd tried—desperately—to remind himself why he couldn't...

Why they shouldn't...

Ah, hell.

When he'd touched her a little while ago, it was everything he could do not to pull her into his arms and find out just how kissable that mouth of hers really was. He absently rubbed his own mouth at the thought. What *was* this? He hadn't even dated since Dianne had left. No time, no interest, no money. Women had come on to him, even knowing about the kids, but not one of them had stirred as much as his pinky.

This one had stirred all sorts of things.

Still, he wasn't ready. Neither was Ashli, he was certain.

Still again, he'd cracked that brittle composure, made her laugh. He'd also, in the space of twenty minutes, made her angry, confused and regard him as if wondering where he'd parked the spaceship.

He'd scared her to death, too. He was sure of it. And that was the last thing he'd intended. He'd seen her furtively wipe first one cheek, then the other, with the tips of her fingers as she'd walked away. He'd said her name, like a prayer, feeling a decided prick right smack in the center of his heart.

Again, he told himself this was stupid, crazy, pointless. To give it up, before he let something happen that would only cause heartache.

Again.

He called the children; instantly, it seemed, they were at the car, hot and panting and breathless with giggles.

Problem was, unlike Elizabeth, Guy could never tell his heart and head apart. Which undoubtedly accounted for some of the more major screwups of his life. But, he pondered as he strapped everybody into their seats—rubbing noses with Ashli, tickling Jake, getting a big kiss from Micah—if even the worst screwup could produce by-products such as these…

Heart, he thought, *do your stuff.*

Avoidance may not have been Elizabeth's usual method for dealing with problems, but Guy brought out the worst in her. She took the long way back into town, trying to convince her stomach to uncoil, praying Guy had an appointment or something and wouldn't have to be at the office the rest of the day. The rest of the week.

No such luck.

They pulled up in front of the office within a breath of each other. There were no other cars in the tiny lot, which meant her mother was out and apparently the new temp had not yet arrived. Her mobile burred next to her just as she reached for the door handle; by the time she'd hung up from the wrong number, Guy had come around to her window, squatting eye level with her.

"We need to talk."

"About what?" She pushed open her door, making him jump out of the way.

"What just happened out there."

They were less than a foot apart, sandwiched between their two cars. In the oppressive humidity, Guy's aftershave enveloped her like a hug.

"I have no idea what you're talking about," she said after too long a pause, then shouldered past him toward the front door.

His fingers on her arm scorched through her sleeve. "Elizabeth—"

She wheeled to him, exasperated. Unnerved. *"What?"*

"I know I'm not imagining this, what's happening here—"

"But that's *exactly* what you're doing," she parried, twisting out of his grasp. "Imagining things. Look, this is very… flattering. You're nice and all that…" She screwed up her mouth. "Very nice. But I'm just not interested, okay?" She started again toward the door.

"Not interested?" she heard behind her as she dug in her purse for the office key. "Or not interested in me?"

Where is that damn key? And who gave you permission to smell so good?

"Both." The key found, she fumbled getting it into the lock.

"Geez, woman… Have you ever, even once, just gone with the flow?"

"No," she said, refusing to look at him. "Now, if you don't mind, this is a pointless conversation."

The humidity-swollen door finally flew open with a *wrrannnk;* she headed straight to her desk. Guy followed, checked the answering machine. She could hear the messages from where she was, and she knew he knew that, but he jotted them down anyway, dropped them on her desk on the way to his.

"Thank you," she mumbled. "You didn't have to do that."

"I know I didn't," Guy said, sliding into the chair behind his desk. "But I did. So could you just accept it and not make a big deal out of it?"

"I'm not making a big deal out of anything—"

The front door opened, giving Elizabeth a convenient excuse to end a conversation likely to get her into more trouble the longer she stayed in it.

"Hello?" called out a rich, dark voice. "Anyone here?"

Elizabeth rose to meet the imposing specimen wearing a Kathie Lee two-piece and a gleaming smile set in a round mahogany-hued face. Eyes a surprising shade of silvery-gray scanned the office, then Guy and Elizabeth, like a metal detector at the airport.

"May we help you?"

"I think you got that backward, honey." The woman extended a hand tipped with pigeon-blood nails. "Cora Mitchell. The agency sent me over."

"Oh...the temp?"

"That's right." She trundled over to the reception desk, began opening and closing drawers. "This my desk?"

"Uh, yes..."

"Okay, it'll do. Now, if one of you can give me twenty minutes to take me through the computer programs and the files, we're in business." The phone rang. Cora immediately answered it, looked over. "If you're Guy Sanford, it's for you."

Elizabeth sighed. At least *something* was going right.

Her peaceful feeling lasted for about ten minutes, until Guy finished his call, sank back against his desk chair, and stared a hole through her as she went about getting Cora settled in. Her face warmed, and she knew he could see her panic, her confusion. Why was she suddenly longing for something she honestly hadn't ever felt she'd needed? And certainly knew she didn't want?

And what in God's name was she supposed to do about it?

Fortunately, her mother soon arrived, followed by the developer and architect for Shadywoods. Immensely grateful for something to focus on besides Guy Sanford, she settled herself at the conference table in her mother's office.

Go with the flow. Good one. With her luck, she'd just end up getting washed out to sea.

The longer the meeting went on, Guy noticed, the more palpable Elizabeth's fury became. This time, however, it wasn't directed at him.

He couldn't believe the travesty of a design himself. *Bim bam boom*—bulldoze the trees, plow under the fields, build where the forests were, rather than in the meadows. And, from what he could see, it was all completely unnecessary. But every alternative Guy suggested that might have preserved the integrity of the space was shot down as being impossible.

"The plans are in place," Will McAfee, the architect—a round little man with colorless hanks of hair hanging over each ear like a faded cocker spaniel—insisted, slamming shut his portfolio. "We're in a time crunch here. Need to get ground broken immediately if we're to get these models up by Labor Day."

Guy had to hand it to the sizzling woman at his elbow— she'd kept quiet much longer than he'd expected her to. Now, however, she popped, like a single, sudden bottle rocket. "Couldn't you at least *consider* Mr. Sanford's suggestions?"

Her mother made a startled sound, something between a gasp and a nervous laugh. "Elizabeth, dear, this isn't our land, you know—"

"But they're ruining it, Mother."

"Elizabeth!" Maureen sucked in a quick breath, flicked a smile at the developer, Hugh Farentino. "We're just being hired to sell the finished product."

"Garbage though it may be."

Her outburst was met with stunned silence. Guy hid his smile behind his hand.

"Well," the developer, a kindly, handsome man in his fifties with whom Guy had previously worked on a project outside Chicago, said at last, "If you have a problem with what we're doing, there's no obligation. I'm sure we could find another Realty company to handle things for us—"

"That won't be necessary," Maureen interjected with a too bright smile, then turned to Elizabeth. "Will it, dear?"

Seconds passed. Tension crackled. Mother and daughter stared at each other. Then, "No," Elizabeth said at last. "I'm sorry for interrupting the meeting." She offered a tight smile to Farentino. "Please...continue."

Whether it was wise or not, Guy squeezed Elizabeth's hand under the table, answering the resultant questions in her eyes with a wink. Not surprisingly, she yanked her hand away. In fact, he could practically hear the growl.

"May I ask what the hell that was all about, young lady?"

McAfee and Farentino had cleared out of her mother's office a few minutes before, Guy right on their heels. Her mother had followed as well—to smooth potentially ruffled feathers, if her current ticked-off state was any indication. Now she was back, twin spots of color staining cheeks underneath eyes hot enough to start a fire.

Unable to settle on any one emotion—eerily similar to trying to decide what to wear to a party—Elizabeth stood, smoothing her skirt. "I'm sorry—"

"Sorry doesn't cut it. You just damn near cost us an account I've been fighting to get for nearly a year!"

"But those plans are preposterous—!"

"Be quiet, Elizabeth." Maureen's hands flew up. "For once in your life, just...be quiet. This may come as a shock, missy, but you can't always make everything go your way." Her mother stepped closer, her flushed skin more pronounced against the pale gray of her blouse. "Once before, I gave up something that meant a great deal to me in order to make you happy. But you were just a kid, and I thought I was doing the right thing. You're not a kid anymore, and I'll be *damned* if I'm going to give in to you this time.''

"I'm not asking you to give in to me, for heaven's sake! It's not as if I'm saying give up the contract—"

"You might as well have. I had to do some mighty fast talking out there just now to convince them we were a hundred percent behind the project.'' She raised one hand to her chest, shaking slightly. ''Now you listen to me—this is *my* baby, and I'm not giving it up. I don't care if there's not a sapling left on that land, Elizabeth. I will not lose this project. Do you hear me? I will *not*.''

Without waiting for a response, her mother stormed out of her office.

It had been easier than Guy had hoped to get the developer to listen to his proposal. As he suspected, if given the right equipment, the man would opt to play fair. But Guy had exactly twenty-four hours to prove his hunch was correct.

Maureen whizzed past him when he came back in, her color high underneath her foundation and powder. He glanced into her office to see Elizabeth staring out the far window at the ivy scrambling up the wall of the dry cleaners next door. Her back was more rigid than usual; didn't take much to figure out she and her mother had had "words," as his own mother would say. He came up behind her, skimming the edge of his tie between his thumb and forefinger to keep from touching her.

"It's just a bunch of trees,'' she said before he could speak, not looking at him. Her voice vibrated with a mélange of emotions—disappointment, frustration, resignation, confusion. "And Michigan has plenty of trees. It's stupid to try to hang on to them.''

"Not if it means that much to you,'' he said quietly.

"Yes, it is. Mother's right. It's going to happen anyway, and there's nothing I can do to stop it.'' Her arms still crossed, she pivoted away from him and briskly crossed to the door, her slip rustling angrily against her legs as she walked. He suspected she was about to cry, didn't want him to see.

"Elizabeth?''

She turned to him, her hand resting against the doorjamb, her only response a slight tilt of her head.

"Can I buy you a cup of coffee?"

Her mouth tightened. "I meant what I said, out by the car."

"It's only coffee, Elizabeth," he said, more irritably than he intended. He calmed himself before he continued. "You're upset, and I just thought getting out of the office for a few minutes would do you some good."

For a moment, something sparked in her eyes, and he thought—hoped—she'd change her mind. But, as if convincing herself, she shook her head. "I…can't," she said, sidestepping Maureen as they crossed paths in the doorway.

Guy just stood there.

"Heavens," Maureen said as she made her way to her desk. "You, too?"

He regarded his employer as if in a fog. "I beg your pardon?"

She started riffling through some papers on her desk, not looking at him. "You going to give me a hard time about the development, too?" She straightened out the papers, laying them carefully on one side of her desk, then leaned both palms on its top. "Are the plans really that bad?"

"What? Actually…" He came to for a second. "Yes, they are. Elizabeth isn't steamed for nothing. But I may have a way of working that out…." The sentence, and his attention, drifted off. Through the open door, he could see Elizabeth sitting at her desk, going through the motions of working.

Maureen came out from behind her desk to stand beside him, her gaze following the path his had taken. "Ah," she said with a little nod, then poked him in the arm before returning to her desk and retrieving her purse from the bottom drawer.

"Come on," she said, slamming shut the drawer. "Time you and I had a little chat."

Chapter 5

Lakeside Diner might've been snazzy once, maybe, in the fifties, but now it was just tired. Vestiges of its former glory lurked everywhere—the gouged red-and-black checkerboard linoleum floor, the chipped Formica soda fountain and booths, the red-vinyl booth seats, replete with the occasional duct-tape patch. But the food was great and the prices were low, according to Maureen, and that's all anyone really cared about.

Guy sat in the booth across from Elizabeth's mother, stirring three packets of sugar into his coffee and trying to ignore the patch on the back of her seat, not sure whether to resent or be grateful for the woman's interference. And interfering was exactly what she was doing. Taking great delight in it, too, if the gleam in those golden eyes accounted for anything.

She ripped open a packet of Sweet 'n' Low and dumped it into her decaf. "My daughter's a real piece of work, isn't she?"

Guy remembered the nettled expression on Elizabeth's face when she saw the two of them leave together, allowed a half smile. "I take it you had a fight?"

"Guy, sometimes I think the only thing that's going to get

through to that girl is a damn two-by-four.'' He had to laugh. ''You know what I'm talking about, don't you?''

''I've noticed she tends to be a touch—''

''Anal,'' Maureen supplied. ''You're attracted to her anyway, aren't you?''

Lack of an answer was as good as one, as far as Maureen was concerned.

Over the tinkle of her spoon against the thick crockery cup, she said, ''And this is a problem because…?''

He felt a rueful grin twist his mouth. ''Because I'm fresh out of two-by-fours. Only…'' Leaning back against the tufted seat, he hissed a sigh between his teeth. ''I think I'm the who needs to be hit upside the head. I'm hardly a prime catch.''

She scrutinized him through expertly mascaraed lashes. ''Meaning the children?''

He nodded. ''Something tells me she doesn't play a clown for kids' birthday parties in her spare time, does she?''

For a long moment, Maureen seemed to be fascinated by the tiny whirlpool of coffee swirling in her cup. Then she replied, ''Nope.''

For a moment, hearing his suspicions confirmed, Guy felt as if the bottom of his stomach had been ripped out. He let his gaze wander out the window next to their booth, concentrating on the mass of white petunias spilling over the sides of the planter on the edge of the sidewalk. ''Three kids is an awful lot to ask someone to take on—''

''Guy.''

He shifted his attention back to Maureen, and saw a combination of concern and devilment dancing in those sparkling eyes. ''Ever since Elizabeth was little, she's had this damnably annoying habit of latching on to preconceived notions, about herself, about other people, too, and hanging on to them like a burr sticks to the underside of a dog.'' Worrying one of the mutilated sweetener packets, she said, ''She's never been around children very much. Being an only child, with no cousins, even, to play with or grow up with, she just doesn't know what to do with them.'' She leaned over, lowering her voice to a conspiratorial hush. "Frankly, I think they simply *scare* her."

"Tell her she's got plenty of company."

"As if anyone could tell that girl anything," Maureen said with a grimace. Now she snagged Guy's wrist with her fingertips. "Sometimes, I have this almost uncontrollable urge to go mess up her desk. Put the paper clips in the top drawer instead of the middle. Push the phone two inches farther to the right." With a bright laugh, she added, "Turn her calendar pages back three days!"

He grinned at the impeccably put-together woman in front of him, feeling a little better. "I had no idea I was working for such a revolutionary."

Toying with her pearls, Maureen's gaze drifted toward the counter for a moment, then back to Guy. "This...*compulsion* of hers to always get her own way..." She shook her head. "It's always been there, I suppose, but ever since her father's death, when she was twelve, she's been driving me nuts. She never just does something—she has to consider all her options, pick everything to death." Her shoulders hitched under her silver silk shell. "It's time somebody shook that girl up a bit."

Guy realized he was accordion-pleating his napkin, pushed it away. His stomach was not taking kindly to the extra acid this conversation was producing. "And why do you think I'm what your daughter needs?"

She angled her head at him. "You don't think so?"

"Hardly."

"Because of the kids?"

"In part."

Her brows lifted, expecting more. Guy didn't deliver. Maureen either understood or decided to bide her time.

"I love my daughter, Guy," she said instead. "But I don't like what she's become, what she's doing to herself. Or what she'll end up being if she doesn't snap out of whatever it is she's in."

"And what is that?"

"Alone."

He stared at his coffee, wondering what he was supposed

to say. He needn't have bothered, because Maureen was more than prepared.

"I was exactly like Elizabeth when I was younger. Determined to be perfect, or what I thought perfect was. I was always punctual, always dressed just so, always had to be in charge. And on the surface, everything *was* perfect. Except for one thing." She took a careful sip of her coffee, then soundlessly settled the cup back onto the saucer. "I was lonelier than the Maytag repairman, because nobody'd put up with my obnoxious compulsiveness for very long."

Maureen Louden was one of the most charming people Guy had ever met. He couldn't imagine her ever being obnoxious or anything close to it. "What happened?"

"The summer between my junior and senior year of college, I was working in the dining room at an upstate resort." She laughed. "I wasn't too proud to waitress, but I kept getting irritated with the customers because they wouldn't finish a particular course in the amount of time *I* thought it should be finished, or place their silverware *properly* on the plates when they were finished. Anyway, one Sunday, a couple and their son, a young man I guessed to be maybe five or so years older than I, stopped for dinner as they were passing through the area. This was in the late sixties, remember. The parents were conservative enough, but their son! Hair to his shoulders, and a shirt loud enough to be heard to Ottawa tucked into a pair of hip-hugging bell bottoms. *And* platform shoes, thank you very much. The boys I dated—when I did date—were all very Ivy League. You know, white shirts, narrow ties, chinos, loafers. And *short* hair." She sliced the air sideways with a flat hand. "*Always.* Well—" she leaned forward "—wouldn't you know, the family sat in my station, so I was forced to wait on this *creature.*"

She sat up straighter in her seat, acting out her part with exaggerated facial expressions and dramatic gestures. "I stomped over to the table, *whipped* out my order pad, and glared at this cretin, fully intending to humiliate him so much he'd feel like vanishing underneath the table." A giggle bubbled up out of her throat. "There was only one flaw in my plan—he looked back. With a pair of the most beautiful green eyes I'd ever seen. And, to make it worse, he smiled. I was completely, totally *gone*.'' She batted her eyes, then chuckled. ''Then *he* was gone, and I was a wreck. All I could think about was those eyes, and his smile, and how I'd probably never see either of them again. Then, the next weekend, what does he do but show up, by himself, and plunk himself down at the same table.'' With a blush, Maureen sighed. ''I didn't glare at him this time.''

Guy smiled. ''This is Elizabeth's father we're talking about, isn't it?''

''Mm-hm,'' Maureen said dreamily, and Guy noticed the woman's face had shed twenty years in the course of the conversation. ''Andrew took me out of myself, showed me what love was, what *life* was.'' She angled her head and said, almost in wonder, ''I didn't change, not really. I simply discovered parts of myself I didn't know were there.''

Suddenly, the dreaminess in her expression vanished like a quickly dispersing fog. ''I'm a firm believer in Fate, Guy. I knew there was a reason you were the only person to answer my ad, although I had no idea what that was. The minute I met you, however, I knew.'' She laughed. ''Or, should I say, the minute I saw Elizabeth's reaction to you, I knew. She sure as hell never looks like that when she talks about Rod.''

''Rod?''

''Some guy she's been 'dating,' if you can call it that, for a couple of years. Hotshot Detroit marketing executive. Cars or something…'' She waved her hand, as if the subject wasn't even worth bringing up. Except she had, hadn't she?

He finished off his coffee, which had coagulated into a cold, sweet syrup at the bottom of his cup, then clattered the cup into the thick saucer in front of him. ''You don't really know me, Mrs. Louden.''

She leaned over, her mouth screwed up. ''The name's Maureen. And honey, the way Elizabeth looks at you, I know all I need to.''

''It's about these three kids…''

It's about the fact that I screwed up one marriage already....

"Oh," Maureen said, her brows pinching together. "Right. Well," she said, snatching up the Guest Check before Guy could get to it, "this just calls for a little creativity, that's all.... Hey! Do the children like museums?"

"Uh, yeah...I suppose..."

"Great," she said, then blinked. "What are you doing on Saturday?"

Guy literally grabbed Elizabeth when she arrived the next morning.

"What are you do—?"

"Come here. I've got something to show you." He dropped his hand from her arm and turned back to his desk, expecting her to follow.

She didn't.

He looked up from the comps spread out on his desk and caught the ambivalence in her eyes, which this morning were nearly the same shade of aqua as her aqua silk suit. He also noticed the circles underneath them. "You feeling okay?"

"What?" Nervous fingers stroked an imaginary wisp of hair from her forehead. "Yes, I'm fine. Why?" She walked deliberately to her desk and tucked her handbag inside the bottom drawer.

"You look tired."

"I am. I...don't sleep well when it's hot."

"You don't have air-conditioning?"

"Of course I have air-conditioning. But the hum keeps me awake sometimes." For a couple of seconds, she pinched the bridge of her nose between her fingers, then let her hand fall to her side. "There was something you wanted to show me?"

"Oh—yes." Guy hesitated, then leaned on his desk in her direction. "If you come over to my desk, I promise I won't snap your bra strap." The minute the words were out of his mouth, he knew he was in big trouble.

Her gaze zinged to his, splinters of aquamarine light sparkling in her eyes. Guy rubbed his hand over his face. "That was a stupid thing to say. I apologize.'' He ventured a glance in her direction. ''But I really do have something to show you, and I really will behave.'' He gestured toward his desk. ''Please?''

Tugging at her jacket hem, she crossed the five feet between their desks as if she expected a canned snake to pop out at her. ''What is it?''

''You sold a couple of homes in Devon Copse last year, right?''

''Yes...''

''And also several over in Brighton Lake.''

She nodded, a hint of a frown playing on her brow. ''What...?''

''What was the difference between the developments?''

''Is this a quiz?''

''Just humor me.''

Suspicion darted from her eyes, but after a moment she said, ''Well...Devon had been developed with land covenants, so much of the natural terrain was preserved. Brighton's land had been clear-cut before building began.''

''Both developments opened six years ago, right?''

''I believe so, yes...''

''And, at the time, the property values were roughly the same.''

Elizabeth shrugged. ''I really don't know. I wasn't around then. Guy, would you please come to the point? I have work to do.''

''They were,'' Guy supplied, waving printouts with the appropriate figures so close to her face she grabbed them in order to keep from getting whacked. Then he handed her another printout.

''These are comps on the homes you sold last year. Same approximate square footage, same basic amenities, comparable neighborhoods. What's different?''

He waited while Elizabeth scanned the lists in front of her. ''The selling prices. Devon's values are, what? Twenty-two, twenty-four percent higher?''

''Twenty-six percent, on average.'' Guy smacked the paper

Elizabeth was holding. "And all because of the landscaping. People will pay more for established, natural terrain. Devon even has a stable and riding and hiking trails, maintained by the community itself. Don't you see? It's to Farentino's financial advantage to preserve as much of the natural surroundings as possible."

With a sigh, Elizabeth sat on the edge of Guy's chair, her hand splayed on her chest. "You're preaching to the converted, Guy. I already know this. But McAfee—"

"Is a greedy fool," Guy interjected, taking no small delight in watching her trim brows sneak up past her glass frames. "I found out he's the planner on three other simultaneous projects spread over several hundred miles. He's virtually duplicated the layout for another development near Lansing in order to save himself some time."

The brows went up even farther. "How on earth do you know this?"

"Sources, my dear," he said, easing a hip onto the corner of his desk. "Lots of sources. And a little searching on the Internet. McAfee has websites on all his projects. Didn't take much to find out the man has those ample little fingers in way too many pies. McAfee is history, if the tone of Farentino's voice tells me anything…what?"

Elizabeth was shaking her head, a smile beginning to tug at lips the color of one of his mother's prize roses. "In one day, you did all this?"

"I am nothing if not amazing, my dear."

"Ah. Modest, too."

"Of course."

She sighed, looking at all the papers spread over his desk. "They're really willing to redesign? That means a substantial delay in the project."

"A month, maybe. Once I pointed out the possibilities of a twenty-percent increase in the property valuation, Farentino couldn't very well find a reason to object. And, as I suspected, the man has no desire to be known as one of 'those' developers who only wants to make a buck." With a grin, Guy added, "This way he gets to make his bucks and make every-body happy, too."

Elizabeth looked away, back at the papers in front of her. "Just like you will."

He hooked one knuckle under her chin and tilted her face toward his. "That's what I do, Elizabeth," he said. "It's what you do, too."

He could practically hear the wheels whirring in her head as she met his gaze. "And who were you trying to make happy here?" she asked after several seconds, then twisted away from his hand, carefully placing the papers on his desk as she rose. "For the sake of the land, for the sake of future generations, I'm thrilled. But, please," she said as she returned to her own desk, "ditch the White Knight routine. It won't work."

Mouth gaping open, hand still poised in the air, he watched her walk away. "Damn, lady," he said, almost amused. "You're impossible, you know that?"

Her eyes glittered when she met his gaze. "And you'll do well to remember that, Mr. Sanford."

She'd done it. She'd broken up with Rod and lived to tell about it. Sorta.

"Hey, blondie—you awake?"

Now all she had to do was face Nancy.

Her head buried underneath the navy blue pillows on Nancy's sofa bed, she lay very still, playing possum. She loved Nancy, she really did. But the woman was going to want to Talk. Elizabeth was not ready.

In truth, she'd been awake for the better part of an hour, wallowing in a quagmire of self-pity. Not that there was any reason, she supposed. After all, she'd should've cut the cord months ago. But Rod's lack of surprise, his mild disappointment had irked her, she had to admit. I mean, *really*—couldn't he have at least made her feel bad about dumping him? But then, that wasn't Rod's style. In fact, he'd even said he was still interested in the Hancock mansion and would Tuesday be convenient to see it?

No muss, no fuss—one useless relationship, neatly excised from her life.

Just in time to face another one just as useless. Even if far more…intriguing.

She silently groaned, not easy to do into a pillow. Guy couldn't help her out by being ugly and gross and mean, *nooo.* Uh-uh, he had to be *nice.* Considerate. Kind. And that's just when he was around.

When he *wasn't* around, she missed him and his eyes and his smiles and even his bizarre *ties,* for God's sake, because…because they made her feel good.

Dumb, dumb, dumb.

Then there was that portrait of the kids on his desk, she thought as she carefully shifted the pillow so she could breathe. Sheesh. Every time she got up to go to the water cooler, they watched her. Those cute little smiles, so hopeful, so ingenuous. Yeah, right—like she didn't know what lay behind those innocent grins. Like the kind of blind trust that makes a child believe her parents will always be there for her, that her love will always be returned, that the pain she feels when that trust is shattered may never go away. The image of that portrait stayed with her as clearly as if she had a copy in her wallet.

She couldn't trust that much. She simply couldn't—

"Hey, get your butt out of bed!" Something flat and hard whacked Elizabeth's bottom through the bedclothes.

"Ouch!" Elizabeth yelped, rubbing her backside but refusing to open her eyes. "Go away. It's still dark."

Nancy yanked the pillow off Elizabeth's head and threw it across the room before she could grab it again. "Whaddya know? The sun just came up."

Elizabeth shimmied down underneath the covers and was rewarded with another thwack. This time, she identified the weapon as the morning paper. "Get *up,* ya bum. It's after nine. I wanna get to the museum before the crowds hit."

Elizabeth yawned and tried to open one eye. When she saw the cup of coffee steaming six inches in front of her nose, she opened the other one, as well. She slowly sat up and took the proffered cup, sighing after the first swallow. Then she squinted at her friend standing in front of her, already dressed in her T-shirt and size five Calvins, an explosion of nearly-black hair fanning around her shoulders. Nancy had landed in Detroit from New Jersey six years ago, courtesy of a husband long since consigned to oblivion. Over thirty and none too pleased about it, the woman was determined to shop, date, and party until she dropped or ran out of people to keep her company, whichever came first. Nancy was far too alive. Far too awake. Far too *here*.

Elizabeth put down the cup and flopped over onto her side again. "Come back next week."

"Nothing doing." Elizabeth could tell Nancy had returned to the kitchen. "It's been three months since we've spent the weekend together," came the disembodied Jersey twang, "and I'll be damned if you're going to spend it on my sofa bed."

She was doomed. Elizabeth tried to focus out the window. The sky, from what she could see through Nancy's partially opened verticals, was crisp blue; the air coming in the open window fairly cool. Chilly, almost. One of those midsummer days hinting of fall. A gorgeous day, a perfect day. A day she wanted to have nothing to do with. "I really don't feel up to the museum today."

"Sure, you do," Nancy said, handing her a bagel with cream cheese. "You're not awake yet. Not even sex sounds good when you're still asleep."

That got a little laugh.

"Yes, folks. She breathes, she eats, she laughs. She even breaks up with guys who aren't her type and lives to tell about it." With that, Nancy sat down on the edge of the bed and raised one dark eyebrow.

"There's nothing to tell, Nance. Although..." Elizabeth took a bite of bagel and warily eyed her friend. "How come you're not all over me about lost opportunities? You couldn't say enough good about the man when I started dating him."

Nancy hid behind her own coffee, her dark-lashed mahogany eyes not quite meeting Elizabeth's. Then she shrugged. "Hey, I married a guy I thought was perfect, then found out

I didn't want perfect. I wanted *right*. You know? Right for *me*. If Rod wasn't right for you, who am I to say differently, huh? Besides, something tells me—'' she wagged her finger ''—your Prince Charming is waiting right around the corner for you.''

Elizabeth smirked. ''And what if I'm not in the market for a Prince Charming?''

This time the eyes met hers straight on. ''Then I'd say your brain needs some serious retooling, *bubelah*.'' Nancy glanced over at the clock on the VCR and swatted Elizabeth's legs. ''Get a move on. We gotta get outta here.''

''It's a museum, not a flight. What's the big hurry?''

Nancy averted her eyes again, and this time Elizabeth thought she saw a smile tweak at the corners of her friend's mouth. ''I just want to avoid the crowds. Like I said.''

Elizabeth stared at her friend until the inevitable blush crept up Nancy's neck. ''Uh-huh. *Now* I get it. This is a setup, isn't it?''

Nancy turned to her, all eyes and innocence. ''Please—give me a *little* credit.'' She did her best to sound offended. Elizabeth didn't buy it for a second. ''Have I ever set you up with someone you didn't know without filling you in first?''

Around a bite of bagel, Elizabeth mumbled, ''Other than your cousin?''

''That doesn't count. He came in unexpectedly. I was desperate.''

''Gee, thanks.''

''Other than that.''

After a deep sigh, Elizabeth shook her head. ''No. I guess not.''

Nancy placed her hand over her heart, bloodred nails shimmering in the morning sunshine. ''I swear I have not arranged a blind date for you, nor will we 'just happen' to run into a friend of mine in the museum. Okay?''

''Blood oath?''

''Blood oath.''

Still skeptical, Elizabeth pushed the last bite of the bagel into her mouth and finally hauled herself out of bed, combing out the tangles in her hair with her fingers as she started toward the bathroom.

"God, I'd kill for hair like yours," she heard over the creaking of the sofa bed mechanism as Nancy closed it up.

Elizabeth pulled her ratted hair out on either side of her face. "*This?* Why?"

"Because, *A,* it's like the color of moonlight, which men find really, really sexy. Don't ask me why, but they do. And, *B,* it's gorgeous. Why do you insist on keeping it up all the time? Come here, come here…"

Nancy took Elizabeth by the shoulders, pushing her into her bedroom and in front of a full-length mirror. "With that mane, you look like a damn princess."

Squinting, Elizabeth tried to make out her blurred image, but all she saw was a pale skinny something with a big yellowish something ballooning around the top of it. "I have no idea what I look like. I can't see a thing."

"And while we're on the subject—when you gonna get contacts?"

"I told you, I can't wear them."

"And how long ago did you try? In junior high? They got these things called disposables nowadays, soft plastic, you can't even feel 'em—"

"I'm perfectly happy with my glasses."

"Uh-huh. Whaddya say after the museum, we go get you some contacts?"

"Oh, sure. Just like that."

"Just like that."

"I don't know…"

"You never do. That's why you have me. So shut up and go take your shower. We gotta get there before eleven."

"And *why* do we have to get there before eleven?"

"I told you—"

"To beat the crowds," they said simultaneously, Elizabeth throwing her hands up into the air. Something was up. She knew it. But Nancy had sworn, and while her friend was as devious as a soap opera villain, she wasn't a liar. As Elizabeth headed for the bathroom, Nancy called out behind her, "And for God's sake, leave your hair loose!"

Elizabeth stood in the middle of the museum lobby, studying the floor plan, periodically shoving her loose hair away from her face. Why had she let Nancy have her way? About the hair, the museum, all of it. She had a headache, her feet hurt because she'd forgotten they were coming to the museum and she only had heels, and she was starving. She banged the floor plan against her leg and let out a *whuh* of air.

"Forget it."

Nancy was shuffling through a batch of postcards she'd just bought at the gift shop. "Forget what?" she asked, not looking at Elizabeth.

"Going another step. I've got to sit down and be fed."

"No!"

Elizabeth looked at her friend. "No?"

"I mean, we've just got to get to the armor exhibit before we leave. That's the whole reason I came. As soon as that's done, I promise, lunch and sit. Okay?"

"Nancy..."

"Please? Just that one thing?" She wagged her hand toward Elizabeth's feet. "Take your shoes off. Who'll notice?"

They'd drifted over to the entrance to the cafeteria, and Elizabeth saw seats and smelled food and refused to budge. "Tell you what. *You* go do armor. *I'm* going in there. Meet me later, okay?"

"Well...I guess that'll work. For me," Nancy quickly added with a too perky smile when Elizabeth raised her eyebrows. "Yeah. That'll be just fine." She started to back away. "Okay, then. I'll just be going and...I'll see you later." Then she turned and disappeared behind a cluster of Japanese tourists.

Now Elizabeth *knew* something was up. But, to tell the truth, her feet hurt too much to care. With a soft groan, she hitched her shoulder bag up onto her shoulder and limped into the cafeteria.

* * *

Twelve-oh-three. Guy slid his hand into his pocket and leaned on the stroller handle. Ashli and Jake had looked at each knight so many times they'd started to give them names, had gone to the bathroom twice, and, due to the proximity of the cafeteria, had asked for lunch at least 162 times. Things were just about to get real dicey when a dark-haired woman weighing all of a hundred pounds roared around the corner as fast as her Nikes could take her, grinding to a dead stop in front of him.

"Ohmigod, you *are* gorgeous!" she blurted out, then grinned, her hand on her chest to calm her panting. "I'm sorry," she managed to gasp between pants, then let out a throaty laugh. "Actually, I'm not sorry at all. You *are* Guy Sanford, I hope?"

He grinned. "And if I'm not?"

"Then I'm going to feel *really* stupid."

He somehow doubted it. "I take it you're Nancy?"

"Yeah." She allowed a quick grin for Micah, who was singing to himself about cars and trucks and "air-panes," then glanced around. "Aren't there supposed to be two more kids?"

Guy smiled and nodded over his shoulder, where floor-to-ceiling Diego Rivera murals took up the entire next room. "They're in there. Absorbing their first lessons in the glorification of the American worker."

"Ah." Guy thought he saw actual relief in the deep-brown eyes. "Look, Elizabeth's in the cafeteria. I'm supposed to be over here enthralled with metal body stockings, so I won't be back for at least fifteen minutes. So go for it." As Ashli and Jake reappeared, Nancy moved away, but not before she whispered, "And for God's sake, act surprised."

Guy parked the stroller underneath one of the arches leading from the hallway to the cafeteria, scanning the sea of tables and bodies in front of them in hope of recognizing one of the bodies as Elizabeth's.

"Can we go in?" Ashli whispered as she latched on to his hand. "It's so pretty."

It was. Bricklike walls and floors, thick antique glass windows, and twinkle-lighted fig trees in huge planters in among the tables had transformed the cafeteria into a Disney-esque version of a medieval church courtyard.

"Just a minute, honey," Guy said, still expecting to find the customary French twist. When he finally recognized her, his breath intake was so sharp, Ashli asked what was wrong.

"What?" he responded, uncomprehending, to the puzzled blue eyes. "Oh, nothing, sweetie." He looked back toward Elizabeth. "Nothing."

Nothing, his foot.

Elizabeth shifted in his direction, but not enough to see him. A salad and a cup of something sat on the table in front of her in which she seemed to be only mildly interested; he noticed her slip her hand underneath the loose, glistening hair and rub the back of her neck, then that she'd slipped her high heels off under the table. He smirked.

"Figures," he muttered to himself, steeling himself to make his move.

Then she removed her glasses, and the sadness in her eyes made him gasp a second time.

"Daddy? What's *wrong?* Why do you keep making those funny noises?"

This time, he didn't even try to answer. Elizabeth's myopic state had softened her features, somehow, as it softened her own focus. When the clouds shifted, sending a shaft of sunlight through the glass ceiling, all Guy could think of was how much he envied the sun, being able to enfold Elizabeth in its warmth. In that creamy pantsuit in some soft, drapey fabric, with that pale-gold hair gleaming down her back, she was...an angel. Okay, so it was trite. Dickens, he wasn't.

She rolled her shoulders as if trying to absorb the sunlight, and he winced slightly at her scowl. Oh, hell—he couldn't do this. Whether it was panic or wisdom that impelled his change of heart, he honestly didn't know. But he did know playing games wasn't fair to her, to him, to anybody. If he was attracted to her—which sure seemed a lame term for what he was feeling right now—then he should just take the bull by the damn horns and go for it and forget about the kids and think about *himself* for the first time in God knows how long, but go about things the right way, the honest way, and then trust that everything would somehow work itself out.

Right?

"Come on, guys," he said, turning the stroller around. "Let's go get lunch."

"But there's food *in there*," Jake protested, yanking on Guy's T-shirt.

"I'm too hungry to go anywhere else!" wailed Ashli, to which Jake added an enthusiastic chorus of "Me, toos" that jerked most heads in the vicinity in their direction. In time-honored parental tradition, Guy pretended they weren't his children and swiftly ushered them away.

The sound of infantile shrieking made Elizabeth replace her glasses and twist around just in time to catch the hasty exit of a short blond girl and a shorter dark-haired boy, and a man about Guy's height with brown shoulder-length hair pushing a stroller.

Her heart plummeted into the pit of her stomach, then bounced right back up into her throat. Before she let herself think about what she was doing, she grabbed her bag and ran, in her stockinged feet, toward the arch through which she'd seen them leave.

But by the time she got there, the family was nowhere to be seen. Panting, Elizabeth leaned against one of the limestone columns and slowly pressed her hand to her lips, squeezing shut her eyes as she realized what was happening. Her heart did that trampoline number all over again when she felt someone put a hand on her wrist; for an instant, she thought—hoped?—to see a certain pair of blue eyes when she opened hers.

But the eyes were brown.

"Hey, honey—you okay?" Nancy asked.

Hysterical laughter rocketed out of her throat. *Okay?*

She didn't even know the meaning of the word anymore.

Chapter 6

He didn't understand. Things were getting worse, not better. Yesterday, Monday, Elizabeth said barely a dozen words to him all day. Even her mother had noticed. And commented, subtly. So had Cora, whose comments weren't the least bit subtle.

Okay, fine, if nothing was going to happen, nothing was going to happen. He could deal with it. And God knows his ego had weathered worse. But they needed to hash this out, to come to some sort of understanding if for no other reason than peace in the workplace. To accomplish even that much, however, she had to at least *look* at him. Pretending to check his messages, he watched Elizabeth cross the room to get a file from the lateral cabinet near the front of the office. A sigh slipped out before he could check it; he thought he saw her tense before bending over the file.

Oh, brother. Wrong move, honey, he thought as the simple little jersey dress hugged her derriere, the slit in back revealing just a touch of white lace from the hem of her slip. Look at her. No one else but Elizabeth could make that dress look that sexy.

A little line of concentration marred her brow as she studied a file on her way back to her desk, her movements disseminating a citrusy perfume that perfectly complimented the pale yellow dress, as cool and appetizing as lemon sherbet, clinging just enough to breasts perfectly proportioned to her diminutiveness, just enough over hips perfect for...any number of things. A substantial quantity of blood raced hell-bent-for-leather toward one particular area of his anatomy.

Yowsa. It had been a helluva long time since *that* had happened.

He stretched out his fingers, wrung his hands to get rid of the tingling, wishing there was something socially acceptable he could do to relieve the tingling in other areas. Then he rubbed his face, hard, and forced himself to think about other things.

Like calling Sybil Bennett. He'd put in the bid on the old house on Wednesday but still hadn't heard. The owner had been out of town and was one of those hopelessly old-fashioned types who didn't believe in E-mail or cellular phones or call forwarding. Of course, since the house had been on the market for three years, Guy could understand why the man wasn't hanging around and waiting for the bids to come pouring in.

He'd bid ridiculously low, leading Sybil to confide that the seller had flatly refused offers that low before. Not that she was trying to get him to up his bid, she'd hastily amended when Guy's eyebrow had raised at her intimation. Of course, she was obligated to lay before the seller any offer that came in, and she would. But still...

He checked his watch again, hoping Elizabeth had an appointment soon so he could call Sybil privately. Yeah, she'd said she wasn't going after the house, but if he did get it, something told him discretion wouldn't exactly be a bad thing.

Look at him. The white linen pants were okay, she supposed, but the rest of the outfit? Please. A poppy-red shirt, a canary-yellow jacket, a black-and-white tie with M. C. Escher birds changing into fish back into birds on it. What most annoyed her was that the clothes weren't cheap—he certainly understood quality; it was just *taste* that seemed to be in such frighteningly short supply....

This was nuts. She could try to find fault with Guy's clothes from now until doomsday and it wouldn't mean a thing. It just didn't matter so much anymore.

And that mattered a great deal.

She'd spent a miserable Saturday night, sitting on the floor in front of Nancy's coffee table and sobbing into her moo-shu pork about Guy and his kids and his blue eyes and the shivers she got when he touched her. About how he was everything she didn't need, didn't want, and how could she have let her feelings get so out of hand?

Nancy had listened and commiserated at appropriate points in the one-sided conversation but had said little, which was suspiciously unusual for Nancy. The next morning, Elizabeth drove back home, then spent a miserable Sunday cleaning her apartment and doing her laundry and thinking about Guy and wondering what to do about him and wondering why she was falling for a guy with three kids—*how* she was falling for a guy with three kids—which just seemed so bloody *unfair*.

But that was nothing compared with how miserable she'd been yesterday. When she got to work, Guy had left an exquisite miniature white rose plant on her desk, not because it some special occasion or anything, but just...because.

He had no idea how close she'd come to throwing the plant at him.

So all she did was to say, "Thank you. It's lovely," as politely and noncommittally as she could. And when she looked, which she tried not to but couldn't avoid entirely, she saw the disappointment in his eyes and she hated being the one who put it there.

Oh, Lordy—this went way past ambivalence. All-out terrified *confusion,* is what this was.

She wished she wasn't confused, that her mother hadn't placed that ad, that Guy hadn't answered it, that he didn't have kids, that she lived on Mars.

And to sweeten the pot, Rod was due to show up for his appointment in less than an hour.

Whoop-de-do.

Elizabeth heard Guy shuffle some papers at his desk, make a couple of calls that sounded promising, and chided herself for realizing—again—how much she liked his laugh. She made a couple of calls herself, shuffled some papers of her own, then made that trip to the filing cabinet, pretending to read the file as she walked back to her desk so she wouldn't have to talk to him or look at him or even acknowledge his presence. Somehow, he'd just have to get over her.

Somehow, she'd have to get over *him.*

He seemed to be checking his watch a lot. Not to mention those furtive little glances in her direction. What were those all about?

She heard him get up and go into the bathroom, immediately returning with a filled watering can. As he passed between the desks to get to the plant, his aftershave nearly curled her toes. *Gunk-gunk-gunk* went the water pouring out of the can, followed by an almost comical gurgling as the thirsty soil slurped it up.

Sinking her head into her palm as she wrote, she wondered why Sybil hadn't called yet about the house. The owner was supposed to have returned yesterday, and Sybil had promised to pass along her offer just as soon as she could get the guy to answer the phone. Thinking about the house, what she'd do with it when it was hers, was the only thing keeping her sane at the moment.

Guy walked back into the bathroom, came back out without the can, sat back down. And dropped his stapler into the metal trash can next to his desk.

Elizabeth yelped and jumped a foot, then whirled around to him, her gaze colliding with his as she pressed both palms against her chest. "Why the hell did you do that?"

"Why the hell won't you look at me?"

Because you have bedroom eyes and I don't want to look at your eyes. I can't think straight when you're looking at me, oh, please, look somewhere else or at least put on some damn sunglasses....

"Nothing personal. I've just been busy," she managed to reply over her bucking heart and returned her attention to her computer, wondering if her nose was growing.

Guy leaned over. "Great little screen saver you got there."

"What? Oh!" She clicked her mouse and the computer woke up. "I better reset it so it doesn't come on so quickly, I guess."

"I guess you'd better."

The phone rang. Cora called across the twenty feet to their desks. "Guy? It's for you, baby."

Pushing...everything out of her brain, she focused again on the computer. Let's see...three bedrooms, two baths, single-car garage...

"Miss Louden?"

Startled, she turned to Guy. His expression unreadable, the phone dangled from his hand. She hadn't missed his deliberate use of her last name. "For you."

Had Cora made a mistake? Odd...Cora never made mistakes. In fact, Cora was the only person Elizabeth knew who was more meticulous than she was.

She picked up her phone, slipping off her gold knot earring. As she watched Guy suddenly take off out the front door, she muttered a puzzled, "Hello?" into the phone.

"Liz? Sybil Bennett."

Guy Sanford and his flight vanished from her brain like a puff of cedar pollen. "Sybil! Did he accept? Did he counter—?"

"Liz...I'm so sorry..."

Elizabeth shut her eyes, cringed. How could she not have gotten it? Damn property had been on the market for three freaking years. "What happened?"

"The weirdest thing. After all this time, yours wasn't the only bid. Unfortunately, neither was it the highest."

"Who...?"

"Now, Liz, you know I can't give you a name until it becomes a matter of record at closing, but I thought it might make you feel better to know the house went to a man with kids who recently moved to the area. He just loves the place and wants to restore it—not tear it down or make hideous apartments out of it. Listen, I'm really bummed, but we'll find something else, won't we?'' As if Elizabeth needed Sybil Bennett to look for houses for her. Really.

But as Elizabeth hung up the phone, her pique with the other agent was overshadowed by threatening tears. This is stupid, she argued with herself—it's just a house. A pile of rotten timbers and creaky floors and missing steps. A rosebush that survived without water or Miracle-Gro, all on its own. An unwieldy wisteria that so desperately needed attention. *Her* attention. A bay window that looked across a great front lawn and let in the morning sun, in front of which she'd envisioned herself standing in her jammies, sipping her first coffee, for so long she'd almost thought she'd done it. It had been her house. *Hers!*

And whose house was it *now?*

It didn't hit all at once, but in bits and pieces, like that strange sensation of slow motion when an avalanche starts. ''Of all the lying…cheating…sneaking, low-down weaselly vermin things to do, you rotten, no-good, opportunistic *creep!* No wonder you were in such a split to get out of here. *Coward!*'' Elizabeth shot up from her desk so fast she banged her thigh, eliciting a string of curses that brought Cora running.

''Miss Elizabeth—what is it, honey?''

''Nothing!'' Eyes brimming, she grabbed a tissue from the boutique box on her desk, carefully dabbing underneath her glasses so her makeup wouldn't smear.

Cora folded her arms across an impressive bosom and cocked her head. ''Uh-huh. What he do this time?''

Elizabeth turned her attention to her banged thigh, then tossed the receptionist a perplexed look. ''Who?''

''The man.''

''What man?''

''You tell me. Nothin' else gets a woman going like you are now except a man, you know what I'm saying?''

Elizabeth shook her head and fell back into her chair. ''You don't understand. It's not a man. I just didn't get something I wanted. That's all."

"And a man had nothing to do with it?"

"Not exactly," Elizabeth allowed.

"Uh-huh. And you mean to tell me that the—let me see if I got this straight—the 'rotten, no-good, opportunistic creep' you just sent to the devil and back again isn't a man?" Her laugh filled the entire office. "Hey, *I* understand, just fine," Cora said with a crisp nod. "It's *you* who doesn't understand." She handed Elizabeth a stack of papers. "Edson Mortgage sent these pre-aps over for the Wagners. Figured you wanted them."

With a sigh, Elizabeth took the papers and lay them on the desk in front of her. It was true—she didn't understand. Anything. At all.

His hands fisted in his pockets, Guy loped down the little Charles Wysockian Main Street toward the park, his expression apparently fierce enough to send the gray-haired woman sweeping the sidewalk outside the florist's scurrying for cover behind a display of mixed bouquets. The midday sun seared his scalp, even through his thick hair; would that it would sear his brain as well, burn some sense into him.

Granted, Sybil hadn't actually *said* Elizabeth got the house, just that the highest bid had come from someone who'd been looking at it for a while. Didn't take a rocket scientist, as they say. Funny thing—after close to two years of having everything disintegrate around him, of having nothing go his way, he thought he'd become inured to constant disappointment. But he wasn't, at all. What he was, was damned tired of it.

And he was even more tired of feeling that everything was his fault.

Still muttering to himself, he found himself at the end of a walking trail, surprised to discover he'd already passed through the woods. For several seconds, he stood staring into the trees as if he expected them to part for him, until a little voice whispered, *Yo, Sanford—this has nothing to do with a house.*

No. He was ticked because nothing he was telling himself about Elizabeth was doing a damn bit of good. So let's go over it again, shall we?

He had kids. He had debts. He had a disastrous matrimonial track record. And Elizabeth had enough sense to stay the hell out of his way. The least he could do was return the favor. He tugged in a sharp breath, let it out, determined he was, indeed, still alive.

He could do this.

Guy turned around and headed back, his pace—and his heart rate—somewhat slower than before. Okay, so he'd lost the house. Big deal. He'd just look for another place, right? As far as Elizabeth was concerned, he was going back to the office, congratulate her and then get on with his sorry life.

When he came in, Elizabeth immediately rose from her desk and crossed in front of him to the files, her expression frosty enough to spit ice cubes. Puzzled, he glanced over at Cora, who just shrugged and offered an enigmatic smile.

Elizabeth started back to her desk, mouth tight, nose hoisted. Guy deliberately stood in her way. The mouth thinned even more.

"Excuse me, Mr. Sanford."

He moved, but he didn't understand. She should be thrilled. Not pissed.

His peripheral vision caught the clock on Cora's desk. He had less than a half hour before he had to leave on his appointment.

He followed Elizabeth back into their office. "So, what did Sybil want?"

Elizabeth spun around so fast she nearly knocked into him. "As if you didn't know!"

Wha—? "It wasn't…good news? About the house?"

"Oh, give me a break, Sanford. I know you like to tease, but I hadn't pegged you as someone who could be deliberately cruel." Tears spilled over her lashes, but she was too angry to notice. Or maybe she had noticed, and that made her even angrier. "After I told you how much I wanted that house, for you to go behind my back and make an offer…and *outbid me* in the bargain—''

"Whoa, Nelly!" Stunned, Guy grabbed Elizabeth's shoulders, her skin smooth, fragile, in his palms. He steeled himself, willed his nerve endings to shut the hell up. "You said you weren't going to make an offer! That's the only reason I did." He paused, then spoke more softly. "But I didn't get it, either. I thought you did."

Her mouth dropped. Closed. Opened again. "You didn't get it?"

"Nope. In fact, I was outside having a good old-fashioned childish pout until I realized it meant more to you than it did to me, that *you* meant more to me than the house did, so I came back to congratulate you. And to invite you to dinner."

Who said that?

Elizabeth, apparently, hadn't heard him. Or whoever.

"You didn't get it?" she repeated over Cora's "Yes!" behind them.

He smiled, then dared to skim his palms along her upper arms. Behind the glasses, her eyes widened as her skin went goose bumpy; he lowered his gaze to find other parts of her body had reacted to his touch as well, the thin fabric of her dress revealing more than he was sure Elizabeth wanted him to know. He couldn't help the grin as he met her gaze—set in a face gone a bright shade of pink—once again. "I think we've already established that."

She cleared her throat. "Then who…?"

"I have no idea. Clearly someone who isn't either one of us."

"Maybe the insane person who just invited you to dinner."

Elizabeth pulled away from Guy and walked back to her desk, then fell into her chair. Guy happened to look up to see Cora circling her hand like a parking lot attendant and mugging, "Go *on,* baby" while rolling her eyes in Elizabeth's direction.

Guy then cautiously approached Elizabeth's desk and slid one hip onto the top. And waited. With any luck, she hadn't heard him, Cora wouldn't open her big mouth, and he could get out of this with his pride more or less intact.

After a few seconds, Elizabeth seemed to come to, as if someone had sprinkled water on her. Now she lifted her face to him, her expression a heart-wrenching mixture of wonder and fear, hope and pain.

She'd heard him.

"Elizabeth?" came a deep masculine voice from just inside the doorway. They both turned, startled. Guy took one look at the tall, distinguished man approaching Elizabeth's desk and decided not to stand. No sense pointing out obvious differences. He glanced at Elizabeth and watched her force a smile to almost colorless lips.

"Rod!"

Rod? As in "dating for the past two years," Rod?

"You're early," she said, standing and smoothing her skirt. "Uh, Rod Braden, I'd like you to meet Guy Sanford, my associate. Rod's interested in the Hancock house," she said, keeping her eyes on Rod instead of Guy. No wonder. Rod Braden was the kind of man that made other men wonder why they bothered getting out of bed in the mornings. And he appeared to be pleasant, too, to add insult to injury.

"Nice to meet you," Guy managed, returning the man's firm handshake. Huh. The man was definitely giving him the once-over, as if trying to figure something out.

"Well." Elizabeth's voice was too high, too perky. "Let me give Mr. Hancock a call, see if he's ready for us," she said, picking up her phone.

Guy and Rod exchanged a few words about absolutely nothing, then Guy returned to his desk, raising one eyebrow at Cora who was gawking at Mr. Suave as if she hadn't seen a man in six years. Elizabeth finished her call, then said, "Okay, let's go," grabbing her purse and fixing a smile to her face as she led her "client" to the front door. As they neared the exit, Guy saw Rod take Elizabeth's elbow, as if he had done so many times before. Just before the door closed behind them, Guy distinctly heard the word *honey*. Something very close to jealousy nipped at his composure with sharp, nasty little teeth.

But Cora looked at Guy and shook her head. "Don't believe everything you hear, baby," she said, then went back to her paperwork.

When Guy returned from his appointment a couple hours later, he found Elizabeth in her mother's office, sitting curled up on the leather love seat and staring out the window. Apparently a favorite pastime.

"Where's everyone else?" he asked from the doorway.

"What?" She offered him where-am-I? eyes. "Oh. Mother's showing properties and Cora's out to lunch." Then, on a deep breath, she let her chin drop onto her folded-up arms. "He bought it. Paying cash. Didn't even quibble about the price."

Guy leaned against her mother's desk. "Then why do you sound as if your cat just died?"

"Because I think I just made a really stupid mistake."

"Okay…" He crossed his arms over his chest, deliberately keeping his distance, knowing this tiny glimmer of trust she was showing was as fragile as a cobweb. "Why?"

Now the eyes clouded with worry. "Because…I think he bought the house to be near me. Which I realize sounds a little egotistical, but I'm not stupid." She sighed, looking out the window again. "Not totally stupid, anyway. We…dated for a while."

"I know. Your mother told me."

She gave a groany little laugh, then said, "She tell you we broke up?"

He shook his head. "Uh, who…?"

"I did. And I thought he was cool with it, but now I'm not so sure. He's one of those men who's used to getting what he wants. Eventually. And that's just going to complicate things even more than they already are."

"I see." Guy shifted his weight on the desk. Swallowed. Hoped he was hearing what he thought he was hearing. "And just how…complicated *are* things?"

He could tell by the set of her jaw she was fighting tears again. After a long moment, she finally said, "Very."

The front door to the office rattled open, and they heard Cora muttering something about the long lines and slow clerks as she put away her purse and went about resettling at her desk like a bird returning to its nest. Guy stepped over to the door, quietly shutting it, keeping his hand on the knob while he continued to hold Elizabeth's gaze in his. Then he said, very slowly and very carefully, "And what can I do to help uncomplicate things for you?"

Elizabeth's laugh startled him. "You are aware, aren't you, that you're a major part of the complication?"

"Flatterer."

Inside that remarkable, intelligent, lovely head of hers, a war raged. He saw it in her flushed cheeks, her panicked eyes. She returned her attention to the quivering ivy.

"Why'd you ask me out?"

"Because I don't have a lick of sense," he admitted, which got a small smile. "And because I like you and would like to get to know you better." Which was true. "Dating seemed like a logical method for accomplishing that goal." Which was also true.

The smile flickered out. "After everything I said to you, you're still…interested?" Her tone was one of wonder more than irritation.

No guts, no glory. "Yes."

She shifted on the love seat to face him, her feet still tucked up under her. "Guy, please, there's no point. I can't be what you want me to be."

"And what is it you think I want you to be?"

She made a tiny gesture that was partly a shrug, partly a shake of her head, and all denial.

He took a step toward her, his hands in his pockets. And said what he felt. Not what he felt he should say. "I'm not looking for a fling, Elizabeth. Or a nanny."

Several seconds passed before she answered. "But that's what I mean. What you want is something…real. Permanent." She aimed a wry smile at her knees. "Like everyone else on this planet, you have your share of faults, Guy Sanford, but somehow, I doubt that fear of commitment is one of them."

"Thank you, I think—"

"I'm not finished. Dammit, Guy. I don't know...I don't think..." She pressed her hand to her mouth, then let it drop back into her lap. "I just can't see myself as a wife. Or a mother. Especially three times over." On an enormous sigh, she added, "And, frankly, if my past experiences are anything to go by, I don't know that I ever will."

Deciding any objection would be pointless, he stood in front of her, looking down at the fine silky head. He could touch her if he wanted to. And he knew that's all it would take. For either of them. He could also leave.

Maybe next time.

"What else?"

She made a short, breathy sound that was a cross between a laugh and a sigh. "That wasn't enough?"

"I just want to know exactly what I'm—we're—dealing with here."

She knotted her hands in her lap, took a deep breath, then another, then said, in a quavery voice: "Okay, since you seem to be a glutton for punishment—we're too...different."

He sat down beside her, hesitating a moment before raising one hand to her cheek, his other one claiming both of hers. Despite the fear and confusion and tears in her eyes, she didn't pull away.

"Maybe that's true, on the surface. And heaven knows, I've told myself a thousand times there's no logical reason for how I feel. But all I know is," he said softly, slipping his hand around to the back of her neck, "whenever I look into your eyes, I feel as if I've come home."

Now one tear, then another, slipped over her lashes. "That's what scares me."

"Why, sweetheart?" His thumb whispered over her cheek, reveling in softness and tears and her delicate beauty.

It took her three tries to get the words out. "Because I feel exactly the same way."

With that, Guy mentally ripped up everything he'd told himself earlier. Slowly, he removed her glasses and set them on the table in front of the love seat, then returned to claim her face with both hands, her mouth with his.

The kiss was everything she hoped for, everything she'd dreaded. His mouth was soft and warm and molded perfectly to hers, his lips conveying a tender urgency that sent a delicious liquid fire, like fine brandy, trickling through her veins. But far more than that, Guy's gentleness and generosity and patience came through that kiss, showing her a world of what-could-bes…if only she wasn't too terrified to accept it.

She nearly sobbed when Guy teased apart her lips, gently caressing her tongue with his, even as it occurred to her that this man knew what he was doing and she'd like nothing more than for him keep doing it for a very long time. When he pulled away, Elizabeth felt as if her life support system had been cut off.

"Wow," Guy said on a whisper, touching his forehead to hers. "You're trembling."

She was. "And you're not playing fair."

"I rarely do."

He imprisoned her hand under his—so warm and strong—slipping it underneath the black-and-white tie, pressing her palm against firm muscles overlying a strong, even heartbeat, dual contrasts to the soft, sensuous fabric of his silk shirt. The trembling grew worse, a frisson of possibilities crackling along her nerve endings like summer lightning.

Piece by piece, he was seducing her. But not just into his bed. Into his heart, his life. If he kissed her again, she'd be lost. And she ached for another kiss, for more, as she'd never ached for anything else in her life.

"Damn," she said.

His mouth, still damp from their kiss, twitched with sad amusement. "Well, there's a first."

Somehow she forced herself to extricate her hand from his, somehow she stood up and actually walked away, albeit none too steadily. To her extreme consternation, his heat followed her like a missile. Even though he hadn't budged from the love seat, he was with her. He was *part* of her.

Just that fast.

"Hey—" Did he sound as shaky as she was? "—since I just got the good-night kiss, you think we could have that date now?"

Oh *brother,* did she not want to do this. But what choice did she have?

"Guy—no. It wouldn't change anything, don't you see?"

She supposed it was just as well she'd left her glasses on the table. This way, she couldn't see his face. The only glitch in this was that now, when she should be making her Dramatic Exit, she couldn't see where she was going. With as much dignity as she could scrape together, she backtracked to the table, to within touching distance of the man who'd just single-handedly overthrown every notion she'd ever had about men and sex and kisses and touching and *needing,* and snatched up her glasses, pushed them back onto her face, and, at last, headed for the office door.

She didn't make it. His arms engulfed her, enfolded her, molding her against his body, wordlessly showing her what she did to him.

She saw hands gentle enough to cradle a baby's head clench into fists at his sides, his chest rise and fall in agonized, ragged breaths. "Tell me," he rasped, the fierce need in his eyes nearly obliterating her resolve, "tell me you felt nothing when I kissed you."

Outside the office, she heard the phone ring, heard Cora answer it, oblivious to the drama unfolding not twenty feet behind her. What should she tell him? To be honest would be foolish, Elizabeth knew; but to lie to Guy was impossible. Now.

"Oh, brother," she said with a rueful laugh. "You have no idea how much I felt."

He suddenly smiled, and she wished she had something to hold on to. "Actually," he said, "I have a pretty good idea. But I want to hear your version." He might have stepped toward her, she wasn't sure. All she saw was the heat in his eyes, all she heard was his voice, as hopeful and persuasive as a child's wish.

She swallowed, fumbled behind her for the doorknob she hoped was where she last saw it. He was definitely closer than he had been five seconds earlier. "If I wasn't who I was," she said, her voice remarkably steady over her thundering heart, "I think we'd be in serious danger of scandalizing Cora."

He actually looked more surprised than triumphant. He backed her against the door, slipped his arms around her waist to insinuate his pelvis against hers, awakening an almost savage need that bled hot in her belly, raced like wildfire through her veins. Her hands landed on his chest—to push away? to surrender?—to feel a heartbeat as out of control as her own.

"*But,* like I said before…" She couldn't let him kiss her. She *couldn't.* "I've never, ever let my heart rule my head." And the last thing she needed was to listen to other, obviously less tractable, areas of her body now intent on throwing in their two cents. "And it wouldn't be in either of our interests to change that policy now."

She watched as the fire in those eyes, those wonderful sweet eyes, simply went out, replaced by a coldness as bitter and unforgiving as a midwinter Lake Michigan wind. His hands tightened around her waist, but only long enough to move her to one side, after which he jerked open the door so hard several papers on her mother's desk fluttered to the floor. He hesitated in the doorway, his intense scrutiny making her cringe. "And where, exactly, has that policy gotten you so far, Miss Louden?"

The instant Guy closed the door behind him, Elizabeth burst into tears.

Chapter 7

The apartment's elderly air conditioner had finally bitten the dust. In its place, an old hassock fan dredged from the bowels of Guy's parents' basement whirred in the middle of the floor, making a pretense of moving the hot air around. A Popsicle wrapper or something plastered to its belly rattled unpleasantly; exhausted, Guy ignored it. He'd washed dishes, folded just enough laundry to get them through to the weekend, bathed two of the three kids, and put them to bed. Praying he was off duty until seven the next morning, he lay sprawled on the couch in a faded Mickey Mouse T-shirt and cutoffs, his bare feet propped on the battered coffee table and a hot scratchy dog's head in his lap, half watching *The Hunt for Red October* for the third time…and half thinking about Elizabeth. Or rather, his stupidity for still burning from her rejection of a week ago. Had he really expected that one kiss would change her mind? Would change *anything?*

All this thinking was overtaxing his brain, he decided as he let his head fall back against the sofa. It had been a long day, and a longer evening. The kids had been particularly crabby; nothing, *nothing,* had made the baby happy, and Ashli's voice had been gravelly, like she might be coming down with a cold. He hoped not. He was scheduled to be out of town during working hours for most of the next three days, checking out properties in outlying communities. He wouldn't be able to pick her up from daycare if she got sick. And his folks were in Grand Rapids, visiting the newest Sanford baby, their fourteenth grandchild. With any luck, he thought with a sigh loud enough to raise Einstein's head, a good night's sleep would clear things up.

He noticed the dog regarding him with a cocked head, concern in his eyes. With a halfhearted chuckle, he wiggled one of Einstein's ears. "It's okay, boy." Satisfied, the dog flopped his chin back onto Guy's lap.

The phone rang; yet another credit card offer. With a curt, "Not interested," he cut the woman off midspiel.

"Daddy?"

Ashli stood in the entrance to the hallway, her sleep-tousled hair soft-focusing her frail shoulders. Repeated washings had faded the flowers on her too small nightgown to almost the same color as the background; he wasn't going to be able to put off shopping for her much longer. Oh, joy.

"What is it, baby?"

She cleared her still-scratchy throat. "I just thought maybe it was Mama."

A fresh wound erupted in Guy's gut. Eighteen—no, nineteen months—and she still hadn't given up. He held out his arms to her; she came running across the carpet and fell across his chest. "No, baby. Just a solicitor," he said into her tangled hair.

"Oh." Ashli clamped a thin arm across his stomach, then lifted liquid blue eyes to him. "You think she's ever coming back?"

How many times had she asked that question? Hundreds? Thousands?

"No," he said with gentle firmness, as he always had. "I don't."

"How can she stop being my mother?"

That was a new one. In self-defense, Guy decided the question was rhetorical. He thought about asking his daughter how she'd feel about maybe having a new mama someday, decided against it. What would be the point, anyway?

Her arm tightened around him enough to feel the faint staccato of her heartbeat against his chest, and he remembered the first time he'd heard it, when she was still inside Dianne. He'd been simply awestruck, at the miracle of this little creature that he'd helped make. He was no less awestruck now.

The phone rang again, making both of them lurch. It was Maureen Louden, with an invitation for dinner the next evening. As Ashli untangled herself and went into the kitchen to get a drink of water, Guy said, "And will Elizabeth be joining us?"

"Since I'd like to see this resolved sometime in my lifetime, what do you think?"

"Maureen," Guy said in a low voice, keeping one eye out on the kitchen and his daughter. "I don't mean any disrespect, but I don't think—"

"*You're* not the problem, you know," she said as if he did. "Or the kids."

He clicked off the TV, tossed the remote onto a stack of newspapers on the table. He wasn't sure he wanted to hear what was coming. "Then what is?"

"She's petrified of failing, would be my guess."

He stared at the remote as if seeing numbers for the first time. "I can't blame her, you know," he finally said.

"Oh, Guy, for goodness' sake—she's not being sold into slavery. Look, she had a couple unfortunate experiences babysitting when she was younger, and she's let them scar her for life. She just needs time to…to…"

"Let my little angels charm the patooties off of her? Yeah right."

"Well, if it doesn't work, at least we could all get on with our lives."

Why couldn't this be just a simple dinner invitation?

He needed—wanted—Elizabeth, insane though it might be. Her energy and fire and her beauty and her barely tapped sense of humor. Even her damn compulsive orderliness. After Dianne, a little regimentation couldn't hurt.

So—what was the right thing to do? Back off, or push a little?

Or push a little *more*.

"Well...I don't know," he said.

"Six-thirty," Maureen said. "Be there." *Click.*

Ah. Salesperson ploy number one: Never give 'em a chance to say no.

He hung up the phone, then tugged on a fold in Ashli's nightgown, trying not to think too hard about what he'd just gotten himself into. "Guess what? You get real food tomorrow night."

Her giggle caught him off guard. "You give us real food."

"Okay, real food that doesn't taste like cardboard."

Another giggle. "You're so silly, Daddy." She was quiet for a second, then asked, "Who's Elizabeth?"

Leave it to Little Miss Beagle Ears. "You know who Elizabeth is, silly. Miss Louden? The lady you met a couple of times the week before last, remember? I work for her mother, who invited us to dinner."

"Oh." She plopped down beside him again, nearly spilling the water. "You like Elizabeth?"

"Sure," Guy said in the most nonchalant tone he could manage, putting his arm around her. "She's a good salesperson. And a nice lady. What's not to like?"

A pair of delicate shoulders hitched under his arm as the child chugged her drink. The water gone, she leaned forward, set the glass on the table, then crashed back against the sofa. "As a friend, though, right? I mean, not like a girlfriend or anything?"

"As a friend, sure," he said, tempted to cross his fingers behind his back.

The child silently regarded him in that wise-woman way of hers, then snuggled back against his ribs once more. "Good," was all she said.

The next morning found Elizabeth sitting at her desk, staring at nothing, twiddling a pencil between her fingers and wondering if there were any openings in the space program. Freeze-dried ice cream, weightlessness, even those hideous spacesuits were preferable to having to face Guy Sanford and hear his laugh and smell his intoxicating fragrance every day.

He was out, thank goodness, digging up more bones. He'd dug up enough in the past two and a half weeks to make a whole damn dinosaur. God, he was good. Almost as good as she was. Bad enough she was so attracted to him. Where was it written she had to *admire* him, too?

Her mother perched in the chair beside her desk; Elizabeth barely twitched her eyes in her direction.

"Your good humor these days is almost more than a body can bear," Maureen said.

Elizabeth harrumphed.

"I bet I know something that'll make you feel better."

"Who says I need to feel better?"

"Everyone who's come into contact with you the past week, that's who. So...got plans for tonight?"

"Why?" Elizabeth said, backing up and giving her mother a sideways glance.

"Oh, for goodness' sake—stop being so all-fired suspicious of everything and everyone, would you? I made a cherry pie this morning before I came in. That's all."

A little elf tugged at the corner of her mouth. "Really?"

"Mm-hm. Interested?"

"You better believe it." Elizabeth was wild for cherry pie. Then she narrowed her eyes and cocked her head at her mother. "*Waait* a minute—what's the catch?"

"That you do the roast beef and veggies to go with the pie."

"That's it?"

"And clean the cellar and do the windows and take down the drapes and don't forget the ashes in the fireplace, Cinderella. Honestly, child. Of course, that's it."

"Sorry."

"You should be."

"I'll be happy to do the rest of the dinner." She was a

much better cook than her mother, although Maureen did more than justice to cherry pie. "I could use the distraction," she admitted. "Besides, I'd like to get out of here early today anyway…"

Before Guy gets back, she almost said.

Her mother raised first one eyebrow, then the other, but thankfully said nothing as she rose from the chair.

This was so silly. Her mother knew. Cora knew. Shoot, old Mrs. Heinz down the street probably knew about the almost-but-not-quite something going on between Guy and Elizabeth. But at least everyone was considerate enough to keep their traps shut. Made things almost tolerable, at least.

"What time would you like to have dinner?"

"Oh, I don't know," Maureen replied, idly skimming one fingernail along the edge of the desk. "Say, about six-thirty?"

"Fine," Elizabeth said, finally turning to some paperwork she should have taken care of yesterday. "Consider it done."

Promptly at six-thirty, Guy rang the doorbell to Maureen's charming little Cape Cod, then waited, as Micah banged his bottle on Guy's shoulder and the other two kids stampeded back and forth on the porch, deliberately squeaking their sneakers on the gray wooden floorboards. Ashli, thank God, had not come down with a cold after all, the scratchiness probably just a reaction from a century's worth of dust embedded in that ratty carpet.

Lord, they had to get out of that apartment. Trouble was, after the Lakeside house, he hadn't seen anything else worth going into hock for. But if he didn't find something else soon, he might have to leave the kids and dog with his folks for a while, which was not something he wanted to do. First, because he couldn't stand the thought of not having those smiles and hugs to wallow in after work every day, and second, because he hadn't returned to Michigan to dump his kids on his parents—

He realized Maureen hadn't answered the bell, so he poked it again.

"Elizabeth!" he heard from inside. "See who that is, would you dear?"

See who that is?

In deference to the two-year-old in his arms who had undoubtedly been a gifted mynah bird in a prior life, Guy bit back the word that flashed through his brain. Had Maureen *tricked* Elizabeth into coming? Before he could even contemplate making a dash for it back to the car, the door swung open.

"Hi," he said, shifting Micah on his hip, already salivating at the scent of roast beef trickling past Elizabeth's perfume. He'd brought a bottle of nonalcoholic wine, which he thought better of handing to her. Arming her would probably not be wise.

"Oh, how nice," he heard Maureen say behind her daughter. Past Elizabeth's trim, white-shorted hips and lusciously smooth legs, he glimpsed a full skirt in some watercolory kinda print. "You made it after all." A bright face peeked over Elizabeth's shoulder.

"Uh, yes," Guy said, not sure what his lines were in Maureen's little production.

Maureen put her hand on her daughter's shoulder. "When I asked Guy if he'd like to have dinner with us tonight, he said he wasn't sure."

Elizabeth smiled, if you could call it that. She hadn't yet unhooked her eyes from Guy. Or asked him inside. "Guess that's why you neglected to tell me you'd invited him, huh?"

"Oh—I guess I did forget to tell you, didn't I?" her mother said, playing the ditzy blonde. "Well, for goodness' sake, honey—where are your manners?"

"Sorry. I must have 'forgotten' them." Still glowering at Guy, Elizabeth stood to one side so they could all troop into Maureen's house.

"Oh…would you look at this *cutie*," Maureen exclaimed as she scooped Micah out of Guy's arms, who parroted, "Cutie?" as he glommed onto Maureen's gold necklace. "And what a lovely young woman you are…Ashli, right?"

He felt his daughter nod from her safe vantage point behind

him. Jake, however, who wouldn't know shy if it bit him, was already inspecting a shelf of knickknacks in one corner of the living room. Guy called him back, firmly clamping one hand on the four-year-old's shoulder. "And this is Jake."

"How do you do, Jake?" Maureen extended her hand, which Jake took.

"You gots any pets?" he asked in his most adorable raspy voice. Guy looked around to see if Elizabeth had heard, but she had vanished.

Maureen smiled. "Well, there are two kitties somewhere around, but they tend to hide. If you're quiet," she said, "they'll come out more quickly."

Jake gave a sober nod, as if he understood completely, then simply sat down on the sofa and folded his hands. Waiting.

"Why don't we all go get our hands washed for dinner?" Maureen suggested, then shot a pointed look at Guy. "Perhaps Elizabeth needs help carving the roast?"

Oh, right. Voluntarily put himself in the same room as an irate woman with a carving knife at her disposal. Tugging at his neckline, he followed the sounds of pans being banged and rattled until he found the kitchen. Elizabeth's face was flushed, and not from cooking, he guessed. Her lips, however, were pressed together so tightly they were colorless. She flashed him the most cursory of looks when he entered, then continued ladling out potatoes as if world peace depended on how precisely she piled them in the serving dish. Guy set the wine on the counter, then stuffed his hands in his pockets and leaned against the doorjamb, a careful four feet away.

"You're really ticked off, aren't you?"

"You're really observant, aren't you?"

"Look, I swear I didn't know she was setting you up."

She shot him another zinger of a look, then picked up the bowl of potatoes and carried them out to the dining table. Thunked them down on the table. Cursed when one fell off the top of the pile and landed in the centerpiece.

Guy stayed where he was. "If it's any consolation, she set me up, too."

Backless sandals slapped against her bare heels as she

tromped back into the kitchen. "Well, it's not," she grumbled, yanking the oven door open so hard it groaned.

When she reached into the oven to pull out the roast, the soft rose fabric of her T-shirt pulled across her back, revealing her braline underneath. He wondered if she wore lace underwear. If she didn't, she should. She would be pretty in lace. She would be pretty in anything. But he'd bet his life savings, if he still had any, she'd be absolutely exquisite in *nothing*.

He came to, lurching toward the oven. "Here…" he said, grabbing a couple of extra pot holders off hooks over the stove. "Let me get that—"

"Never mind. I've already got it." Guy backed away and let Elizabeth lug the beef up onto the counter as she slammed the oven door shut with her knee. She threw down the oven mitts she'd been using, then shoved back an escaped strand of hair off her forehead with the back of her hand. She swallowed repeatedly, close to tears.

"Would you like us to leave?" he asked softly.

Clutching the edge of the counter, she shut her eyes, tightly, and shook her head.

"You're sure?"

She let out a long, wobbly sigh and shook her head again. "No," she said in a small voice. He watched in embarrassed agony as she fought to regain her composure, which she did after several seconds. Then, with a grimace, she said, "But this isn't your fault. I'm not sending you back out in the street with three hungry kids to feed."

"You're a kind woman, Elizabeth Louden—"

She yanked a small skillet off the overhead rack, clattered it onto the burner. "Damn her," she muttered. "I should have seen it coming."

"Does she often play matchmaker?"

Elizabeth chopped up half a stick of butter into the skillet, turned the flame on underneath. "This seems to be a recently acquired hobby," she said with a wry twist to her mouth, poking at the chunks of butter with a wooden spoon until it melted and started to sizzle. Guy watched in fascination as she dumped out a little glass dish of chopped nuts into the butter and stirred them around for a few seconds, then turned off the flame and removed the skillet from the burner. "Do the kids eat broccoli?"

"What? Oh…Ashli will, Jake won't, Micah might."

She actually smiled. Sorta kinda.

"You've never had dinner with kids before, have you?"

"Not this many and not this young," she said, pushing her glasses up onto the bridge of her nose as she drizzled the butter-drenched nuts over the steamed broccoli, and Guy realized in horror she'd just effectively killed any chance of any of the kids eating the broccoli. They'd even pick nuts out of brownies.

She caught his look. "What's wrong?" Her eyes followed his to the broccoli. "Oh. They hate nuts?"

"Maybe they won't tonight…"

"Hey, don't worry about it," she said in that tone women use when what they say isn't necessarily what they mean, so a man had best be on his toes if he knows what's good for him. "Either they eat it—" she picked up the casserole, then shrugged "—or they don't. Ain't no skin off my nose, that's for sure." She nodded toward the cupboard over the counter. "Plates are up there, silverware in the drawer underneath. I guess we need four more place settings."

She swept out of the kitchen before she could hear Guy's chuckle.

Damned if she didn't sound exactly like his mother.

Nobody had warned her.

No one had warned her how sexy a man tending to his children could be, or how much she'd envy a crabby two-year-old his father's comforting voice, a broad chest to lean against, the tender stroke of a strong masculine hand against a cheek.

Neither had anyone warned her how easily kids—some kids—could steal your heart. Or if they had, she hadn't listened. More than once that evening, in spite of relentless squabbling and messiness and loudness and pickiness, they'd caught her off guard, made her laugh out loud. Nudged to life something deep inside her, something she really hadn't thought was there. Had been afraid to admit to, at any rate.

None of which altered the fact that she was still gonna kill her mother.

"Mrs. Louden, I'm finished," Ashli said. "May I be excused?"

"Of course, dear," Maureen said. "You, too, Jake, if you like. There are some games and dolls in Elizabeth's old room upstairs." She winked. "And the kitties often take naps on the bed in there."

Jake was gone like a shot. Ashli, however, remained seated, familiar blue eyes pinned to Elizabeth's. "Mrs. Louden says you cooked the dinner."

Elizabeth managed a smile, painfully aware it was not being returned. "I sure did," she replied, keeping her voice light.

"It was very good," she said, but there was a distance between the child and the words, leaving Elizabeth with the distinct impression she'd been prompted. "Thank you." Then she, too, left the room.

Guy set Micah down with a huff of surprise. "Wow. You never know when civilization is going to kick in."

"Their manners are wonderful for such young children," Maureen said, tickling the baby, who was pounding on her lap. Then to Elizabeth, "Weren't they, dear?"

She thought better of mentioning the guarded expression on Ashli's young-old features. But then, what did she know about kids and their moods?

Micah careened around the table, coming to a halt in front of her with his hands tucked down into his overalls. He studied her for several seconds, his enormous gray eyes luminous in the candlelight. Then he slammed into her knees, giggling.

"Yes," she finally agreed, unable to keep from touching the baby's soft wavy hair. With a squeal, he scampered back to his father, burying his face in Guy's lap. Elizabeth met Guy's smile with a tentative one of her own. "They even ate the nuts."

Then they just sat there. Grinning at each other. Frozen.

Maureen popped up from the table and started blowing out

candles, clanking silverware and dishes and generally knocking everybody back to earth. "Why don't you two have your coffee in the living room while I get the kitchen straightened away?" Any protest Elizabeth might have had was immediately quashed by one of her mother's "looks." Then she held out her hand to the baby. "Wanna see what we've got in the kitchen to play with?"

"P'ay wif?" the toddler squeaked, happily letting Maureen lead him away.

Elizabeth and Guy stood as well. She wiped her hands on the front of her shorts until she realized he might think she looked nervous, so she crammed them into her pockets. "Go on." She tried a smile. "I'll bring in the coffee?"

Her voice squeaked at the end of the question.

Guy walked around the table to stand in front of her. He tugged on her wrist until he'd freed one hand from her pocket, which he then turned over and forced her to uncoil. "I almost think I'd rather have you mad," he said, bringing her palm to his lips for a gentle, brief kiss. Then, after a wink, he sauntered out to the living room.

Took a full minute before she could link brain function to muscles enough to move.

When she brought the coffee in a few minutes later, Guy was standing in the middle of the room stroking his chin, contemplating the old spinet tucked against the wall next to the stairs, while childish bickering reverberated in the stairwell. Hoping he didn't notice how badly the cups were rattling, she set the tray down on the cherrywood table fronting the blue-flowered sofa that had been in the same spot since forever.

"Who plays?" he asked.

"Oh, I took lessons, but only until I was about fourteen. And no, I don't remember a blessed thing, so don't ask." He chuckled, accepting a cup of coffee from her. She took care not to let their fingers touch, but ignoring the snug fit of his black T-shirt—declaring Plays Well with Others in white letters—was something else again.

"Cut it out!" shrieked a feminine voice overhead, followed by sandpapery, tormenting giggles.

Elizabeth glanced toward the stairs like a heroine in a horror flick. "Shouldn't you intervene or something?"

"Nope." Guy took a sip of coffee, creaking the keyboard cover when he lifted it, then lightly raking his fingertips over the keys. "Is it in tune?"

"I have no idea." Elizabeth settled onto the sofa with her coffee, nearly spilling it when a loud thump overhead trembled the ceiling light fixture. Guy still seemed oblivious to the battle, so she tried to assume a similar nonchalance. "Uh...why don't you find out for yourself?"

He turned to her, grinning like a kid just picked for the best playground baseball team. "You wouldn't mind?"

"I don't know. I haven't heard you yet." Another thump, this one accompanied by a scream. She was about to say that, really, perhaps he should do *something* before blood was shed, but Guy was already at the foot of the stairs.

"Ashli! Jake! Get your fannies out here!"

She heard scuffling, her bedroom door opening, then: "He keeps throwing the dolls at me and I keep telling him to stop but he won't listen...." over Jake's whine of, "She won't let me play with the Lite Brite—"

"Enough!" The tone of Guy's voice even made Elizabeth straighten up. "Either figure out how to play together, *quietly,* or we go home. *And,* if you mess up my evening, you will go to bed the minute we get in the door." He paused, one hand braced on his hip. "Understood?"

There was some mumbling followed by two contrite, "Yes, Daddys," then the bedroom door quietly closed.

"I'm impressed."

Guy rubbed his face and searched for someplace to set his coffee, finally choosing a high shelf on a nearby bookcase. "Don't be. It doesn't always work."

"Do they...fight like that a lot?"

"Constantly. Now—" Guy slid onto the piano bench "—if my little darlings will cooperate for five minutes, would you like some music?"

She nodded, a little dazed.

He ran his fingers up and down the keys for several seconds, then began to coax a soft jazz ballad from keys that had never known anything other than mediocre renditions of Bach minuets. Carrying her cup with her, Elizabeth moved over to the piano, leaning against it so she could watch those lean, capable hands pull such incredible sound from the neglected instrument. The thought filtered through her brain that she wouldn't mind trading places with the piano right about now.

The corners of his mouth curved up. "You like jazz?"

"I prefer classical," she admitted. "But I've never heard jazz played like this before. This is so…so…"

"Sexy," he supplied, not looking at her.

The cooling system in her mother's house didn't work worth beans here, either. Her skin nearly crackled from the sudden heat flooding her…everything. "Yes."

Neither spoke until he'd finished the piece. When he lifted his eyes to her, the characteristic grin she'd expected wasn't there. Instead, she saw something else. Or, more accurately, several something elses.

"You still ticked?" he asked.

"About tonight, you mean?"

He nodded.

"I don't know…." She took another sip of coffee. "No. Well…maybe a little." When he chuckled, she repeated limply, "I don't know."

He reached up, briefly squeezed her wrist, then began playing again.

Through a haze of what she finally recognized—admitted?—was desire, she studied him, unable to think past anything save the gentle masculinity seated in front of her. Unable, even, to bring up images of his children to blot out the writhing tendrils of longing curling inside her gut, keeping the fear uneasy company. He wore his hair loose tonight, the glow from the piano lamp tingeing the molasses-colored waves with gold, defining his beard-shadowed face into angles she hadn't before noticed. Muscles rippled rhythmically across his shoulders, back, upper arms as he played, leading her eyes down to his hands as they danced across the keys. She recalled watching those hands caress Micah's little back, cup his daughter's head, tickle Jake....

She looked up. He was watching her, still not smiling.

"Why don't you play anymore?" she asked in a rush, unable to unhook herself from his gaze, thinking how foolish it was not to. "You're very good."

"Thank you," he acknowledged with a quick nod. "I used to play in some of the lesser Chicago clubs, before Ashli came. I minored in music in college."

"So...you do classical, too?"

There was the grin, like an old friend. "I do classical. I prefer jazz."

She understood. The mellow sound and sensuous, asymmetric rhythms suited him. "You didn't answer my question...." she began, but he shook his head.

"When Dianne took off, she left me with a pile of bills and two empty bank accounts. The piano was the first thing to go. And playing gigs isn't an option when you have three kids to take care of every night." He spoke with the dispassion of someone looking for understanding, not sympathy. Someone with not so much pride that he can't admit his mistakes, but with enough to prevent an admission of how much he's hurting.

She'd forgotten, in her zeal to avoid complications in her cozy little existence, how lonely Guy probably was. And the guts it took for him to hold his little family together, all by himself. That he was a single father, rather than a single mother, made his situation no less difficult. He had the same day care nightmares, the same sleepless nights and dinners to fix every evening and all the household madness to deal with, just like her mother had after Elizabeth's father's death. At that moment, her heart—or at least part of it—went out to him, even if she still kept her hands tightly gripped around her empty coffee cup.

"What happened?" she asked.

"With me and Dianne, you mean?"

"Yes."

He thought a moment. "We married too young, I suppose. Didn't know who we were, what we expected from each other or life." He shook his head, not looking at her. "I had no idea I had it in me, to be a father, to be responsible for someone else's well-being. Or that when you sacrifice some of your old notions about happiness to ensure someone else's, you haven't sacrificed anything at all. Nothing worthwhile, anyway."

Elizabeth circled the rim of her coffee cup with one finger. "I take it Dianne didn't see it that way."

A half laugh stumbled out of his throat. "Yeah. You could say that."

For several seconds, Elizabeth again fought the urge to touch him. Then, she finally murmured, "Tell me about it. Her leaving."

His eyes lifted to her, the blue darkened to a dull slate. "You sure?"

She nodded.

He began to play again, softly. "Micah had just turned six months old. The kids had been spending a week with my folks, but I'd been insanely busy that week and hadn't been home very much. I came home one night, late, to find a cryptic note on the kitchen table, a half-empty closet, and the bedroom drapes missing." He pushed out a short, rueful laugh. "Never did figure that one out."

Elizabeth leaned her cheek in her palm. "Was it true, what Ashli said? About her never contacting you after that?"

"Not even once. I gave it six months, then filed for divorce." He rubbed his face, the lines on either side of his mouth suddenly deeper. "I knew she was having a hard time." He turned to her, briefly. "Micah was a 'surprise,' as they say. But I figured, once the baby came, she'd be fine."

"I take it she wasn't?"

He shook his head. "She cried constantly, it seemed. Had no interest in anything we used to do. She took care of the kids okay, but she was perpetually cranky." He leaned both hands against the spinet's top and shook his head again. "My mother said she just had the baby blues, that I should bring her flowers, pay her more attention, things like that. So I did. She said she needed time away from the kids, so I made sure she got it. When she said she wanted to take some art classes, I brought home some catalogs and encouraged her to go.''

She heard guilt in the ensuing silence. Unfounded, probably, but there all the same. *No matter what I did,* he was saying, *it wasn't enough. I couldn't save my marriage.*

"At the end of the semester," he finished, "she ran away with one of her instructors. Some Italian guy. As in, *from* Italy. Far as I know, she's still there."

Elizabeth's comment was decidedly unladylike, and Guy chuckled.

"And she never once contacted the children?"

Guy looked at her.

"Sorry," she said on a sigh. "I just can't…" She frowned into her coffee. "How could someone abandon their own children?"

"A question I ask myself at least a dozen times a day," Guy said, weariness dulling his words. Suddenly, though, he patted the bench beside him, that damn grin flickering to life like the flame that got the moth. "Come on—keep me company."

She pulled her cup closer to her chest. "I'm keeping you company just fine up here."

"Scaredy cat."

"Am not!"

Guy laughed, softly, shaking his head. And lifted his hand to her.

Which, after maybe a half second's deliberation, she took, wordlessly slipping onto the seat beside him. She withdrew her hand as soon as she was seated, but she still sat close enough for her skin to prickle from his body heat. She tried to inch away from him without being obvious. "Happy now?"

He just smiled and began another piece.

"Now *that,* I know," she said with a grin of her own. "Joplin, isn't it?"

"It is. Does that mean ragtime is on your list?"

"Absolutely. I could never play it, though. Couldn't get the hang of the syncopation."

"I'm not surprised."

She blinked. "Excuse me?"

"To hear the offbeat rhythm, you have to let go of all those classical conventions. What you were taught was the norm. You see?"

She saw. "Can I ask you something?"

"Sure."

"You obviously love doing this...." She swept one hand to indicate the piano. "Having to give it up, to get rid of even the piano... Did you resent it?"

"Of course I did," he countered immediately. "Making music was a very large part of my life." Then he stopped playing, right in the middle of a phrase, and turned to her, his hands resting on his thighs. "But never, not even once, have I blamed the kids. That's what you're asking, isn't it?"

It was, and it unsettled her that he should cut to the heart of her question so easily. She flushed again, averting her eyes.

"It's a perfectly natural question, Elizabeth," he said mildly, picking up the piece exactly where he'd left off. "And I'm glad you asked."

She waited for the rest of the explanation, but apparently there wasn't one.

The kids' fight had shaken her, but not too badly. In fact, she seemed...impressed. She'd even laughed when Jake said the red "cremations" in the centerpiece were prettier than the white ones. So—maybe?—there was hope.

Maybe even more. Something happened a few minutes ago, right before she'd joined him on the bench. A shift of some sort. He could hear it in her voice, in the way her laughter had lost some of its defensiveness. He sensed she'd stopped running. Not that she was moving *toward* him, exactly. But maybe she was at least...standing still? And was this a good thing? Or an invitation to disaster?

In any case, he didn't dare push it.

He checked his watch. "I really hate to do this," he said,

twisting to face her on the bench, need jolting through him when he found his lips barely six inches from hers. "But if I don't get Micah into bed by nine he'll keep the other two up until midnight."

His heart leaped at the look of actual disappointment in those green eyes. But heaven forbid she should admit it. She slid out from the bench, tugging at the hem of her shorts. "Of course. I'll just gather Micah's things for you."

Guy got up from the piano and carefully lowered the key cover. "You'd better let me do it. I've got the routine down pat." He began gathering bottles and toys and assorted infant paraphernalia into the oversize diaper bag, pausing only to yell, "Jake! Ashli! Time to go!" up the stairs.

Jake came barreling down so fast he "slipped" on the sixth step from the bottom and bumped the rest of the way, which earned him a sharp look of disapproval. But Ashli wasn't following. He started to call again, but Elizabeth briefly touched his arm.

"Let me get her."

Elizabeth paused at the top of the stairs, her hand on the banister, giving her heart a chance to settle back down. Guy could easily have kissed her a few minutes ago; she couldn't decide whether she was more surprised or disappointed that he hadn't.

She also couldn't decide whether approaching Ashli right now was a smart move or not.

She stopped at the door, watching the fragile-looking little girl sitting cross-legged on her bed with one of her old dolls in her lap, a very contented calico cat snuggled against her thigh. The room didn't look too bad, considering. The dolls from the big bookshelf were scattered to kingdom come, and millions of little plastic Lite Brite pegs lay all over the pastel hooked rug, but the walls still stood and there was no blood.

Except, maybe, for what was leeching from Elizabeth's heart.

"Ashli?" she said softly, achingly aware she was seeing herself as a child, huddled on her bed, grieving a loss she spoke of seldom and thought about nearly constantly. "Your daddy's calling you. Time to go home."

Hugging the doll, the child scanned the room. "It's so pretty in here."

Elizabeth ground a few Lite Brites into the rug as she drifted over to the bed, then cautiously sat on the white eyelet bedspread. Her eyes flicked over the soft periwinkle-blue walls with white crown molding and trim around the windows, the well-worn rug which she'd come to hate once she started wearing high heels, the maple twin four-poster. "I suppose it is—"

"My room's *horrible*," Ashli suddenly volunteered, though more to the doll than Elizabeth. "I have to share with my brothers, and the apartment we're living in right now is really awful. It's way too small, and it smells, and there's only one bathroom."

With a smile, Elizabeth said, "Oooh...only one bathroom?"

"Yeah."

"Bummer."

She saw the little mouth twitch, fighting either a smile or tears, she couldn't tell. Then, clasping the doll more tightly, she asked, "Do you like my Daddy?"

Elizabeth tried not to react. "Sure."

"He hasn't liked another woman since Mama left. Did you know that?"

"No. No, I didn't."

The child eyed her warily. "How *much* do you like Daddy?"

"We're..." She paused. What *were* they? "Friends," she finished. "Just friends."

"That's good," Ashli said with a sigh of relief, carefully setting the doll back on the pillows. "Because you can't marry him, you know. 'Cause if he gets married again, Mama won't come back—"

"Ashli!"

They both jumped. How long had Guy been standing there?

"We need to go." His words vibrated with a mixture of embarrassment and controlled anger, answering Elizabeth's unspoken question. "*Now*."

Chapter 8

Elizabeth stood by in silence as Guy piled the kids into the Volvo, shut the doors, then straightened up to face her. "I had no idea she'd say that to you—"

"Guy, it's okay, really. She's still hurting, that's all."

He leaned one elbow on the car's roof and huffed into his palm, then slid his hand around to the back of his neck, rubbing it for a minute. "Yeah, I know."

After a moment's hesitation, Elizabeth touched his arm. "Just like her father."

This time, she saw pain flash through eyes now deepened to cobalt in the dim porch light. But he shook his head. "It's not the same," he said in a low voice, looking out over Maureen's front yard. "I don't expect Dianne to come back." He paused, then faced Elizabeth again. "I don't *want* Dianne to come back. Not for me, at least."

"Maybe not. But Ashli does."

Guy dug his fingers into the back of his neck, rolled his head around. Then: "We really need to be going." But he didn't move.

She nodded, then let her hand find its way to the side of an evening-roughened face. "What are you doing to me, Guy Sanford?" she whispered.

He started, his eyes widening. He grabbed her hand and pressed his lips, hard, into her palm, then clasped her hand to his chest. "You tell me."

You're making me need you, she finally admitted to herself. *Because you're making me feel needed.*

But she would not allow the thought a voice. Not yet. Possibly not ever. Instead, her only reply was to push herself up on tiptoe and rasp her lips over his cheek, then back away to let herself float on that sea of rich, sensuous blue. Too quickly, he opened his car door, got in, drove away. When she went back into the house to collect her things, her mother met her with a stupid grin and a pair of arched eyebrows.

"Let me guess." Elizabeth grabbed her purse off the table by the front door. "You were watching."

"Of course."

She fished in her clutch bag for her keys and headed back out the door.

"That's it?" her mother asked behind her.

"For the moment," was all she'd say, figuring that should be sufficient to torture the woman for at least the next few hours. Served her right.

The car drove itself back to her place, while unfinished, unfocused thoughts swarmed in her head, *longing* the only concept to finally emerge cohesive enough to recognize. But longing for *what?*

Elizabeth tossed her purse and keys on the table by her front door, clicked on the entry light, then slipped off her sandals while she flipped through her mail. On autopilot, she drifted into her shadowy kitchen and threw most of the mail into the garbage can under the sink, checked her messages, put her breakfast dishes away.

Finally, a few more thoughts began to settle enough to pick out one or two to chew on. For one thing, she just didn't know what to do about this idea of *needing* someone—a concept she thought she'd cured herself of years ago. This wasn't just physical need, either—having never had sex, she literally had no idea what she was missing—although she'd never ached to be…close to a man the way she ached for Guy.

Crazy, wasn't it? To be needed and wanted and cherished by one person for the rest of her days—the prize that every human being who ever placed a personal ad or walked into a singles bar or signed up for a video dating service vied for— was hers for the taking, if she wanted it. But that was the problem—*did* she want it?

Did she dare let her guard down that much again?

With a great sigh, she leaned heavily onto the counter, briefly cupping her face in her hands, then jerked up her head, staring into her dark living room. It had been easy before, to stay uninvolved. Guy, though, was unlike any man she'd ever known, his emotions right out there for everyone to see and touch and experience right along with him.

But it was this very openness that unnerved her, too. Being around Guy forced things out of her psyche she hadn't felt since she was a child, feelings she'd purposely put away when her father died. Feelings that rendered her vulnerable, out of control. Making her *human,* she realized with a start. Human, with all the potential screwups concomitant to that state of existence. And all the potential joy, as well.

Of course, there were the children. Still. Well, she thought, wandering into the living room and flopping down on her stomach onto her sofa, they weren't so bad. Actually, notwithstanding the fighting and pickiness and lack of volume control, his kids were pretty neat. Funny, bright, outgoing… But there was a big difference between enjoying their company for a couple of hours and living with them. Mothering them.

Putting herself in direct line for being hurt. Or *to* hurt, which was far, far worse.

She huffed a sigh, twisted onto her back. Choices. So many choices. She could continue to keep her distance, running the risk of missing out on what could be the most wonderful thing to ever happen to her. Or she could let things develop, maybe, give Guy and a relationship with him—and his kids—a chance, and risk drowning in responsibilities beyond her ability to handle.

Drowning in something that, once let loose, she knew she'd never be able to control.

The next morning—still numb from a worry-filled, sleepless night—Guy stepped into the hallway at the title company to see Elizabeth sitting in the reception area, flipping through a year-old *House and Garden* and trying to hide a yawn. His heart flipped clear to Wisconsin.

And when he caught her startled gaze, and the delighted-but-tenuous smile that went with it, he couldn't get rid of his clients fast enough.

The Foleys ushered out, he slid into the chair beside hers. "The Hancock house?"

"How—?"

"Cora."

"Oh. Of course."

"I thought you were scheduled for ten-thirty?"

"We moved it up."

He claimed her wrist, felt her pulse escalate. "Sleep well?"

She just laughed.

He grinned, squeezed her wrist, then let it go. "Good. Neither did I."

Silence stretched between them, making Guy uncharacteristically self-conscious. He was petrified to speak, to break the spell. But he did anyway.

"So—" Guy shifted his weight; she removed her hand to her lap. He noticed. Smiled. "You're meeting Rod Braden?"

"Yes!" She'd practically thrown the word at him. "Yes, I am," she repeated, her voice calmer.

"You okay with that?"

"Why wouldn't I be?"

"Because...you said..." The what-*are*-you-talking-about look in her eyes derailed his sentence.

"We only dated casually, Guy," she said, then her eyes flickered to her black skirt, where she brushed off a nonexistent something-or-other. "I never...I mean we didn't..." She was blushing furiously, but damned if he was going to help her out. "We weren't…intimate." She went completely still, as if afraid of his reaction.

He leaned over as closely as he dared. "It's okay," he whispered three inches from her ear. "Your secret's safe."

Then he forced himself to stand, forced hands that wanted to touch her so badly they screamed into his pants pockets. "I'll be out of cellular range the rest of the day again," he said, hearing the strain in his voice. "Make sure Cora takes messages for me?"

"Sure."

He hesitated, then quickly walked away before he embarrassed the hell out of both of them, half expecting to see the men with the nets the minute he set foot outside the door.

"Well. Now I know the lay of the land," Rod said with a smile around a mouthful of hot roast beef sandwich.

He'd insisted on taking her to lunch; Elizabeth had been in no mood to argue, even if she wasn't particularly hungry. "Excuse me?"

"But at least you could have been straight with me."

She blinked into golden eyes. "Excuse me?"

"Your associate. Stanford, Sanford…what was it? You two have something going, don't you?"

"Where…? What…?" Oh, brother.

His deep laugh filled the restaurant. "I saw you, at the title office. When I came in the other door? You were so, mmm, intent on your conversation, you didn't see me."

"Oh."

"I'm right, aren't I?"

Elizabeth stared at her chef's salad for several seconds, then finally let out, "Let's just say the possibilities are there."

Let's just say the idea of letting Guy Sanford do anything he wants with my body doesn't exactly repel me.

Rod chuckled softly. "I saw a lot more going on than *possibilities*, Elizabeth." As she blushed—again!—he added kindly, "You sure never looked at me that way."

She couldn't speak, petrified the tears would start if she did.

"You never cried for me, either, I'll bet."

She shook her head, swallowed several times, then took a deep breath. "You know, at least half the population of lower Michigan said I was an idiot to let you go. I now understand why they thought that."

"But not enough to change your mind?"

"Rod, I—"

"No justification necessary, honey. I didn't expect an affirmative reply." Rod then leaned toward her, holding back his tie so it wouldn't land in the gravy. "I'm a patient man, Elizabeth, but not a stupid one. So go for it. Let your heart tell you what's right."

"For a change," she mumbled. Then she asked, "Were you in love with me?"

"I was—am—very fond of you." He smiled, shrugged. "You're bright and witty and very, very classy. *And* stunning," he allowed with a mock toast of his iced tea.

"I'd've made a good wife, in other words."

"You'd make a helluva wife. But not mine."

She opened her mouth, only to realize she had nothing to say.

"There's a Miss Frawley from Mr. Guy's day care center on the phone," Cora said when Elizabeth came out of the rest room after lunch. "Seems Ashli's sick and says she wants to come home, but I can't get him on his cellular." She held out the phone. "You want to talk to them?"

Since she had no choice, Elizabeth took the phone, identifying herself and repeating Cora's explanation for why they couldn't reach Guy.

"Did you say Elizabeth Louden?" asked the pleasant female voice on the other end. One that didn't sound *too* worried, so Elizabeth guessed—hoped—she wasn't dealing with anything life-threatening.

"That's right."

"Oh, good. Mr. Sanford has you listed as an emergency contact. If he isn't available, maybe you could pick up Ashli?"

"He has *me* listed?"

"Yes." A pause. "You...didn't know?"

"No. I didn't."

"Oh, I see." The woman now sounded flustered. "See, if we can't reach Mr. Sanford, then we go to one of the people on his emergency list. We already tried his parents, but they're not around, either. But if he listed you without your consent—"

"Oh, just a minute," Elizabeth said on an exasperated sigh. "How...sick is she?"

"She's more uncomfortable than sick, would be my guess. Just a cold, but it's a heavy one and she's not breathing too well 'cause her nose is all stuffed up. Poor baby," the woman added. Deliberately.

Elizabeth felt a little twinge around her heart. "Does she have a fever?"

"No, uh-uh. Says her throat isn't sore, either. She just wants—needs—to be in a nice soft *quiet* bed somewhere and be fed some soup, that's all." Ms. Frawley's voice was sounding more hopeful.

Elizabeth pinched her nose, her heart thudding in her chest. Her afternoon was clear, she already knew.... "Okay, okay...I'll come get her."

"Oh, thank you so much. You know where we are?"

The directions scribbled on the back of an envelope, Elizabeth assured the woman she'd be there in ten minutes, hung up and panicked. "What did I just do?" she asked Cora in a tight voice. "What on earth do I know about taking care of a sick little girl?"

A pencil clamped between her teeth while she riffled through one of the file drawers, Cora darted her a look that was pure pity. "Child," she said with remarkable clarity around the pencil, "I never did see anyone take on so about stuff that other people just go ahead and *do,* you know that?" She yanked a file out of the drawer, then the pencil out of her mouth. Fastening one broad hand on a broader, floral polyester-clad hip she asked, "You never got sick as a kid?"

"Of course I did."

"And what did your mama do for you?"

Elizabeth thought about this for a minute, then shrugged. "I don't know. Gave me stuff I liked to eat, kept me warm. Or cool, whatever. Read to me."

"Well, honey, this child isn't a different species." She stood up and walked with great deliberateness back to her desk. "Odds are she'd like the same things you did."

Cora had a point. But boy oh boy, the last thing she'd expected today was a pop quiz in Mothering for the Woefully Inept. With another sigh, she collected her handbag from her desk and headed for the door. Just as she opened it, she heard Cora say, "I bet there's one more thing your mother gave you when you were sick."

She twisted around, eyebrows raised. "And what's that?"

"A mountain of love, honey."

Elizabeth nodded and shut the door behind her, gasping in the muggy heat. Chicken soup, orange juice, a comfortable bed—those, she had.

The last item she wasn't so sure about.

The first few minutes in the car were awkward at best. Neither one of them was sure what to say, what to do, Ashli's declaration of the night before hanging between them like a poisonous gas. Resentment that Elizabeth, instead of her father, had come to pick her up simmered behind the moist eyes, but Elizabeth refused to take it personally.

She glanced over at the sniffling little girl, a pang of empathy pricking her heart. She was sure Ashli racked this up as one more indignity, one more demonstration of how rotten her life was. Never mind how devoted her father was, or even how much her extended family probably loved her. When you were eight, priorities were different. Elizabeth remembered, all too clearly, how much a child's world is made up of a slew of little things that may seem insignificant to a grown-up. A well-loved doll to hug. A favorite TV show, on at the same time every day. Your own bed in your own house, and the *right* voice to soothe you when you don't feel well. When those things are yanked away, it can seem as if the world itself is disintegrating around you. Change—any change—becomes almost impossible to bear, and even the most unpracticed survival instinct will fight to preserve a fragile status quo.

Oh, yes. Elizabeth remembered. And the memories evoked a totally unexpected feeling of connectedness to this little girl.

The child clutched some papers to a chest covered by a wisp of a sundress over a short-sleeved T-shirt, her bare legs jutting straight off the edge of the front seat, positioning her jelly-sandaled feet inches away from the car's air-conditioning vent. Which, at last, was working again.

"Is that air too cold on you?"

Ashli's only response was a negative jerk of her head, corn-silk hair swishing over shoulders so slender one of the dress's spaghetti straps kept slipping off.

"Cora's going to keep trying to get your daddy, honey. He'll come get you as soon as he can, I'm sure."

Ashli just nodded and sniffed.

"Need a tissue?"

She shook her head again, not so emphatically, shifting the papers against her chest. Not knowing what else to do, Elizabeth kept talking. "Are those art projects?"

No answer.

"I'd love to see them later. Your daddy told me how talented you were."

He hadn't, but Elizabeth figured he probably would have had the subject come up. Sure enough, that merited at least a modicum of response.

"He did?"

"Mm-hm.

A pause. "Could I have that tissue now?"

"Oh, sure, sweetie. There's a box between the seats, there. See it?"

A second later, she heard the sound of a small, stuffed nose unsuccessfully trying to blow, followed by a very shaky sigh. Tears, she knew, were imminent. Sure enough, when she looked over, a great big fat one was slithering down a soft pink cheek.

"We're almost there," she said gently, and received a sad shrug in response.

A few minutes later, Elizabeth unlocked her front door and ushered the child inside, checking the thermostat to make sure the air-conditioning wasn't too high, then going into the kitchen. "Let's see..." She opened the refrigerator, scanning the contents. "Would you like some juice? There's orange, apple-grape, and cran-raspberry." She looked up to find a pair of watery blue eyes peering over the counter at her.

"What's cran-raspberry taste like?" Ashli asked, so faintly Elizabeth could hardly hear her.

"Here..." Elizabeth poured a half-inch of the ruby-red liquid into a glass and handed it to her. "Try it."

Ashli took a tentative sip, her brow puckered in concentration for a full thirty seconds. Then she nodded, handing back the glass.

"Want some more?"

Another nod, this one accompanied by a tiny smile.

She handed the child a full glass of the juice with instructions to finish it either in the kitchen or at the dining table, then told her she'd be right back as soon as she prepared the bed.

She'd never taken care of as much as a goldfish before, Elizabeth realized as she turned back the comforter and fluffed up the pillows. Now she was taking care of a *child*. Someone else's child, at that. A little human being who would undoubtedly give her father a blow-by-blow description of the afternoon's events.

How did she get herself into these fixes?

Elizabeth pawed through her nightgown drawer and pulled out a shortie cotton gown that would probably serve for Ashli to sleep in, laying it out on the bed. She straightened up, hands on hips, trying to remember what her mother had done for her when she'd been sick. A bath. She bet Ashli would like nice, warm, frothy bubble bath.

She quickly changed out of her black linen dress into a pair of shorts and an oversize T-shirt, then hurried into the living room, where she found the little girl sitting disconsolately on the white sofa with the papers still clasped to her chest, staring at the crystal collection. The tears, such as they were, had

dried; but more than a cold was making that little face s
incredibly sad.

Elizabeth hesitated, not sure what to do, then followe
Ashli's gaze to the crystal. Wordlessly, she crossed to the éta
gère and turned on the lights underneath each shelf, watching
the big blue eyes grow even larger.

"They look like something a princess should have," Ashl
croaked.

"Hardly." She beckoned with her hand. "Come take
closer look."

Ashli leaned forward and set her papers on the glass-toppe
coffee table, then slid down off the sofa and cautiously ap
proached the display, as if afraid the vision might disappear
When she got right up to the shelves, she reached out, the
snatched back her hand and tucked it behind her back.

Elizabeth smiled. "I bet someone hears 'don't touch' a lo
doesn't she?"

The child nodded, a hairline frown creasing her brow. "
think Daddy really means it more for the boys, 'cause the
wreck everything they get close to."

"And you?"

Elizabeth had never seen a more rueful smile. "If I don'
touch stuff, then I can't get blamed when something gets bro
ken."

"Good thinking." Elizabeth slipped her arm around thos
fragile shoulders, catching a whiff of baby shampoo as sh
did. She imagined Guy doing the honors, and her heart kin
of did this little pingy thing in her chest. "Okay. The rule is
you can't pick up any of the pieces, because they're glass. I
they drop, they might break and I'd be afraid the sharp piece
would hurt you. But you can't hurt them or you if you jus
touch them with one finger, like this...." Elizabeth demon
strated, skimming her index finger over the faceted design o
a Waterford vase just at Ashli's level. "See?"

Still cautious, Ashli imitated Elizabeth, her tiny finger ska
ing along the surface of the crystal. Slowly, a faint smil
tugged at the corners of the little girl's mouth, and she sighe

A sigh of contentment this time, Elizabeth thought. Then, without warning, Ashli sneezed. Loudly and messily.

Mortification streaked across her features. ''Oh, no...I got the glass all yucky.''

''Hey, forget it. It's not like it can get your cold or anything.'' As tentatively as Ashli had reached out to the crystal, Elizabeth now brushed back a few silky strands of hair from the little girl's face. The flinch was almost, but not completely, imperceptible.

''That's it—'' She looped one arm around the child's shoulders and marched her back to the sofa. ''Time you and I had a little woman-to-woman chat.''

Wordlessly, Ashli let herself be led, easing herself onto the sofa. Not surprisingly, she wouldn't look at Elizabeth.

''Okay, honey—out with it. Why don't you like me?''

The blond head whipped around. ''But I do like you!''

''Yeah?'' Elizabeth handed Ashli a tissue. ''Coulda fooled me.''

The child blew her nose, then stared at her knees, wadding the tissue up in long, thin fingers. ''I just don't want you to take Mama's place.''

''Ah.'' Elizabeth sank back into the sofa, her arms crossed. ''Why do you think that's something to worry about?''

''Because I see the way Daddy looks at you,'' she said. ''And he talks about you *all* the time.'' This last comment was accompanied by an exasperated roll of the eyes. Before Elizabeth could think of what to say, Ashli twisted around to her. ''Do you want to marry Daddy?''

She commended herself for not reacting. But she'd somehow expected to hash this out with the father before discussing it with the daughter. When—if—the time came. ''We haven't talked about it,'' was all she could think of to say.

The blue eyes flooded; clearly, the little girl expected— wanted—a flat-out no.

From somewhere, from nowhere, it came to Elizabeth to take the little hand in hers. ''Ashli, listen to me. I can't take your mother's place, okay? She'll always be your mama, no matter what.''

"But, see, if Daddy gets married again, she won't ever come back!"

Elizabeth shut her eyes, praying for the right words. God! How do you convince a child to let go, when the only solution she'll accept is a return to the way things were?

"Honey, I know you don't know me very well, but trust me. Whether your daddy gets married again has nothing to do with whether or not your Mama comes back. No one would ever keep you from seeing her."

After a long moment, Ashli said, "You sure?"

"There are two things I don't do, Ashli. I don't tell lies, and I don't break my promises."

The blue eyes turned to her. "Ever?"

"Cross my heart."

Ashli continued to scrutinize Elizabeth for several seconds more, then asked, "Will you promise me something, then?"

"If I can, sure."

"If you and Daddy decide to become, you know, boyfriend and girlfriend, will you tell me?"

The question startled Elizabeth. But what surprised her more was that she wasn't sure how to answer. "Why do you think we wouldn't tell you?" she asked, knowing she was sidestepping the issue.

She shrugged. "Because grown-ups..." She stopped sucked in a little breath, started again. "They just do whatever they want and leave the kids to find out on their own. And that stinks."

"You better believe that stinks. But I'd never hurt you honey. And neither would your father."

Ashli sneezed again, and again, then gave a cursory nod of acceptance.

It seemed the conversation was over. "How about...a bubble bath?" Elizabeth ventured, to be rewarded with a real smile.

"Well, come on, then." She stood up, holding out a hand to Ashli. "Let's get you into the tub."

"I'm so sorry," Guy said the moment Elizabeth opened the door, his senses sent into immediate overdrive from her per fume, the scent of roast chicken and the sight of those killer legs peeking out from underneath a huge sage-green shirt. "I swear she was fine this morning when I dropped her off."

"Yeah, that was a real low-down thing you did." One pink-tipped finger pushed her glasses back into place. "Letting your kid get a cold." She backed up, letting Micah and Jake barrel into the apartment, but cut Guy off with that same finger, now jabbed into his chest. "Although what's the deal with not telling me you gave my name to the day care center to use in an emergency?"

She could probably feel the heat from his blush from where she stood. "I really meant to, I did, but I've been so busy and I kept forgetting, and actually, I never thought they'd ever have to call you...."

"It's okay," she interrupted. "It just would have been nice to have some warning, though." She squeezed his arm, then stood to one side so he could enter, whereupon his life flashed before his eyes.

"Don't touch!" he bellowed, and, for once, four little hands immediately reversed from a collision course with some very fragile-looking crystal in a lit étagère. In a single two-second scan of the apartment, he saw all the makings for potential catastrophe. Oh, geez—a *white* sofa?

"Come here." When they obeyed, he pointed to the dining table, the only piece of furniture in this apartment that would probably take them longer than five minutes to stain, break or gouge. "Sit over there, and do not move unless I tell you." He caught Jake's chin in his hand and met his eyes. "Understand?"

"Yes," came the overly enthusiastic reply accompanied by a bobbing head. He turned his gaze to a mimicking Micah, knowing full well a promise elicited from a two-year-old was more worthless than Confederate greenbacks. "Okay, you two—sit."

They sat.

"Impressive, again," Elizabeth said from the kitchen.

Guy leaned over the counter, speaking in a hushed voice.

"If I'm lucky, they'll stay out of trouble just long enough to collect my daughter and get back out of here before they realize it's all bluff."

"You know…" Elizabeth opened the oven door to check on the chicken, the fragrance setting Guy's stomach to growling like an angry cat. "I was thinking." She spooned up the juices from bottom of the pan; they hit that crisp skin with a tantalizing sizzle that made his knees weak. She closed the oven door, leaned back against the far counter with her arms crossed, a pair of pot holders clutched in one hand. "Maybe you shouldn't take Ashli back tonight. She's gotten really settled in here, and being as she shares a room with the boys…"

Out of the corner of his eye, Guy could see said boys were already fidgeting. "Oh, I was going to let her stay in my room. I'll sleep on the couch."

He couldn't read the expression in those green eyes, but he could see some sort of struggle going on behind them. "Well," she said after a moment, "why don't you all have dinner here, and afterward, ask Ashli what she wants to do?"

Guy straightened up, bracing his hands on the edge of the counter. "You're volunteering to take care of a sick child all night?"

"Yes."

"Why?"

"Because…I want to."

Anxiety and hope fought it out in her eyes, and something clutched in his chest. What she was offering, for her, took a lot of guts. And he'd've given anything to be able to accept her dinner invitation, as well, but…

"You don't know how good that sounds, staying here for dinner. Unfortunately, Micah's on his last diaper and I think Jake's coming down with something, too, so I don't think staying would be a good idea."

Her eyes clouded, setting off a small burst of delight in his brain. "Well, okay then, I suppose…but let me give you half that chicken, and some potatoes and salad—"

"And my daughter?"

"Stays here."

He knew better than to argue. Or to press her for her reasons.

"Go on into the bedroom and see her," she said. When he cast a wary glance at his sons, she smiled. "It's okay. I may be little, but they're littler."

Guy had to walk through the rest of the apartment to get to the bedroom, an extremely enlightening twenty-foot journey. The orderly placement of everything down to the stone-blue damask throw pillows on the white sofa, the pale carpet and ice-blue walls and glittering crystal, was as soothing and pretty as a pristine winter landscape. If a little chilly for his taste.

Her bedroom, on the other hand, was anything but.

Brilliant late-day sunshine filtered through half-closed miniblinds, flooding walls the color of ripe cantaloupe. Flowers— huge and vibrant and out of control—were everywhere. Corals. Crimsons. Gaudy, blinding yellows. Splashed across a comforter neatly folded at the foot of the bed, undulating in the folds of matching draperies looped across a brass rod and puddling on the carpet on either side of the windows, rippling along the dust ruffle. He glimpsed white laminate bookcases crammed with paperbacks; a tightly woven rattan chair with an emerald-green cushion; a white French provincial vanity, similar to the set in Elizabeth's childhood bedroom, cluttered—yes, cluttered!—with assorted, undefinable female…stuff.

Guy chuckled. It was all here, in this room. All the warmth and sunshine and passion the woman was so afraid to let anyone see, hidden in a place where she could keep perfect control over it. This was the Elizabeth no one knew. This was the Elizabeth he'd known, somehow, was there all along.

Ashli was asleep on bright-yellow sheets, like a fairy child laid inside a buttercup. Her nose was still clogged, he guessed from the little snuffling sounds she made as she slept, but her color looked normal—if glowing—and she seemed, for the first time in ages, at peace. She awoke when he approached the bed, immediately springing up and throwing her arms around his neck.

"Heyya, munchkin..." He kissed her forehead, which he gratefully noted was cool. "How ya feelin'?"

"Better," she said with a grin. "Elizabeth gave me lots of juice and soup, and that made my nose feel better. And I got to take a bubble bath. And she read to me, and this bed is *sooo* comfortable." She giggled. "And look what she gave me. She said I could take it home with me, when I leave."

She'd removed from a little wire stand on the bed table next to her an intricately carved crystal heart, maybe three inches across, laying it in his open palm. The delicacy of the ornament was belied by the weight and substance of the crystal; it was, he thought, an inherently feminine object, and a perfect symbol for his daughter. Not to mention the woman who'd given it to her.

He fingered the pink satin ribbon attached to its top, then carefully rehung it on its stand, where it quivered for a moment or two, sparkling in the diffused sunshine creeping through the blinds.

"Isn't it pretty?" Ashli asked, leaning back against the pillows.

"Very," Guy agreed, then turned back to her with a grin. "Hey—I thought you were supposed to be sick. Sounds like you've been having an awful lot of fun to me."

Another giggle skipped out of Ashli's throat. Guy could have kissed Elizabeth, just for that. "Elizabeth said I needed to be..." Her brow creased for a second as she fought to remember the word. Then she brightened. "Pampered."

Guy sighed. "I haven't been able to do much in the pampering department lately, I guess, huh?"

Ashli wiggled in the bed, pulling her knees up to her chin. "Elizabeth said how hard it is for you to take care of us all by yourself and still have to work and that she remembered feeling bad when her daddy died when she was a little girl, 'cause her mother couldn't be around as much anymore." Plucking at a fold in the sheet, she said with lowered eyes, "She said she got lonely, too."

Guy swallowed, then touched his forehead to hers. "Elizabeth asked me if you could stay overnight. Would you like to do that?''

"A night away from the boys?" Ashli rolled her eyes, and Guy had to suppress a laugh. "You better believe it." Staking her claim, she snuggled back down under the covers, folding her arms across her chest.

He bent over and kissed her forehead, brushing back her bangs with his fingers. "I'll call you later tonight, okay? After I get the boys in bed."

She nodded so hard the bed shook.

When he returned to the kitchen, Micah was happily stacking a dozen Tupperware bowls and lids, emitting squeals of delight when Jake knocked them down and he got to do it all over again.

"And you said you didn't know what to do with kids."

Elizabeth was cutting up the chicken and transferring the pieces to a large piece of aluminum foil. She tossed a brief glance in his direction, but no comment.

"Ah. The noise is driving you batty, isn't it?"

"Completely," she admitted, efficiently tucking the foil around the chicken. She sighed. "How on earth do you stand it?" Once again, the tower crashed onto the floor; both boys let out whoops of laughter that made her cringe.

"Believe me, I get my share of headaches," Guy said. "And bedtime never comes quickly enough." He shrugged. "But it comes with the territory."

"You get used to it, is what you're saying."

"No. You get used to *dealing* with it. Big difference."

She seemed to consider this for a minute, then snapped shut the lid on a jade-green Tupperware bowl and slipped it into a plastic sack, setting the chicken on top. "There. That should do it. And there are three potatoes in with the chicken...."

"Sure wish I could stay," Guy said, inching closer.

Elizabeth lifted her eyes to his, and Guy realized just how close he was. "I do, too," she said softly, and with clear invitation.

There were four beady little eyes riveted to them, watching every move. He remembered what it had been like, part of what had driven Dianne nuts. No privacy, always having to schedule, always having to wait until little people were in bed or away, always having to consider how certain actions might be construed. Then he thought of his parents, who never hid their desire for each other, and what an inspiration their openness had been to their children, four of whom were in extremely happy marriages.

Slipping one hand around Elizabeth's waist, he accepted that invitation. Enthusiastically. He kissed her until he felt her heart speed up, right along with his, until a tiny telltale moan rumbled deep in her throat. He kissed her until he nearly forgot the boys were even there. And when he pulled away, she looked into his eyes and said, "I think I'm beginning to understand how parents do this."

"Yep," he agreed, grinning like a danged fool. "What makes the little varmints in the first place also helps keep you sane after they get here."

Two pairs of arms clamped around their legs. "Up!" said Micah. "Hug!"

Laughing, Guy reached down and hauled the baby up onto his hip, then reclaimed Elizabeth's waist as Micah planted a wet kiss first on his lips, then leaned toward Elizabeth. With a laugh, she gamely accepted the sloppy embrace. Guy let the baby down, then repeated the procedure with Jake, who declined, however, to kiss Elizabeth. Then he, too, wriggled down, returning to the game on the kitchen floor.

"Of course, spontaneity can be a problem."

Elizabeth laughed and looped her arms around *his* waist. "Forewarned is forearmed, huh?"

Did he dare believe…? He smoothed a strand of hair from her cheek. "Am I imagining things, or have you stopped running?"

Her forehead fell forward, onto his chest. "It's…hard to run when you keep tripping over your heart."

She was like a butterfly he hadn't really expected to light on his hand—he dared not breathe for fear it would flit away. "Scared?"

"Oh, Lord," she said, rubbing her cheek against his shirt. *"Petrified."*

"But...?"

She lifted her head and smiled. The way she had for the Gundersons. No, not that way, because this was for him, and him alone, and it was even more heart-stopping than he thought it would be. "I can only take one step at a time."

"I wouldn't expect anything more." His heart ramming against his ribs, he brushed her lips with his once more, then gathered up his troops and turned to leave. Turned back.

"I'll call."

"You'd better," she said.

Chapter 9

From somewhere deep in a dream, Elizabeth heard a funny trilling sound. Then it stopped. Then it sounded again.

Scrambling across the sofa bed, she grappled for the phone, knocked it off the end table, caught it before it hit the floor. "Hello?" she grumbled, hanging half off the bed.

"Lord and Taylor is having a humongous sale at Twelve Oaks, we gotta go."

Shoving her mop out of her face, Elizabeth hauled herself into a sitting position, grabbed her watch off the end table and squinted at it, then mumbled, "Nancy, unless Detroit is now in a different time zone than Spruce Lake, it's 7:00 a.m. At this hour, I don't care if Lord and Taylor's *giving* stuff away—"

"Listen, listen, listen…" A newspaper or something rattled on the other end of the line. "Liz Claiborne, half off. Anne Klein, thirty-five percent. Ellen Tracy, select group, up to forty percent off. I tell you, we *gotta* go."

She yawned. "Uh-uh. *You* gotta go. *I* don't gotta go nowhere."

"Oh, come on…it's so much more fun shopping with you.

I hate shopping by myself. Hey—we can cruise for cute boys and everything.''

With a weary laugh, Elizabeth fell back against the sofa cushions. It really had been a long time since they'd bummed around together....

Behind her, the bathroom door closed, soon followed by a toilet flush.

Oh, right.

"Actually—'' she yawned again ''—the idea doesn't sound half bad, now that my heart is beating again. But I'm not alone.''

A *looong* silence followed.

"Oh, yeah? Wait, wait, wait—I gotta get comfortable for this—''

"Don't get excited. I was on nursing duty for an eight-year-old last night.''

This pause was longer than the last. *"You?"*

"What's so weird about that?''

"What *isn't* weird about that, you mean,'' came the flabbergasted reply. "How the hell did you get roped into that?''

"I volunteered,'' Elizabeth sighed, then grinned as her little charge climbed up on the bed with her. "But in any case, I'm not a free agent this morning.''

"So bring her along.''

"Hello? She's not feeling well. Which is why I was nursing her?…What?'' This last word was directed at Ashli, who was emphatically shaking her head.

"I feel fine this morning.''

Elizabeth put a hand on the child's forehead. "No sniffles?''

"Uh-uh.''

"Throat okay?''

"Uh-huh.''

"You're sure?''

She nodded again.

"I heard,'' Nancy said. "So bring her along.''

"Well…I don't know…'' Elizabeth shifted her gaze to Ashli's questioning one, then tucked the phone against her collarbone. "Wanna go shopping?''

"Yes! Can I?"

"We have to ask your father."

Ashli didn't seem to think this would be a problem, so Elizabeth put the phone back to her ear. "We have to check with Dad, but, okay, sure. We'll meet you at ten in front of Lord and Taylor."

Not only was there no problem, Elizabeth didn't think she'd ever heard anyone sound more grateful. She quickly gathered that shopping for little-girl stuff was not high on Guy's list of favorite things to do. Did she mind, he asked, picking up a few things and he'd pay her back?

Somewhere around one, the three of them plopped down around a table in front of one of the mall restaurants, shopping bags falling every which way around them. "Hungry?" Elizabeth asked Ashli, too tired to even care if she got her white shorts dirty on the seat.

The child nodded, her primary response to most questions the entire morning.

"Does this kid ever talk?" Nancy asked good-naturedly, shoving the hem of her ankle-length sundress out of the way to rub an aching instep.

"Yeah, when she can get a word in edgewise, yammer-mouth."

Over Ashli's giggles, Nancy pulled a face, then said to her, "You hear how she talks to me? Her best friend, she says. Hah!"

Ashli giggled again.

Elizabeth leaned her chin in her hand and smiled at the little girl, who'd been grinning and/or giggling the entire morning. Come to think of it, Elizabeth had been grinning and giggling a good bit herself. It felt good. *Damn* good. She pulled a five-dollar bill out of her purse, gestured toward the open-doored restaurant. "Here. Live."

The blue eyes widened. "I can get anything I want?"

"As long as it comes to less than five bucks, sure."

"Even if it isn't healthy?"

"I don't think they serve anything that will kill you. At least not after one meal."

As Elizabeth carefully watched Ashli head straight for the cinnamon rolls, she heard Nancy ask, "Is this called a step in the right direction?"

She flicked a glance at the brunette, then looked right back at Ashli. "Meaning?"

"Seeing how you get along with one of his kids?"

"It wasn't planned, Nance, if that's what you mean."

"But…?"

"But…I'd have to admit, so far, so good. To tell you the truth, I haven't had this much fun in a very long time."

"Yep, that's me…old chopped liver herself." Nancy started in on the other instep.

"And if Ashli were Guy's only child," she said, ignoring Nancy's editorializing, "*and* if mothering meant nothing more than fun outings and buying pretties all the time…" She sighed. "But I'm not a total fool. Okay, so I'm enjoying playing the indulgent auntie for the day. That doesn't mean I'm ready to sign up for the long haul."

Nancy let out an exasperated huff, then waved her hand around in a gesture of acquiescence. "Yeah, I see your point. It's tough, dealing with another woman's kids. In your place, I'm not sure I wouldn't do the same thing. Even if the guy did have the hottest blue eyes this side of Sweden."

Slowly, Elizabeth veered her eyes to her friend's face. "Nancy?"

"Yeah?"

"How'd you know what color Guy's eyes were?"

Nancy instantly snatched up one of the shopping bags and started pawing through it. "Whaddya think of putting this top—" she hauled out a red rayon shell "—with—" she dropped the first bag, grabbed a second and pulled out a floral skirt "—this skirt?"

"Nance…"

The woman cracked like an overripe pecan. "Okay. In the museum. You were right. That *was* Guy and the kids." She sighed, stuffing everything back into the shopping bags. "Your mother and I were trying to arrange something, that Guy would 'run into' you there.'' She shrugged. ''I don't know what happened. I told him where you were, and but he must've chickened out or something. I don't know…'' Another shrug.

Before Elizabeth could analyze this latest tidbit, Ashli returned to the table with two enormous cinnamon rolls and a cup of orange juice. ''Let's see…'' Elizabeth pretended to scrutinize her purchase. ''Orange juice. That's a fruit, right? And the cinnamon roll hits your bread group, definitely. Probably eggs, which is what, dairy? And, oh! Look…there's some nuts, too. Hey, four out of four. Is this healthy or what?''

All this time, Ashli giggled. ''You sound just like Daddy,'' she said, and Elizabeth's heart did that little pingy thing again.

''Well, I'm off to the john,'' Nancy unceremoniously announced. ''Don't talk about me while I'm gone.''

Ashli wanted to peruse her booty while she ate, but Elizabeth said not while her fingers were so sticky. There was, she realized, a lot to peruse. A half-dozen pairs of panties, several nighties and a summer robe, socks in at least ten appalling hues— the child had clearly inherited her father's color sense—shorts and T-shirts and two little jersey sundresses they'd found on sale and couldn't pass up, and enough hair geegaws to last until the child reached college. Guy was going to kill her.

Guy would just have to deal with it.

Nancy returned, looking much relieved, and the two of them grabbed burgers and Diet Cokes before tackling the *upper* level of the mall, which had, if Elizabeth's memory served, a dress shop that specialized in petites.

And a bookstore.

While Nancy kept Ashli otherwise occupied, Elizabeth checked out the section on child care. Which just happened to be an aisle away from a certain other area in which Elizabeth's expertise was even more limited. Her arms full of how-to books on raising kids, she sidled over to this section as casually as she could manage. Ten minutes later, after skimming the contents of perhaps a half-dozen ''tastefully illustrated'' volumes, she realized to her acute embarrassment she was extremely aroused.

She chose two of the most "tasteful" of the selections and hoped the clerk wouldn't look at her as she paid for her purchases.

"What took you so long?" Nancy demanded when Elizabeth caught up with them in front of The Gap.

Elizabeth blushed, which made Nancy grab the bookstore shopping bag before Elizabeth could do anything about it. Five seconds later, Nancy broke out into a cackle that carried all the way to the lower level.

That did it. Pushing her glasses up onto her nose, Elizabeth announced, "I think it's time we went home, Ashli, don't you?"

"Not yet," Nancy said with a firm shake of her head, taking her by the arm and dragging her along, Ashli scurrying in their wake.

"Nancy! What on earth are you doing…?"

"You *will* go in here, and you *will* try these on."

Elizabeth looked up. Somebody-or-other's Complete Vision Center. She grimaced at her friend. "Contacts?"

"Contacts."

"What if I say no?"

"It's usually easier to do the eye exam if the patient hasn't been knocked unconscious."

"Elizabeth?" piped a soft voice at her elbow.

"Yeah, honey?"

"Are contacts those things people wear instead of glasses?"

"Yes."

Ashli thought about this for a moment, then said, "When you don't have your glasses on, you can't see very well, can you?"

"That's putting it mildly."

"So you can't see yourself in a mirror?"

"No…"

"I thought so," the child said with a sage nod. "Then you can't see that you're much prettier without your glasses." She shrugged. "Just thought you should know."

Elizabeth exchanged an I'm-doomed glance with Nancy's blatantly triumphant one and stepped across the threshold to the optometry office. In less than an hour, for the first time since she was nine years old, she could see clearly without having to constantly shove those damn glasses back up on her nose.

They sat on the pond's bank, watching, through a humid coral haze, the children scamper at the water's edge twenty feet away. Despite having spent hours at the mall—an activity which would have rendered Guy crippled and crazed—Elizabeth had whipped up a "little" stir-fry dinner for them all, helped Ashli change about a million times so she could model her loot—for which she refused to accept reimbursement—and still had energy left to go for a walk afterward. This was no ordinary woman.

"I haven't seen Ashli this relaxed and happy in months," Guy said. "Thank you."

With both hands, she piled her hair loosely on top of her head, looking both surprised and pleased. "You're welcome, I suppose," she said. "Mind you, though—I have no idea what I did."

A few damp tendrils curled over the base of her neck, glistening in the waning light. Chuckling, Guy leaned over and brushed his lips over the salty moisture, making her shudder. And giggle.

"What are you thinking?" she asked, letting the hair tumble back down.

He leaned back on the grass, his head propped in his hand. She stretched out on her side next to him, resting her hand on his chest; he interlaced their fingers, stroking her palm with his thumb. "That for the first time in ages I'm sorry my kids are around."

She glanced over at the pond, as if to make sure they weren't being watched, then smiled. "Hmm. Whatever happened to dating?"

"This will do."

She laughed, freely, from deep in her throat. "Opportunist."

"Absolutely."

"And what was all that about only wanting the best?"

"Let's see," he mused, watching her fingers tease his shirt buttons. "It's sunset, I'm lying next to a wonderful, gorgeous woman who's just fed me a wonderful, gorgeous meal, my three wonderful, gorgeous kids are happily giving ducks indigestion a few feet away... It doesn't get much better than this."

Her grin turned positively wicked. "It doesn't?"

She was turning him inside out. He stared at her tiny hand captured in his, then brought it to his lips. "Who are you, Elizabeth Louden?"

The grin softened, he thought, into something more introspective. "I'm not sure anymore," she said quietly. "But I do know one thing..." At his raised eyebrow, she supplied, "It's much more fun being me when I'm around you."

A curious way of putting it, but he understood. "Yeah," he said. "Me, too."

Two of the ducks apparently decided they weren't being fed quickly enough and had waddled up onto the bank to press their case, sending Jake and Micah scurrying for their lives and Ashli into peals of laughter. Elizabeth sat up, hugging her knees.

"Wusses," Ashli accused, and Elizabeth laughed as well. Guy, however, for the first time in more than a year, wasn't interested in his children's antics.

"I have to tell you something."

Still laughing, Elizabeth twisted around and looked at him.

He hauled himself up onto his elbow, skimming his palm up and down her forearm. "After Dianne left, I made a vow that whether or not I ever slept with anyone again, I would not parade women in and out of my children's lives."

She looked away. "And have you?"

"Kept that vow?"

"Slept with anyone since your divorce?"

"Other than the occasional freaked out child, no."

Elizabeth chuckled, then let herself fall back against the sloping bank, stretching her arms over her head. "Then I think you're *waaay* overdue."

She wasn't wearing a bra, he suddenly realized, the evidence blatantly pressed against the thin fabric of her white shirt. Guy shifted his attention to the kids, to the pond, to the ducks, but it was too late. His body had reacted, and he wanted Elizabeth with an urgency like he'd never known before. He felt her hand on his arm.

"I don't mean to be a tease," she said softly when he turned to her. "And like you said. It's not just us we're thinking about here."

He studied her for a moment, then carefully stroked her cheek with one finger. "Until I met you, celibacy was no sacrifice."

After what seemed like an eternity, Elizabeth pushed herself up onto her elbow to face him, her hair festooned with bits of grass. "Could your parents take the kids on Friday night?"

Guy searched those lovely green eyes and realized he wasn't breathing. "What are you saying?"

She looked down, but her fingers found their way to his arm, skating up and down so that all the hairs stood on end. Then her eyes drifted back up to his.

"Exactly what you think I'm saying."

Thank God he was already sitting down, because he sure as hell would've fallen over otherwise. He wasn't sure if her proposition or his reaction to it stunned him more. Whatever it was, he couldn't speak.

"Daddy! The bread's all gone!" Jake hollered from what seemed like a universe away.

"Did I misread your signals?" Elizabeth asked at the same time.

For a second, Guy was confused. "What?"

"I'm not very good at any of this," she said, again pulling herself into a sitting position. "I thought you…were interested in taking things further."

"Daaad!"

"*What?*" Guy glowered at his son over Elizabeth's head.

"There's no more bread."

"So just sit and *talk* to the ducks, for crying out loud!"

"Micah pooped his pants," was Ashli's addition to the conversation.

"He'll live for a few minutes," Guy called back.

"But he really stinks!"

"Ashli! It's okay! Just…cope for a minute, all right?"

Ashli made a great dramatic gesture of holding her nose with one hand and waving with the other, but she ceased her barrage for the moment.

Guy fell backward with a groan, covering his eyes with his hands, only to hear Elizabeth laughing.

"What's so funny?" he asked, his eyes still covered.

"You. This. Us."

He lowered his hands, sat up to kiss her lightly on the mouth. "You did not misread the signals," he said quietly, threading his fingers through that unbelievably soft hair. "But jumping into bed just to relieve a hormonal itch isn't my thing, you got that?" He grasped a handful of hair, gave it a gentle tug. "The only reason I want to make love to you is because I care about you. Very deeply."

She flushed at that. And smiled, just a little, plucked something out of his hair.

He studied her, hard. "Did you hear what I said?"

"Yes."

"And you're still here?"

"Oh, yes."

"A week ago," he said over his thudding heart, "I couldn't even buy you coffee."

"A week ago…" She just shook her head. "Things were different."

He turned his attention to his children. "Are they?"

She followed his gaze; he saw the ambivalence resurface, saw her push it back.

"I have to play devil's advocate, sweetheart."

Her eyes once again his, she said, "One step at a time, Guy. One step at a time."

Before he could point out that what they were about to do was a doozy of a step, Micah sailed into his arms and knocked him over onto the grass.

By Friday, Elizabeth was close to total incoherence. She'd find herself reading the same spec three times before being able to decide if the house might be right for a client. She made phone calls only to forget who she was calling. She spaced appointments. She even crabbed at Cora about something so minor she'd forgotten it ten minutes later.

All because she was going to let Guy make love to her? Honestly—what was the big deal? It was just…sex. Women had sex all the time.

Other women, maybe.

"Going to lunch, Miss Elizabeth," Cora called from the outer office. "Make sure you give your mother those messages if she calls in."

Elizabeth mumbled something, frowning at some graph or something on her computer screen. A bar chart. A bar chart which, no matter how she tried to convince herself otherwise, looked like a bunch of primary colored, rectangular phallic symbols marching across her screen—

She eeked when Guy grabbed her by the wrist, pulled her to her feet, and dragged her to her mother's office, then more or less threw her down onto the couch.

"What are you do—? Mmph!"

His kiss swallowed her question. Answered it, too. Quite clearly. Her arms twined around his neck as Guy lay on top of her, their bodies pressed so tightly together you couldn't have slipped a credit card between them.

She shivered, she sparked, she whimpered and gasped and hoped to God Cora hadn't forgotten anything. From somewhere, the thought scuttled through her brain that she was having an incredibly good time. Her hands flew up to his hair, yanking so hard on the rubber band holding his ponytail he winced. Then he laughed and renewed his assault on her mouth, her senses, her long-neglected libido. When he paused to snatch some air, she managed to gasp a breathless, "Is this supposed to be calming me down?"

"Now why would I want to do that?" he mumbled from the base of her neck.

Before she could think of a reply, he'd claimed her mouth again. Her blood roared in her ears as his tongue searched out hers and made it his own, as their pelvises fused together and she could feel his arousal. She ached for him, wanted him, knew why she'd waited. Wondered how she'd managed to wait this long.

He read her mind. "Maybe," he suggested in her ear as he fingered the top button of her blouse, "We should nip over to your apartment and speed things up a bit."

All she could manage was a moan.

"Was that a 'yes'?"

"No, that was a moan."

One side of that delicious mouth hitched up. "So...?" He skimmed one finger down the front of her blouse, teasing the top of her breast. "Whaddya say?"

"Hah! If you think I'm gonna settle for a quickie for our first time together—" she sat up, shoving him off of her in the process "—you've got another think coming, buster." She pulled herself up off the couch and walked away, one hand tugging her skirt back where it belonged while the other smoothed her hair.

With a low laugh, Guy caught her from behind, his hands melting into her shoulders, massaging them. "I suppose you're right, honey-bunch—"

"Please. You're making my teeth hurt...ohhh...yes, right there."

"Hmmm...was that a moan?"

"That was a 'don't stop.' Brother. You really have to learn to listen better."

He chuckled. "You *sure* you want to wait?"

She moaned again, figured he could take it any way he damn well chose, then noticed the stack of mail on her mother's desk. She shimmied out from underneath his hands and crossed the room. "Hey—when did this get here?"

"Here I am," she heard Guy mutter, "trying my best to seduce the woman, and she notices the *mail,* for God's sake...."

"Oh, hush. Here—this one's for you."

She handed him the envelope, returned to poking through the rest of the mail. Several seconds had passed before she realized he'd been silent.

On instant alert, she looked up. He sagged against the conference table, staring at a letter pinched in his right hand. Light-blue, tissuey. A foreign air letter.

Her stomach wrenched. "Guy? Everything okay?"

He turned to her, so pale she thought he'd become ill. *"What?"*

In the silence, she could hear the erratic ticking of the tiny clock on her mother's desk. "It's from Dianne," he said, handing her the letter. "She's coming back."

Chapter 10

She skimmed the flowery-scripted letter, handed it back.

"No comment?" he asked.

"Should there be?"

He shrugged, then said, "If the dates jive, she'll be back in about a week."

A sudden chill brought Elizabeth's hands to her bare arms. Chafing herself, she got up from her mother's desk and wandered over to the window. "When are you going to tell the children?"

"I don't know that I am."

She turned. "What?"

He smacked the letter against his palm, a vein throbbing in his temple. "Why should I? For all I know, she may not even make it back. Maybe she'll meet some Swedish hunk in the airport and decide to shack up with *him*—"

"Guy!"

Looking into his eyes was like standing at the brink of a volcano mistakenly considered extinct. Behind the serene blue, bitterness glowed with red-hot fury.

"So she said she broke up with Guido or Gonzo or whatever his name is. Like I'm supposed to *believe* her? Dianne's not exactly high on my list of reliable people, Elizabeth. Not a word in more than a year…'' He shook his head, glaring at the thin blue paper. ''She left me, left her own *children,* for God's sake—''

''Which she regrets, if her letter is to be believed.''

''Yeah, right.''

''You really don't believe she wants to make amends?''

Anguish twisted his features. ''I really don't believe she's capable of that.''

''Ah.''

He snapped his head around. ''Ah?''

Twin darts of pain jabbed her temples. ''You still love her, don't you?''

''*What?* Don't be ridiculous—''

''I'm not.'' Her own calmness surprised her. ''No, no…it's all quite clear. As long as she was away, you could choke it down, pretend you no longer felt anything. But now it's all coming to the surface, isn't it?''

''Elizabeth, don't. This doesn't change what's happening between us—''

''But it does change what you thought you felt about Dianne, Guy.''

He said nothing, and her calm shattered. How could she have been such a fool? She suddenly felt trapped. Suffocated. She spun around, fled outside.

''Elizabeth!'' she heard behind her, but she ran up the street, oblivious to the heads whipping around in her direction. She kept running, into the woods at the end of the block, hearing Guy's footfalls quickly close the gap between them.

''Elizabeth! For God's sake—stop!''

He caught her wrist, nearly pulling her shoulder out of joint as he spun her around, his breathing ragged. ''What the hell is the matter with you—?''

''You are!'' she shrieked, trying to twist free of his clasp. It didn't work. ''Why do you keep pretending you don't still feel something? I dare you to tell me that you're not hurting right now!'' With her free hand, she scrubbed dust and tears off her cheeks. "That hearing from Dianne just rip through your gut! My *God*, Guy—she gave you three children! And now she's coming back—"

"Yes, Elizabeth! My ex-wife is coming back! Sound the trumpets!" His free hand slipped around the back of her neck so that she had no choice but to look at him. "Yes, I loved Dianne. *Loved*. Past tense, got it? The woman abandoned my children, *her* children, ripped me off, with absolutely no attempt to work things out. *She ran away*—"

"And you're not hurt by that?"

Fury blazed in his eyes. "Of course I'm hurt! Not a single day goes by that I don't feel like someone carved out my heart with a dull knife!"

"A someone who's returning to the scene of the crime!"

He choked out something that sounded like a laugh. "And this means...?"

Her mouth open, Elizabeth shook her head, realizing she had no idea what she meant. A weathered English garden seat crouched under a shuddering-leafed maple tree a few feet away. Her now throbbing head cradled in her palms, she stumbled to the bench, sank onto the slatted wooden seat.

Guy followed, sat beside her. "I can handle this, honey. But the one thing I can't take is your pity."

"*Pity?*" Her brows flew up. "Where did that come from? I don't pity *anyone*, which I would think would be perfectly obvious by now! Far as I'm concerned, when something bad happens, a person either copes with it and goes on, or gives up and lets circumstances win. You've got my support, my sympathy, and heaven *knows* my libido, but pity is not on my list of giveaways, okay? But—" She stopped, catching her lip between her teeth, knowing what she had to say.

"But...?"

She lifted one hand, skimming her fingers across his jaw. "But I think I need to back off for a bit."

"*What?*"

"Guy, listen to me. Since Dianne left, I'll bet you've been so busy trying to keep Ashli and the boys from falling apart, you probably haven't given yourself ten minutes to really work out how you feel about...everything. Right?''

His mouth set, he raised his head, contemplated the willow a few feet away. She shifted, forcing that hot blue gaze to meet hers. "Right?''

"Maybe, but that doesn't mean..."

"There's too much about Dianne and your marriage I can't help you with. Or fix. Or even deal with, to be blunt. I'm here for you—'' she placed her hand on her heart ''—but I can't be in your head. This, you have to work out on your own.''

"And just what do you think I've been doing for the last year and a half?''

She shook her head. "Not the same thing.''

"Says who?''

"Guy, if you just think about it for a minute...''

He raised one hand, cutting her off, but said nothing for a long moment. Then he leaned forward, framing his head in his hands; she watched the muscles in his back expand, contract as he breathed. "So you're walking out on me, too?''

"Oh, Guy,'' she said softly, aching for the bitterness in his voice, "you really are an idiot, you know that?''

That got a short, brittle laugh. "I've never doubted that for a minute.'' He fisted his hands together, propped his chin on top. "You're canceling tonight, in other words.''

"Under the circumstances, I think that's best, don't you?''

"Dammit, Elizabeth!'' He shot up from the bench, strode away, came back. Iced fire seared her from underneath dark brows plunged in an angry V. "Taking this relationship to the next step was your idea, remember? Yours! Now, suddenly, *you've* decided the timing is wrong, and what I might think obviously means squat. Never mind that I might not feel the same way, that I could use your support in this. For the love of God, woman—where the hell is it written that you get to call all the shots?''

But before she could open her mouth, he tramped off, startling a flock of sparrows out of a nearby quince.

Figured. The storm exploded out of nowhere just as he was about to put the kids to bed. A single thunderclap ripped open the skies, hammering iron-hard raindrops into the shingled roof and angrily sluicing across tenuously mullioned window-panes. Even so, the kids' wails—the boys' about the thunder and lightning and noise, Ashli's about the boys being such wusses—cut right through the din and straight to Guy's temples. Sympathetic, he wasn't.

"It's just a lousy little thunderstorm," he implored from the doorway to their bedroom, his head throbbing even more from having just raced around the apartment shutting windows. A disembodied howl floated down the hall—Einstein didn't like thunderstorms, either.

"It'll be over in fifteen minutes, for goodness' sake. Just lie down—"

The walls shook with the next heart-stopping thundercrack, bringing with it a new round of "Dad-*deee...!*"

The howling grew louder, too.

Guy gave up, crossed the room and swept Micah up out of his crib, no sooner sitting down on Jake's youth bed than lightning strobed through the room, setting off a long, ominous rumble of thunder that crescendoed into another teeth-rattling ka-*boom!* Micah screamed and banged his hard little skull into Guy's mouth in an attempt to crawl on top of his head. The children's caterwauling covered—he hoped—his swearing.

He felt the bed sag by his other hip. "You, too?" he managed to ask his daughter over Micah's sobs.

The next blinding flash brought her closer. "Case you needed help with the boys."

Fresh out of arms, he could only plant a kiss on her head. "Thanks, baby."

He got them to sing some Barney songs, his pounding head keeping excellent time with the inane ditties, until at last both kids and storm settled down. Even Einstein had ceased his serenade. He tucked them all back in, gave them all drinks of water and kisses and hugs—again—and finally escaped to the putrid living room and his thoughts.

The rain had let up enough to reopen some of the windows, letting in a sticky—but cool, at least—breeze. He slipped the screen out of one window, setting it carelessly on the floor at his feet, and leaned out, only to pull back in to avoid being drenched by a miniature waterfall from a cracked gutter overhead.

It was suddenly all too much. He collapsed onto the sofa, no energy to even protest when the dog crawled up beside him and plastered his prickly torso against Guy's bare leg. For a year and a half, he'd done it all himself, day after day after day, his only breaks occasional visits to his parents' for a holiday. Admittedly, as he'd chosen to stay in Chicago until recently, the choice to do it all himself had been his, as well. But still...

He shifted on the sofa, trying to distance himself from hot panting fur, letting his arm fall across his forehead. The previous three hours had been hell. For starters, Jake and Ashli had not taken well the news that their weekend with Nana and Papa had been postponed, which Guy had done so as to not impose on his parents any more than necessary—after forty-five years of marriage, the couple deserved their freedom. However, Jake had wailed, Ashli sulked, their mutual bad moods rendering them even more intolerant of each other. They had fought about everything. The TV. Their toys. Whose turn it was to feed the dog, water the dog, walk the dog. Whether *Family Matters* came on at seven or eight and whether Urkel was a real person or not. To top it off, they were stuck with spaghetti. Again.

Had Elizabeth been there, he realized, things would have been no different. The nasty, noisy, unreasonable children who had just cost him at least another year of his life would have been just as nasty, noisy and unreasonable with company present. They were very egalitarian that way.

This was a woman unused to children, to noise, to dirt, to chaos—

Wait a minute—was that what the craziness with Elizabeth this afternoon had really been about? That she'd gotten herself in too deep and had panicked, using Dianne's imminent return as a convenient out? What else could it be, since all that rubbish about his needing to come to terms about Dianne was just that—rubbish. Hey—if anyone had a problem to work out here, it sure wasn't *him*.

Sweating, he shoved the dog onto the floor; his head shrieked. That's it—need drugs *now*.

He stood, hanging on to his head so it wouldn't fall off, then stumbled to the kitchen, where the aspirin lived beyond the reach of even the most nimble two-year-old. As if performing some sort of penance, he forced himself to swallow two tablets without water. Grimacing, he snapped the cap back onto the bottle, his eyes drifting to the hall closet, inside of which were photo albums he'd simply boxed up when they left Chicago and crammed up there without looking at them. Albums filled with pictures of Dianne.

Unresolved issues…pfhh. Couldn't get much more resolved than hating the woman's guts.

Guy frowned up at the box, then dragged it down. One corner of it ripped as he clumsily hauled it over to the kitchen table and dumped it, batting at the resulting cloud of dust. He pulled out the most recent album, jerking back when a spider bungee-jumped off one corner and skittered across the kitchen table.

He shook the album in case the spider had friends, then scraped back a chair and lowered himself onto it. As he slowly turned the pages, he looked at Dianne's photos almost as if he'd never seen them, waiting for something—anything—to happen.

Hadn't been a bad marriage, really, up until the end. But Dianne had as good as died for him when she left. No one forced her to run away with Umberto or Roberto or whatever his name was. No one turned her out of her house, or told her to never make contact with her children again. And what happened to all the money? Had she really been so naive as to turn it over to lover boy? Even so, last he heard, they had phones in Italy. If she'd really wanted to come home, she could have called collect. He would have done anything, at the beginning, when he still loved her—or at least, still believed he loved her—to make her happy. To bring her home. To make amends.

He stopped at an eight-by-ten taken right after they'd gotten married. Funny how she never considered herself particularly photogenic. She'd been pretty enough, as far as Guy was concerned. Big brown eyes, a good smile, long curly hair the color of tarnished brass. Puke blonde, she'd called it, even though she refused to change the color. Ashli's hair would probably darken like that. She'd probably hate it, too.

He flipped more pages, still slowly, reliving anniversaries, Christmases, births and birthdays. Good times, good memories. All soured, irrevocably.

He slammed shut the album, batting at another dust cloud.

The rapping sound confused him for a minute, especially as the dog hadn't twitched as much as an eyebrow. Then it came again, more insistent, mingled with the pattering rain.

"Guy?" came the faint voice through the door. "I know you're in there. Open the door, wouldja?"

Slightly cotton-brained, he obeyed. There stood Elizabeth, dripping wet and grinning, clutching a tote bag, a bottle of wine and a Wal-Mart bag.

"Sheesh, buddy, it's about time," she said, pushing past him into the apartment. "Good *Lord,* it's wet out there. Got a towel?"

Immobile, he watched as she dumped everything on the counter, then tracked water across the floor to the kitchen sink, where she began to wring out her hair. "The kids asleep?" she asked, whispering.

"Uh, yeah, I suppose, but the fan's on in their room—they probably can't hear us. Elizabeth—what on earth are you doing here?"

She just smiled, shaking drops of water off her hands into the sink. "Guy?"

"Huh?"

"A towel?"

"Oh...I'm..." He fetched one from a nearby closet and handed it to her. "Confused."

Her laugh sounded rusty. "Probably no more than I am...oh!" She had bent over to towel dry her hair, popping up like a jack-in-the-box when Einstein poked his nose into er head. She backed up against the sink as the dog yawned, then shook his head as if trying to rattle something loose. "What is *that?*"

Guy regarded the animal for a moment. "The vet said *dog,* but I lean toward the missing link theory myself. His name's Einstein, by the way."

Her hair a tangled mass around her face, Elizabeth pulled her mouth into a wry smile. "Why am I not surprised there's a dog, too?" She dipped forward again, swiftly turbaning her hair with the towel, her blouse fused to her back like a second skin.

"Elizabeth, for God's sake…" He stepped back to the linen closet, yanked out another towel. "You're soaked!"

"Yeah, well, that's what happens—thanks—" she accepted the second towel, patting her face with it "—when you stand outside a man's door for ten minutes in the pouring rain because you can't make up your mind if what you're about to do is completely stupid or not."

After a moment, he said, "I take it you decided."

"What to do, yeah. How smart it is, no."

He had no comment for that. Instead, he asked, "Ever hear of umbrellas?"

She shook her head cautiously, like it hurt, as she wrung out the bottom of her blouse. "Not a cloud in the sky when I left the apartment."

Guy began to come to. "Can I get you something? Tea? Coffee? A dry shirt?"

"Which works better with headaches?"

"Aspirin."

She didn't quite laugh. "Can't take it. It screws up my stomach. Got any Tylenol?"

"No," he said. "It screws up my budget."

She decided on tea and the dry shirt. While Guy let the microwave handle the tea, he blindly grabbed a shirt from his dresser in his darkened room, then offered both tea and shirt to her simultaneously. She set the tea on the counter, carried the shirt into the bathroom, reappearing a minute later. The

faded U of M garment fell noncommitally to midthigh, excep
for the way it cupped her breasts like a pair of eager hands.

"I hung the wet stuff over the shower rod." She sort o
floated over to the counter to get her tea. Damn shirt snuggle
right up to her cute little fanny, too. "That okay?"

Guy realized he had the edge of the counter in a death grip
"Yeah. Fine."

Making tiny slurping noises as she sipped the tea, sh
walked into the living room. Enough unanswered question
hung between them to make up a week's worth of *Jeopardy*
but it was her serve.

"This really is terrible," she said. "Ashli wasn't exagger
ating."

Heat raced up his neck. "I didn't exactly expect com
pany—"

"Guy, for heaven's sake," she said with a laugh. "You'r
a working single father with three kids. I didn't expect th
place to look as though Martha Stewart had just struck." Sh
padded barefoot across the offensive carpet to the half-ope
window, wiping a quarter-size puddle off the grungy sill wit
the shirt's hem. "No, what I meant was, it really is too ba
about the Lakewood house. It would've been perfect for all o
you. Ashli told me how much she loved it. Said she'd eve
picked out her bedroom."

Guy finally released the counter and ventured into the livin
room, sliding one hip against the arm of the sofa. "Yeah,
know. But there'll be other houses."

The soft green eyes regarded him thoughtfully over anothe
swallow of tea, then darted away. After a moment, she toe
the carpet, cradling the mug to her chest as if it were a priz
she'd just won. "Does your…bedroom have this same car
peting?"

His heart started *ka-thonking* in his chest like a car with
flat tire. "No," he said from his perch on the sofa, afraid–
unable—to move. "The floor is bare."

Color washed up her neck, staining her cheeks. "Then…
take it we're not talking serious soundproofing here."

His headache miraculously vanished. He levered himself off the sofa arm, stepped closer to her. "Not an ounce."

Her hands tensed around the mug. "How soundly do the kids sleep?"

"Very." He lifted a hand to her cheek, felt her breath— warm, moist—on his knuckles. "How's your headache?"

She closed her eyes. "Nearly…gone."

"Elizabeth—"

She backed up so quickly she bumped into the end table, nearly knocking over the lamp. "Guy, I have absolutely no idea what I'm doing. You were right—I *am* used to calling the shots, to being absolutely in control. See, that's the only way I feel safe, if I'm the one in charge. Because basically, I don't trust anyone but myself, usually. Except that, for some reason, I trust you, so I should just stop being so scared, right? I mean, what kind of life am I going to have if I don't take a risk now and then, right? So. Here I am, in all my soggy glory, about to…to…"

Her hand flew to her face, as if checking her own temperature. "Oh, hell—I have no idea what I'm about to do…and stop laughing at me! I'm trying to apologize—I think—and you're not making things any easier."

"I'm sorry, honey," he said over another bout of chuckles, fitting his hands to her waist. And a bit lower.

She was wearing bikini underpants. *Tiny* bikini underpants.

"But you realize, of course," he said over the knot in his throat, "you're still doing it."

"Doing what?"

"Calling the shots."

Her eyes grew large. "And how do you figure that?"

He tugged her closer. "Who decided we shouldn't be together tonight?"

"Well, me, but—"

"And then who decides to just show up on my doorstep?"

"Oh. I see what you mean." Then she sighed. "I guess old habits are hard to break." She peered up at him from underneath her lashes. "You mad at me?"

"Let's just say...I'm considering various ways of getting you back."

A smile flirted with her lips. "As in, your being ruthless and all that."

"As in."

The smile faltered; she peered into her cup, apparently discovering it was empty. She slipped out of his arms and returned to the kitchen, rinsed it out, set it on top of the mountain of dishes in the drainer.

"Elizabeth?"

She turned, her eyes answering his question before he asked it.

"*Are* you afraid?"

She laced her arms together over her stomach, then lifted one shoulder. "I'm not really sure. It's been a long time since I felt like this."

"Like what?"

"Vulnerable."

His heart swelled as he realized what a gift she was giving him—her honesty. Dianne and he had shared eight years, a bed, and three children, but she had never once opened up to him the way Elizabeth had just done. There would be no guessing games with this woman, no wondering what to do, what he'd done wrong, whether or not he should tread lightly. He remembered the day they met, wondering what it would take to erase the worry lines in her face. Although he still didn't know what that might be—or whether, no matter how much he *wanted* her, he *deserved* her—he knew he'd do anything in his power to ensure her happiness.

Even if that meant eventually letting her go.

He leaned over the counter, held out his hands, palms up; after a moment, she obeyed his silent request, resting her small, smooth hands in his. "What you said before," he said quietly, caressing her knuckles with his thumbs, "about trusting me?"

She nodded.

"Hang on to that, okay?"

She nodded, again, then turned away, noticing the album

on the table, which she opened without invitation. When she came to the eight-by-ten of Dianne, she sucked in a breath.

"Wow. She's pretty."

Guy came up behind her, threaded his arms around her waist, resting his chin in the crook between her neck and shoulder. "She never thought so."

"Really?" She stared at the portrait another moment or two, then turned the page as he drew her earlobe between his lips. A little shiver made her flinch, but otherwise, no reaction. "That's too bad."

"Elizabeth?" He nestled most closely against that soft, adorable rear end.

"Mmm?" she said, passing to the next page. "This Ashli as a baby?"

"Uh, yes…her second birthday. Elizabeth."

"Yes?"

"In case you hadn't noticed, I'm trying to seduce you."

She leaned back, skimming his forearms with her fingertips. "Oh, yeah?"

If anyone under five feet tall woke up right now, he'd die. Very slowly, very carefully, he slipped his hands underneath the shirt, skirting them inch by inch over her waist, up one delectable rib at a time, teasing the underside of her breasts. She made a tiny sound, like a purr, deep in her throat.

"You smell so good," he murmured, nuzzling her neck, keeping one eye on the hallway. Holding his breath. "Like…lemon meringue pie." The purr turned into a startled giggle. "And you're so smooth—" He traced one petal-soft areola with a fingertip, smiling when it puckered. Ever so lightly, he grazed the sensitive skin, avoiding her nipples. A shudder rippled through her; he knew they'd be taut. Aching. Desperate for his touch. "Been a while, has it?"

All she did was moan.

"Is that a yes?" he whispered, claiming her breasts at last. She gasped, pushing into his hands. Oh, yeah—honest to a fault.

"That was," she said breathlessly, "most definitely a yes."

"I thought it might be." He slipped his hands out from

underneath the shirt—at great personal cost, mind—then leaned against the counter, arms crossed.

It took a second. Or three. When she at last turned around, he could see arousal had left her groggy as a drunk. And as disoriented. "Why'd you stop?"

He made a show of checking his watch. "Just put the kids down a half hour ago. Takes 'em a good hour to fall into a deep sleep."

Her eyes narrowed. "Let me guess—you just got even."

He grinned.

She was going to kill him.

In one smooth motion, she tore the damp towel off her head and smacked him with it before he could even lift his arms. "You are a cruel, cruel man."

He grabbed the towel out of her hands, laughing. "Wish you could see the look on your face right now." Then he somehow looped the towel around her back and jerked her to him, planting a hard kiss on her mouth. "Fulfill a frustrated man's fantasies," he said when he lifted his mouth from hers. "Where's your hairbrush?"

Her heart went *thud.* "Why?" she squeaked.

His brow creased for a second, then he let out a laugh, tangled one hand in her matted hair. "To brush your hair, goof. What'd you think I meant?"

Her face warmed. Again. "You don't want to know," she mumbled, retrieving her hairbrush from her purse.

Guy pulled out a kitchen chair, pointed to it. "Sit, woman."

She sat, straddling the chair backward, and leaned her head on her arms. When Guy moved behind her, her heart shifted into a *molto vivace* beat she was sure he could probably hear.

Well. You never know, do you? God knows this wasn't what she'd imagined her first time to be like. She'd always pictured candlelight, silk lingerie, roses, Nat King Cole. Or maybe Vivaldi. Not sitting in some tired kitchen with peeling linoleum, underneath a butt-ugly ceiling fixture which gave off a stark, yellowish light that was at once flat and unflattering. Not wearing some man's old college T-shirt, or looking at photos of his ex-wife and kids. Not waiting to make absolutely sure those kids were sound asleep before things went any further. Nosirree, not at all what she'd planned.

But it would do.

As Guy carefully brushed out the tangles, her breasts tingled, remembering his touch, like liquid lightning, his patience, his smile, his laughter—

Apprehension shunted through her, threatening a happiness at once tenuous and strong: there was no guarantee what she felt for Guy was enough. Or that it ever would be.

She shifted, pushing aside the unwanted thought. "Mmm. You're good at this."

She felt him lift her hair, press his lips against her neck. Her nipples tightened, pleaded, begged. "I have a little girl, remember?" he said. "I've had lots of practice."

"Speaking of whom...how'd Ashli take the news?"

The brushing halted, for a moment, then resumed. "I told you. I don't know that I'm going to tell her."

Yanking her hair out of his hands, Elizabeth reversed herself on the chair. "Are you nuts?"

"I'm not finished—"

"Neither am I," she said, snatching the brush away from him. "Guy—you can't put this off." Her eyes flicked to the hallway, back to that stubbornly set mouth. Geez—were they a good match or what? "Dianne could be back any day. What if she calls and Ashli answers the phone?"

"Dammit, Elizabeth!" A scowl darkened his features as he sank back into his own chair. "This is real life, not a theoretical episode from one of your books."

"What *are* you talking about?"

"The books you've got scattered all over your apartment? Mixed in with *The Single Woman's Guide to Investment Strategy* and *The Crystal Collector's Guidebook*? You've been reading up."

Her brows shot up. "Well, gee whiz—call the Feds, why doncha?"

"Books can't tell you how to be a parent, Elizabeth. Only falling flat on your face a coupla thousand times can do that."

"At least it's a place to start," she found herself saying to his back as he got up, walked over to the sink.

He poured himself a glass of water, downing it before facing her again. "Sweetheart, I read every damn book I could get my mitts on after Dianne left, trying to figure out how to convince Ashli her mother didn't leave because of something *she* did. Absolutely nothing worked. She still asks me, every single day, when her mother's coming back. It's almost as if, I don't know, like she wants a second chance to somehow make it up to her." He leaned against the sink, flattening one palm to his chest. "Trust me—I have no problem in the reality-dispensing department. I've been totally up-front with her, telling her from the start that her mother probably wasn't coming back, figuring that was a damn sight better than giving her false hope. And in the past few weeks I thought—*hoped*—Ashli was finally coming to terms with that and beginning to put it all behind her. And since she's met you…"

"Oh, no, uh-uh." Elizabeth waved both hands in front of her face. "Don't you go putting that kind of pressure on me—"

"Oh, for the love of…" Guy knelt in front of her, capturing her wrists. "Would you get this through that lovely but steel-like head of yours—there is no pressure about this. None. All I'm saying is, she's been happier since you came into her life." He folded her hand, kissed her knuckles. "We all have. So deal with it, dammit."

Elizabeth melted for a second, then yanked her hands out of his, flinging one of them out in exasperation. "So what are you going to do? Wait until Dianne shows up at your front door? *That* would do her a whole lot of good—"

"And what's the alternative?" He stood, walking back to the sink. "If I do, and Dianne doesn't return, I'm right back to square one. She'll either think her mother's betrayed her again, or that she's still being punished for some imaginary infraction. I just can't put her through that a second time." He slammed his hand into the counter. "I can't put *myself* through that a second time."

Light-dawning time. Of course he couldn't. Lord—talk

about being slow. "Oh, Guy. I'm sorry.... What do I know about any of this? You're right—no book is going to provide the answers...I had no business—"

"And there she goes again, folks," he said on a quiet laugh, then held out his arms. In a breath she was in them, nestling into that strong chest like a child herself. "Do you have any idea what a kick it was to find all those books at your place to begin with?" he murmured into her hair.

A blush stung her cheeks as she thought of the books he *hadn't* seen. "I just wanted to—"

"I know. Be in control." But she could hear the grin in his voice.

After a while, she said, measuring her words, "All my life, whenever I wanted to know about something, or how to do something, I'd read up on it. Take courses. Go to seminars. When things started... When it looked like..." She stopped, took a breath and held on to Guy more tightly. "I just want to live up to your expectations, that's all."

His hands captured her jaw and lifted her face to his. "Expectations?" he asked, his brows hooding his eyes. "What on earth are you talking about?"

"Remember? Out at the Shadywoods site that day? When you said you only wanted the best for your kids?"

"No one's expecting you to be perfect, for Pete's sake!" He pressed cool lips to her forehead, then said on a half laugh, "You might as well get used to the idea right now that you're gonna screw up as much as the rest of the human race. One of those genetic flaws no one's figured out how to fix yet."

"So I'm wasting my time, is that what you're saying?"

"Pretty much." His smile washed over her. "And I think there are much better ways to spend your time."

"Like what?"

She felt his hands insinuate themselves against her ribs, slide upward along her spinal column as he lowered his mouth for a lingering kiss. A buttery warmth spread through her various appendages, lapped at her belly, lower.

"It's been an hour," he said, drawing her more tightly to

him, his fingers wreaking havoc with a hitherto unknown sensitive spot at the base of her spine.

"Are you sure?...Oh!" she asked on a gasp as his tongue slowly snaked down her neck. Then she dug her hands into his shoulders— Well, *dug* probably wasn't the right word, since those muscles could've bent spoons—and tried her best to glare at him. "You still getting even?"

Heat flared in those storm-blue eyes, as his hands found their way underneath the shirt for the second time that evening, flickering sparks over her bare back, her ribs, her breasts... "Oh, honey, trust me—*even* is not what I hope to get tonight."

Her nipple jolted to attention against his thumb and she suddenly realized she wasn't seeing clearly even *with* her contacts in.

"Besides..." He captured her unfocused eyes in his own. "Before you get all fired up about parenthood, there's a prerequisite course you have to take."

She was fired up, all right. And woefully weak of limb. "Oh?" she said, wilting fast. "What's that?"

Grinning, Guy swung an arm underneath her trembling legs and picked her up as if she weighed no more than a matchstick. "Here's a clue," he whispered, carrying her down the hall. "There's no text for this course." He pushed open his bedroom door, flicking the switch next to the door, which turned on the bed table lamp. "Welcome to your first class."

Through demurely lowered lashes, Elizabeth stole a glimpse of Guy's bed—and burst out laughing, clamping her hand to her mouth to stifle the sound.

Chapter 11

"What's...?" Guy followed her gaze, then let his head fall back with a groan. "Oh, *hell.*" Whereupon he basically dropped her so fast her heels bumped against the wooden floor. Elizabeth stumbled for a second before collapsing against the doorjamb, holding her stomach as she shook with helpless, overwrought laughter. Ignoring her, Guy yanked a red plastic laundry basket off the floor, into which he began shoveling the mountain of clothes towering on the center of the sheetless bed.

He stopped, waving something pink and ruffly at her. Accusingly. "I suppose *you* would fold them. And for crying out loud," he said, pretending to glare over a twitching mouth, "stop giggling, wouldja? What is this—a pajama party?"

Now laughing so hard her ribs hurt, she staggered across the room and snatched the basket—and the pink ruffly something—out of his hands. She dumped the basket on the floor, and then, with one gargantuan lunge, swept everything into it. "There. Done." She blew a strand of hair out of her face. "So, where are the sheets?"

Five minutes later, there they stood, hot, horny and out of

breath, staring at the bed as though it were a minefield. Elizabeth could hear her heart's *whump-whump* over the dog's arrhythmic panting out in the hall. At this rate, the kids would be wanting breakfast before they finally got down to business. She cleared her throat—

"Yes?" Guy asked, too quickly.

"Why don't you, uh, go get that bottle of wine and a couple of glasses? And that package in the Wal-Mart bag while you're at it."

"Aye, aye sir," Guy said with a mock salute, then disappeared. Quickly, Elizabeth slipped off the T-shirt and panties and into bed, modestly tucking the sheet over her breasts. She lay back, then pulled her head forward and quickly combed out her hair with her hands so that it fanned out around her shoulders, feeling like a Victorian maiden on her wedding night. Guy quickly returned, quietly closed the door, then set the wine and glasses—and a pair of candles—on the dresser. And held out the package, grimacing.

"You don't trust me to take care of this?" Her already being in bed didn't seem to affect him one way or the other.

"I just thought—"

"—that if you didn't take care of it, I wouldn't either?"

She squirmed. "I just didn't want to leave anything to chance."

With a sigh, Guy set the package of condoms on the nightstand and lowered himself to the bed. "Neither do I, sweetheart," he said softly. "We'd already planned this, remember? Besides, I already have three kids. Don't need another one."

She was surprised how much his comment bothered her. "Ever?"

Now it was his turn to be surprised. "Certainly not nine months from now," he said, giving her a brief kiss. Trying to swallow down the panic screaming through her veins, she glanced over at the dresser. "Candles?"

He stood, lighting them with a match. "Only the best for my little control freak." He clicked off the bedside lamp, undressed without ceremony and lay down beside her, the mattress sagging—but not, thank God, squeaking—under his weight. The candlelight danced over his muscled body, delineating a broad, darkly haired chest, narrow waist and hips, flat stomach, and...*oh, my.*

Now, she'd never had much experience with "oh, my" before. Oh, yeah, she'd felt the occasional arousal digging into her hip during a hot make-out session, but she'd never seen one. She wasn't sure whether to be fascinated, impressed or thrilled to bits.

Unconsciously, she tugged the sheet a fraction higher. "I, um, can't exactly compete with *that.*"

She saw Guy stifle the laugh that rose from his throat, tamping it down to a low, sensuous chuckle. "If you could, we'd be in *big* trouble." Then he kissed her, slowly, sweetly. "And this is one time I swear I won't say *don't touch.*"

Every single muscle tensed, from her neck to her toes. A breathy, masculine laugh tickled her base of her neck. "Or whatever. It's okay."

"Oh, uh...I will if you want me to..."

He pressed two fingers to her lips. "Listen, since it means so much to you, how about we just let you run the show tonight, okay?"

"You...you wouldn't mind?"

"Is that immense relief I detect?"

"Is it that evident?"

He chuckled. "Might say that. So, I'll tell you what—"

But she captured that lovely face in her hands and shook her head. "I trust you, Guy," she whispered. "It's just that I'm a little..."

"Out of practice?"

"Virginal."

His smile froze in place. "What?"

She was grateful, at least, to hear only surprise, not incredulity, in his voice. "Remember what you said about 'my first lesson?'"

Fifteen different expressions flashed across his face as he seemed to regroup. "But I didn't think..." He gave a weak laugh. "Well. This is new territory for me, too." He lay back on the pillows, pressing her hand against his chest. "You've never had sex. I've never had sex with someone who hasn't."

She hitched herself onto one elbow and slid her hand out from under his. And down. Past his chest…his stomach…skimming a hip…until…

"In fifteen minutes," she whispered, "neither of those things will be true anymore."

"Honey, you keep doing that, we'll be lucky to make it to five." Then he hooked two fingers underneath the sheet and drew it away from her body. And just looked. Even in the dim, oscillating light, she could see his expression soften.

He didn't say a word. He didn't have to. For just a second, realizing what was about to happen, her stomach went haywire. Then he smiled at her, and nothing else mattered. She lifted her arms, welcoming him, and felt, for the first time in her life, the delicious sensation of a lover's bare skin against hers.

So much for the "using Dianne's return as an excuse to back out" theory. Not to mention any last-minute maybe-we-shouldn't-do-this panic on his part, either. Oh, the doubts were still there. In spades. But his ability—and willingness—to act on them vanished the second Elizabeth walked dripping wet through his door.

Now she lay naked and trusting in his arms, in his bed, and he knew there was no turning back. Not from her, not from what she meant to him. And certainly not from whatever mistakes they were destined to make down the road.

"Make love to me," she whispered, touching his mouth. Then grinned. "And make it good. I've waited a long time for this."

Fully intending to honor the lady's wishes, he had planned on taking things slowly, gently, carefully, for both their sakes. What he hadn't planned on was his little virgin's catching fire like dry kindling.

She was so soft, so smooth and fragrant and exquisitely responsive, her pale rose nipples sweet nuggets of pleasure against his tongue as she arched toward him, clawed at him, wordlessly petitioning him to give her as much as he had. Her fingers tangled themselves in his hair in order to claim his mouth, over and over and over, and he luxuriated in her contented mewling noises as he discovered each highly charged erogenous zone in its turn.

Then she was on top of him, her weightless hair shielding them both from the cool misty breeze that sporadically shivered the metal miniblinds over the open window. Surprised, delighted, he followed her lead, straining against her pliant moistness, not wanting to rush, not sure how long he could wait. She sat up, straddling him, lifting his hands to down-soft breasts.

"I love it when you touch me," she said simply, and the ingenuousness of her words, her low, desire-roughened voice, made him catch his breath. Her eyes were wide-open and fastened to his, and he could see a thousand thoughts behind them. With the pads of his thumbs, he teased her nipples; her eyes fluttered closed as she covered his hands with hers. "More," she murmured, her lips curving into a smile.

No other man had ever evoked that response from her, he realized. No other man had given her what he would. The responsibility scared him, thrilled him. Awed him.

"Patience, honey," he whispered, letting his fingers trail down her ribs, over her thighs, back around to her buttocks.

He felt her tiny, smooth hands test his chest and nipples until his response matched hers, then slide up his neck to sift through his hair so she could offer sweetly aggressive kisses which he took with no argument. He found her slight awkwardness, her freshness, unbelievably arousing, and he realized with a start they'd arrived at that place in her eyes he'd sensed weeks before, that rare place where intimacy means far more than being naked with each other. Smiling, silently grazing her back with his hand, he lay still while she continued to search and taste and tease until he heard his own gasp of approval, her delighted laugh in response.

She laughed again when he flipped her onto her back and kneeled above her. One arm stretched, coyly, over her head, her small, beautiful breasts nearly flattened against her rib cage. She cupped the side of his face with her other hand and whispered, "Told you I wasn't a prude."

"Shh," he teased, placing one finger against ripe, erotically parted lips. "No talking in class." His gaze roamed her body, pale perfection against the plain white sheet. Then he followed with his mouth.

First her throat, his tongue taunting that special spot just over her clavicle until she quivered. Then back to her breasts, his mouth courting one, his fingers mercilessly teasing the other, suckling and raking the nipples while she clutched his head to her, blissful sighs suddenly yielding to an astonished cry—his cue to continue his journey, irrevocably downward, downward, to a spot he knew was probably already throbbing, screaming for release. He hesitated, considering his next move, as he spread her with his fingers. She was so slick and swollen, so ready. He explored and stroked and caressed, deliberately tormenting her while he watched that delicate face, knowing her ache was becoming deliciously unbearable. She pushed against his hand, moaning, begging, her face contorted in sweet agony.

At last he positioned himself over her, still daring to push the limit, kissing her breasts, her belly and the moist golden curls at its base, seeing just how high he could take her.

"Guy!" Surprisingly strong fingers dug into his shoulders as she lifted her head, panting. "You trying to kill me here or what? For the love of—*oh!*"

He'd started to slip inside, forgetting. "I'm sorry! Here, let me just—"

She clamped her hands on his backside, yanked him back. "Leave now," she said in a fierce whisper, "and you're dead meat."

So he stayed, moving carefully now, giving her time to open and accept. He knew better than to ask her if she was okay—the candlesticks were within reach; she'd probably bean him with one. After only a few seconds, though, she nodded, and he let himself fill her, his thrusts deep, gentle, controlled. Her tightness was exciting. Excruciatingly so. But he watched her face, lit with joy and surprise, and thought his heart would break. His breath caught from trying to hang on—to not steal her glory, he thought with an agonized smile.

And glorious it was. With a gasp equal parts shock and pleasure, Elizabeth clutched him, burying her face in his shoulder to muffle her cries as she shattered underneath him, her contractions vice-strong and seemingly never-ending.

With a guttural cry of relief, he let himself go.

She'd never lain with a man's chest hair tickling her ear, her bare breasts pressed against someone's rib cage, listening to a pounding heart after having just made love. She'd never shivered in a breeze skimming bare skin still flushed and damp from lovemaking, never felt the profound contentment of being wrapped in a lover's arms, or the anticipation of being able to do this *again,* and this time, she knew what to expect.

A little bit of heaven, this.

It was a night filled with "never befores" after years of "same-old, same-old." She'd always wondered what she'd feel, afterward. Well, and *during,* too, she supposed. But whether or not she'd feel different somehow had always intrigued her. Not enough to find out for its own sake, obviously, but still, she'd wondered. Now, she knew.

She was not the same person she was a half hour ago.

And thank God for that.

Guy kissed the top of her head, his fingers gently stroking the arm possessively encircling his rib cage. "I'm surprised I'm not glowing," she murmured, replete.

His chuckle rumbled in her ear. Then, with his breath teasing her hair he said, "I have to tell you—unless you were faking, you just had a humdinger of a first time."

She grinned again, pleased with herself. "Oh, yeah? Well, buster, as I wouldn't have a clue how to fake anything, I'll just have to take your word for it."

"It gets better."

"Oh, please," she said, laughing quietly. "I don't think I could live through *better.*"

"Not only will you live, honey-bunch, you'll thank me, too."

The breeze turned suddenly cooler; Guy reached down and pulled the sheet up over them, then gathered her back into his arms. Just that fast, reality intruded. *Damn.*

"Wanna talk?" Guy asked, lazily stroking her shoulder.

Tears suddenly pricking her eyes, she flipped onto her other side, facing away from him. She'd never felt this, either—the brutally sharp fear that could easily destroy the first real happiness she'd felt since she was a child. When Guy spooned himself against her back and draped his arm over her shoulder, she clasped his hand, kissed it. "What did we just do?" she asked in a tiny voice.

He nuzzled her neck, laughing softly. "I know you're a novice, sweetie, but I didn't think I'd have to spell it out."

"Very funny." She could hear the tears in her voice, knew he could hear them, too. She felt him shift, raise himself up onto one elbow. His hand caressed her bare arm. "Having second thoughts?"

"Shoot—I'm on at least my twelfth by now." She squeezed shut her eyes, fighting. "I just didn't know…" Unbidden tears slipped over her lashes. She tried, unsuccessfully, to wipe them away with her fingertips. "What made me think that becoming lovers would make everything okay?"

Guy turned her back around; she crumpled into his chest. "Nobody said it did."

But she wasn't listening. "All I could think about until five minutes ago was me," she said, pushing her clenched fist into her heart. "What *I* wanted. And I wanted you. I became obsessed with the idea, like a craving that's been ignored too long. So all reason flew out the window while Elizabeth Louden let her libido run riot—"

"While Elizabeth Louden discovered she was human," Guy interrupted her, tenderly stroking her hair from her face. "Don't you dare start this head-over-the-heart nonsense again."

The passion temporarily spent and set aside, doubt came roaring to the surface. "But think about it, Guy. Okay, so we had a good time in bed. I mean, I suppose we did—I don't exactly have a backlog of experience for comparison. That doesn't automatically make me a good mother. And your children have been hurt once before. What if I screw up? If their own mother screwed up, who's to say that I wouldn't, too?''

Guy stayed ominously quiet for a long moment, then said, "Hell, lady…you sure know how to kill the afterglow."

The stinging grew worse. "I'm sorry—"

"Dammit, Elizabeth—listen to me," he said in a fierce whisper. "We didn't go to bed on a lark, remember? We planned this. We knew there were no guarantees, but we care about each other and we know what we're doing. And the kids adore you, you little twit." He thumbed her eyebrow, her temple. "*I* adore you."

But none of that was enough, and she could tell he knew it as well as she did, even as he lay here bewitching her with those lethal blue eyes. Eyes that, she realized, were not being entirely truthful.

"Damn you, Guy," she expelled on a long shaky sigh. "A half hour ago, I wanted to sleep with you. Now I wonder how I could live without you. And that scares the living daylights out of me, because it's been a long, long time since I felt that way about another human being."

She saw both sadness and wonder in his expression as he drew his knuckles down her cheek. "Then how do you think I feel?"

She shifted on the pillow, looked hard at him. "What do you mean?"

"See, part of me knows you'd make a great mother. And don't give me that look…I'm serious. Hell, if I can keep the kids alive, anyone can. But there's another part of me, the practical side—you're giving me that look again—who wonders…"

"Spit it out, Guy."

He linked their fingers, studied them, then kissed her fingertips. "If I…if you'd really be happy. If you really *could* stand the constant messes and noise and confusion." Air whooshed through his lips. "I'm not a fool, honey. I've been through this before."

With that, there was no stopping the tears.

Guy reached over and plucked a tissue from the box on his nightstand, handed it to her, then hauled himself to a sitting position. He retrieved the wine, poured it into the glasses. "Here," he said when she'd pulled herself upright, as well. "Might as well."

Elizabeth blew her nose before carefully arranging two pillows at her back. Holding the sheet to her breasts again, she took the glass of wine. At Guy's smirk, she said, "So, when I'm not in the throes of ecstasy, I'm still modest. So sue me."

He settled his own pillows behind him, then slipped an arm around her shoulders. "Actually," he said, kissing the top of her head. "It's rather endearing."

She grunted. "So…have we solved anything?"

Guy took a thoughtful sip of wine. "I don't think so."

"Yeah, that's what I would have said, too." She more or less gulped down her wine, set her glass on her nightstand, then wiggled down into the pillows.

"Okay…" She stroked his arm with the back of her hand. "What now?"

He scrutinized her for a moment, then said, "Isn't this the part where you jump out of bed, yank on your clothes and take off like a bat out of hell?"

She tilted her head at him. "That what you expect me to do?"

"Let's just say I wouldn't be surprised."

"Let's just say then, that, no matter what my head is saying, the rest of me cannot leave." She touched his face, feeling the fire begin to build again, needing him to quench both the inferno and the fear that came with it. A tentative smile tugged at her mouth. "Not until my clothes dry, at least. Oh, Guy…this is dumb, I know. Sex isn't going to solve one blessed thing, but I can't seem to move out of this bed. And this from the woman who never, ever, in her entire life just lived for the moment."

Guy now ditched his own glass, then rolled over and kissed her. "Sometimes," he said, "the moment is all you have. So you take it. And enjoy it. And trust it has lots of friends in the wings waiting to come keep it company." He slipped his hand underneath the sheet and cupped her breast, smiling as her nipple sprang to attention. "And I discovered a long time ago this is a lot more fun than getting drunk."

"I see," she said, between kisses of her own down his neck, thinking she was probably a little drunk anyway from downing that glass of wine so quickly. "So you're saying…that this is a good way…to avoid dealing with…things?" Which was precisely what they were doing. Nobody was even trying to untie the knots they'd just pulled more tightly. This went against every instinct Elizabeth had, but she was in no state to argue. Instead, she drew his earlobe between her lips, tasting the dull tang of gold.

"The best," he said, pulling back the sheet, his palm lightly whisking over her breasts and belly, making her shiver.

"I'm not sure I like that philosophy."

"Prude." He kissed her, stroked her face.

"What?" she said, feigning hurt feelings, as she let her hands rake through his hair. His wonderful, long hair. The wine—and rekindled sexual desire—was warming every molecule in her body, producing what she knew was an artificial state of peace. She didn't care. She couldn't. "I didn't pass the class?"

"Mmm," he murmured, starting in on her neck. "Didn't I tell you?"

"Oooh…uh, what?"

"This is at least a four-year course."

"I see," she said, closing her eyes. Feeling. Loving. Ignoring the pain his words were causing, the pain of pretending everything was settled. "And then?"

"There's graduate school…" His lips found their way to her breasts, gently tugging at her right nipple, then suckling it, before tasting the other one. "Then postgraduate work…" He traced her navel with his tongue and she groaned. "And, if you're lucky…" Then a series of slow, delicate kisses down her belly wiped out what little sense she had left. "…unlimited extention courses for the rest of your life."

Once again, she let Guy stoke the embers of her need into searing, consuming flames, for a precious few minutes quenching all reason, sanity, logic. But this time, just as the blaze devoured the last vestige of reality, her own tears put out the fire.

Guy pried open his eyes, as much as he could after barely two hours of sleep, and realized two things. One, it was still dark. And two, unless Elizabeth had morphed into a werewolf, that was the dog sprawled on the other half of the bed.

He stumbled into a pair of shorts and toward the kitchen, the dog literally on his heels, where he found her scurrying about stuffing things into her tote bag like a chipmunk who'd waited until the last minute to stock up for winter. "May I keep the shirt?" she asked. "Mine's still wet."

"Uh, yeah…sure. What are you doing?"

"Attempting to sneak out before the kids wake up."

"They're not chickens, Elizabeth. They don't herald the approaching dawn."

"Yeah, well, you're the one who said whatever you expect them to do, they don't. Remember? I'm the lady who doesn't take chances."

The panic in her voice tore at his heart. In spite of everything he'd said, everything they'd done, fear—and remorse, he thought—shackled her words. Not that he didn't understand, all too well, what she was feeling. He sidestepped the counter into the kitchen, hugging her to him. "After last night, I'd say that no longer applies."

"We were safe…"

"That's not what I meant."

She smiled over glittering peridot eyes, red-rimmed from tears and lack of sleep. "I know it isn't," she whispered, then extricated herself, hefting the tote bag up onto her shoulder.

"Sweetheart," he said softly, "please don't run from this."

She turned to him, her eyes wide. "Who says I'm running?"

He pointed to her tote bag.

"Considering the circumstances," she said, "I think a hasty exit would be prudent, don't you?"

"Love 'em and leave 'em, huh?"

Her eyes welled up again and he felt like a cad. "Oh, hell…" He pulled her into his arms again, tucking her head under his chin. "Let's just think this through for a minute, okay? Utilize some of the famous Louden logic."

He felt a nod, then something close to a giggle, against his chest.

"Fact—we only want what's best for everyone, here." He backed away and looked into her face. "We agreed on that?"

Another nod.

"Good," he said, resettling her in his arms. "Okay, fact—you're afraid you can't take care of my kids."

"That I won't be any good at it," she corrected.

"Let's not argue semantics. The result is the same, right?"

"Yeah. I guess."

Her grudging acquiescence prompted a smile in spite of the situation. He continued. "Fact—I'm afraid you won't be *happy* taking care of my kids."

"Which we decided was the same thing—"

"Hush. If I can't argue your point, you can't argue mine."

She hushed.

"Fact—in order for this relationship to progress, we have to somehow either convince ourselves our fears are groundless or overcome them."

After a moment, she said, "That makes sense."

"Of course it makes sense. I can, when pushed to the wall, use my brain just as efficiently as you can."

She gently thumped his arm with the underside of her fist.

"So…" He raised her chin and pecked her on the lips. "I have an idea. And no comments until I'm finished."

That got the raised-eyebrow routine and a very suspicious, "What?"

"The family has a cabin about a hundred miles north of here. Pretty spot, by a lake. Rustic, but not primitive." He grinned. "Mom insisted on electricity and running water. But simple, secluded. There's even a pier you can fish off of."

Her mouth pulled into a smirk. "*You* can fish off of. And, no, I don't scale 'em, bone 'em, or gut 'em, either, so don't ask." Frowning, she plopped the tote bag back onto the counter. "Guy, honey—what's fishing got to do with our situation?"

"Would you just ride this one out with me, please? My folks said the cabin's gone begging because everyone's been so busy. So…why don't we take the kids up there for the weekend? Sort of a trial run."

"Trial by fire is more like it."

"Think of it along the lines of a crash course in being a family."

She stared at him for a moment, and he could see apprehension wrestling with hope in the green depths. Then she walked over to the living room window with one hand over her mouth, the other planted on her hip. After staring outside for a full minute, she turned to him. "What would the sleeping arrangements be?"

"Kids in the loft, me on the sofa, you in the bedroom."

She gave him an "uh-huh" look, then turned back to the window, brow puckered. "For two days?"

"Three. I'm including Monday. And I'm sure your mother will understand, so close your mouth."

The eyebrows went up again but the mouth closed. But then she said, "Okay—if we do this? We *both* have to promise to ride the whole weekend out."

He crossed his arms, fighting the smile. "I will if you will."

The dog yawned, flapped his ears, collapsed on the kitchen floor with a groan. After another minute of silent consultation with his backyard, Elizabeth gave a sharp nod of her head. "Fine. Let's do it." Then, like a commanding officer who's just been giving marching orders, she went into action. "That means a trip to the store for supplies—do you have a cooler? And how much milk will the kids drink in three days? Let's see…I have to call Mother…"

"Geez, lady—you just hear a starting pistol go off or something? Relax. You call your mother—no. *I'll* call your mother. You just go home, pack your own stuff. I'll handle the food and the kids and the dog and we'll swing by your place about nine."

"The dog?"

"I can't very well leave him here for three days, honey."

She looked over at Einstein, stretched out across half the kitchen floor. Sensing he'd become the object of human conversation, he rolled the skyward eye in their direction, half-heartedly thumped his long tail. "Oh...I suppose not."

"I...take it you're not a dog person."

"Figured that right out, didja?"

"He's part of the package, you know."

"I know."

"So...?"

"Sooo..." She sort of moseyed on over to him, giving him a broad smile. "I suggest, if you want *that* and me to cohabitate living space for any reasonable length of time, you give him a bath at your earliest opportunity."

"Or...what?"

Instead of answering, she simply laid her palm against his bare chest, kissed him, then vanished out the door, her espadrilles nearly soundless against the metal treads of the stairs. At the bottom, she turned. "Nine?" she said.

He nodded, watched her go, then sucked in a knife-sharp breath of weighted, humid air as he turned back into the apartment.

Ashli stood in the middle of the living room, already dressed.

"What're you doing up so early, baby?" he asked, only then noticing the tear-streaked face. "Ashli?" He crossed to her, tried to touch her shoulder. "What's wrong—?"

But she jerked away, her eyes boiling with accusation.

"You *lied* to me! You both lied to me!"

Chapter 12

"She knows."

Still trying to decide whether one pair of jeans would be sufficient, Elizabeth turned her attention from the soft-sided suitcase lying spread-eagled on her bed to Guy.

"Knows what?" she asked, impatiently pushing back a floating strand of hair off her forehead, trying not to feel rushed. Guy and the kids had arrived fifteen minutes early; she was running fifteen minutes late.

"About us. About…" he lowered his voice "…last night."

Her gaze shot to his, disbelieving. That would explain Ashli's borderline rudeness when they'd arrived this morning, but still…

"That's crazy," she said, pulling a second pair of jeans from her dresser drawer. "They were all sound asleep." She faced him. "Weren't they?"

He walked over, took the jeans out of her hands. "So were we."

"For what? Two hours?"

"She got up to go, saw my door was closed…and opened it."

"Opened it? You mean, she *saw* us?"

"Asleep," he said in a futile attempt to reassure her. He neatly tucked the jeans into her suitcase. "That it?"

"What? Yes," Elizabeth said with a distracted wave of her hand. "And she still wants to go on this trip?"

"Actually…" He zipped the case, yanked it upright. "No."

Elizabeth dropped onto the edge of the bed so hard the skirt of her sundress poofed out over her thighs. "Guy, maybe we're pushing things. Maybe it's too soon.…"

"And what good would waiting do?" He skimmed a fingertip over her shoulder.

With a resigned sigh, she covered his hand with hers and looked into his eyes. Her lover's eyes, she realized with a little start. "I'm so sorry.…" she said, shaking her head. "Now I *know* I shouldn't have come over last night—"

He snagged her chin in his hand, impaling her with his eyes. "And I'd be a far more miserable man this morning if you hadn't." Squatting in front of her, he took both her hands in his. "Look, I know there's a lot to work through, but I refuse to accept that what happened last night wasn't a good thing."

"For us, maybe," Elizabeth said. "But not for your daughter. Less than two weeks after telling her I never lied, never broke my promises, I do both right under her nose."

"What are you talking about?"

A ragged sigh somehow escaped her lungs. "When Ashli was here, we had a long talk, about how she didn't want me to marry you because then Dianne couldn't come back. When I assured her…" She closed her eyes, took a deep, steadying breath. "When I told her nothing that happened between you and me could affect whether her mother returned or not, she seemed to back down a little. But she also made me promise that we wouldn't…go further in our relationship without telling her. Said she hated when grown-ups did whatever they wanted as if the kids didn't count. Or words to that effect." She shook her head. "If she does know, then, as far as she's concerned, I just blew my promise big-time." Lifting her gaze, she said to her window, "Now what do I do?"

Guy squeezed her hands, stood, then nodded toward the suitcase. "Ready?"

"Uh, yeah." She rose as well, trying to rub the tension from the small of her back.

He lugged the case off the mattress, planted a quick kiss on Elizabeth's forehead. "It's what do *we* do. And the answer is, we'll muddle through the best we can. But for the moment, let's just get this show on the road, okay?"

Elizabeth nodded, then sadly retrieved her tote bag from the dresser. Maybe she'd passed one test last night, but she'd failed another, even more important one, big-time.

Forcing everyone to go through with this definitely put him in the running for Idiot of the Year. Crying shame, too, because it was an exquisite day for a ride. The morning haze had dissipated to reveal an unbroken expanse of silken turquoise sky, the only cloud around the little one with dark blond hair in the seat directly behind him.

Elizabeth, bless her heart, was trying her best to remain upbeat, even though every attempt she made to talk to Ashli was met with instant recoil. Several times, Guy had been tempted to rebuke the child, but each time a light touch on his arm shut him up. Somehow, Elizabeth seemed to understand what was going on more than he did. Which was just as well, since he sure as hell didn't have a clue what to do.

At the moment, peace reigned: Micah had fallen asleep, Jake and Ashli were silently staring out their respective car windows. He glanced at Elizabeth, at that regal serenity that had knocked him for a loop in the first place. The passion blazing underneath the coolness, however, would definitely keep him on his toes. Not to mention the turmoil that kept her busy making folds in the full skirt of her pastel-flowered sundress.

"You remember to pack a bathing suit?" he asked, out of nowhere.

She jumped when he spoke. "What? Oh. That would be tricky. I don't own one."

He looked at her as if she'd just admitted to worshiping trees. "How can you not own a bathing suit?"

"As I don't swim," she said coolly, "or moonlight as a swimsuit model, one would be superfluous."

"You can't swim?"

"I didn't say I *couldn't* swim; I said I *don't* swim."

"I don't understand…"

"See this skin?" She pointed to her arm. "I'd have to marinate myself for twenty-four hours in SPF 30 sunscreen before I dared go out in the sun. And since I can't see without my glasses, which are just a wee bit problematic to wear in the water, I never found swimming all that much fun." She shrugged. "I took lessons a while back, just because I figured if I was ever invited to a yacht party and fell overboard, I'd like to least give the sharks a run for their money. But it's not something I'd do voluntarily."

"Daddy?"

Guy looked at Jake in the rear view mirror. "Yeah, buddy?"

"C'n we get in the water as soon as we get there?"

"Not until I can be out there with you, okay?"

"Daddy, Einstein smells." This from Ashli, the first words she'd said—other than "Tell Jake to be quiet!" a dozen times—in the past half hour.

"He's a dog. They do that."

"Yuck."

Elizabeth smirked and turned toward her window, her chin in her hand.

"I promise," he said. "First thing when we get back, the dog gets a bath."

Guy and the two older kids took off for the lake before the car motor even cooled down, leaving Elizabeth to watch Micah chase assorted foolhardy squirrels up the sixty-foot pines flanking the cabin. Wobbling on the thick, fragrant pine-needle cushions, the baby gleefully yammered at his new friends, oblivious to their scolding.

Elizabeth leaned back on her elbows on the porch steps,

raising her face to the tender breeze, wishing it could somehow whisk away her anxiety. Surprise, surprise—the closer she and Guy got, the more complicated things got. She hated the way Ashli looked at her, all that doubt and mistrust seething just underneath the surface, much worse now than that day when she'd been sick. Somehow, she had to regain the child's faith, though she had no idea how to go about doing that. And they had to get to the bottom of this business about Dianne. She knew what Guy kept saying, what Ashli kept saying, but gut instinct told Elizabeth that there was more to Ashli's resistance than simply her conviction that her mother wouldn't return if Guy remarried.

So. Here she was, stuck in the middle of the woods for three days, still having no idea whether or not this was going to pan out, desperately wanting to try, petrified even her best efforts would fall short. She pressed her fist into the knot of tension lodged in her stomach. How in God's name had she managed to become entangled in exactly what she'd so assiduously avoided in her relationship with Rod? With anyone, for that matter, since she was twelve years old?

Damn blue eyes.

She jerked her head in an attempt to unseat the worries, then focused again on Micah, absorbing the birdsong shimmering through the forest, the squirrels' fierce chitterings, the wind's teasing rustle through the tops of the pines, soft-focused splashing and muffled laughter a hundred yards away. Guy's and Jake's, at least. Ashli's sparkling giggle was conspicuously, painfully absent.

Micah brought her a pinecone, which he tossed in her lap with a huge grin and wide eyes. The ache shifted, eased, as she touched it. "What a great pinecone!"

He held out his hand, demanding it back. "Pi'cone," he repeated, and she laughed, delighted.

"That's right." She pointed to another squirrel, bravely making the foray toward the cabin. "Squirrel?"

"Girl!" he squealed, taking off after the poor beast. When it scampered up the tree, he turned to her, tiny face crumpled. "Where girl go, 'Libbef?"

It took her a second to realize he'd said her name. The clutch at her heart took her by surprise. "Up the tree," she said.

"Twee?"

"Uh-huh."

"Oh." The baby regarded the tree for a moment, then said, "Girl go home?"

"Yes," she said, smiling. "That's right—the squirrel lives in the tree."

Micah marched right up to the trunk, twisting himself to peer up into the branches, then waved. "Bye-bye, girl." Apparently satisfied he'd fulfilled his social obligations, he pranced back to Elizabeth, climbing up on the steps beside her and mimicking her pose, elbows on the top step and all.

Elizabeth giggled, then pulled the toddler onto her lap. To her amazement, Micah immediately cuddled against her chest with his thumb in his mouth. Her breath hitched in her lungs at the sensation of this tiny person nestled in her arms. She lay her cheek on top of his fine, curly hair and shut her eyes, breathing in his...*oh.*

"Hmm—I think someone needs his diaper changed—"

"*No!*" Micah wiggled out of her arms, backing away from her.

Elizabeth glanced out toward the lake—toward Guy—then realized the Time had Come. She stood up and grabbed for Micah, who took off inside the house as fast as a pair of two-year-old legs could go. Which, Elizabeth soon discovered, was incredibly fast. She chased him to the middle of the main room, then played catch-me-if-you-can around the big plaid sofa until, with a back-wrenching lunge, she latched onto the back of the baby's shirt. Feeling a little like a rodeo wrangler, she heaved the now howling child into her arms, only to narrowly miss being clipped in the chin by a banging head.

"Micah! Cut it out!"

The howls turned to screams.

Tucking him under her arm like a sack of possessed potatoes, she hauled him into the bedroom and dropped him onto the bed, taking care to keep him pinned with one hand while she grabbed his diaper bag off the dresser. Somehow, she spread a changing pad underneath the kicking legs; somehow, she got a diaper and wipes out of the bag without losing either the baby or a limb; somehow, she got his shorts off without having to remove little sneakers, a feat for which she mentally patted herself on the back.

Then she took a deep breath—figuring it would be a few minutes before she dared breathe again—and ripped open the diaper.

She immediately knew how Hercules must have felt about the Augean stables. "Sheesh, baby—this three days' worth?"

Micah wailed and tried to flip over; with faster reflexes than she knew she had, she caught him and flipped him back. She pulled out a wipe, reassessed the load, grabbed a half dozen more. Still trying to dodge flailing limbs—which she now realized would be less lethal if she'd removed the shoes—she gingerly patted at the muck.

Micah shrieked.

"*What?*" she said, jumping, during which time the baby's hands shot down and tried to—

"Oh, no you don't," Elizabeth muttered, grabbing his hands just in time. Now she had one hand cuffing the baby's wrists, the other one holding a wipe and trying to keep her teeth from getting knocked out by turbocharged Sesame Street sneakers. This was not enough hands. How did people *do* this?

"Use the front of the diaper to wipe most of it off," she heard behind her.

"What?" she said again, twisting around to see a grinning Guy standing in the doorway, wiping his damp hair with a towel. Distractedly, she noticed lake water trickling down his matted chest hair. "If you're determined, you can usually get most of it into the diaper. Then use the wipes to clean up the residue."

That he hadn't offered to rescue her was not lost on her. But at least he wasn't laughing. Laughing would have justified murder.

She did as instructed, surprised how well it worked. Two wipes later, the baby was clean. A little powder, a fresh diaper, and she was done. She slipped Micah's shorts back up, gave him a hug and a kiss, and set him on the floor.

"What do you do with the used diapers?" she then asked. "Call the EPA for toxic waste disposal?"

Now he laughed. "Here." He picked up the offensive thing and efficiently folded everything disgusting to the inside, cleanly taping it into a neat bundle. "They go into those little bags in the diaper bag, then into the garbage. Look sharp," he said, tossing it back to her. She jumped, fumbled, caught it, then heard, "Lunch ready? We're starved."

Letting loose with an indignant howl, she jerked the diaper over her head and chased him all the way into the kitchen.

After lunch, Ashli went outside to play while Guy put Micah and Jake down for naps on the bed. And had promptly, Elizabeth discovered when she peeked into the room a few minutes later, conked out himself beside them.

For a few moments, she wasn't quite sure what to do with herself. Unaware she was scratching the dog's head, she surveyed the plainly furnished main room: sleeper sofa, couple of chairs, a braided rug, tables, lamps, all in shades of brown. In the corner, a wrought-iron staircase spiraled to the walled-in loft where the kids would sleep, containing a pair of cots and a well-used Portacrib. That was it.

Nothing highfalutin' about the kitchen, either, Elizabeth thought as she rinsed off the few lunch dishes and stacked them on the slanted drainboard next to the utilitarian sink. The highlight—literally—of the room was a vintage refrigerator in an amazing shade of aqua, snuggled next to an equally geriatric electric stove. A long plank table and six mismatched chairs took up most of the center of the smallish room, which also managed to harbor a fairly decent maple hutch and a couple of cupboards.

But Guy's *family* was in this house, each piece clearly having been donated by various branches of the clan, and because of that, she found the hodgepodge effect humorously peaceful. And God knew, she needed *peaceful* right now.

With Einstein silently rooting her on, she squatted down to

riffle through the two grocery bags and the cooler, trying to figure out how, exactly, Guy intended for them to manage anything resembling a real meal out of this. He'd brought peanut butter, bologna, American cheese, three loaves of bread, Miracle Whip, bacon, eggs, a half head of lettuce, two tomatoes, a nearly gone cucumber, some frozen chicken pieces, a box of Minute Rice, two packages of macaroni and cheese, three boxes of dry cereal, and a package of hot dogs with two already missing.

Gotta love the man. With a half laugh, she shoved the dog's face away from hers, then wondered how close the nearest grocery store was as she straightened up, glancing out the window. Across the front yard, Ashli sat twisting herself around in the tire swing suspended from an impressive oak about twenty feet from the cabin.

So much for *that* peaceful moment.

She frowned, swiping a strand of hair off her cheek. The chicken's way out—which held no small appeal at the moment—would be to do nothing. Just stay here until Guy woke up, keep an eye on Ashli from an impersonal distance.

But Elizabeth's chicken days were over.

The perishables safely tucked into the refrigerator, she stepped out onto the porch, grasping the splintery banister to steady herself for a moment before forcing gelatinous legs down the steps.

"Get a grip, Louden," she muttered as she started toward the child, tucking her arms underneath her breasts. Bubbles of stomach acid pushed reminders of recently consumed bologna sandwich into her throat, but she refused to become ill. Ashli looked briefly in her direction, then away, as if she hadn't seen her.

No surprise there.

Elizabeth stopped several feet from the swing, her arms still crossed. She considered her body language, made herself unlock her arms only to stuff her hands into the dress's front pockets. "Hey, sweetie," she said through a bologna-tinged catch in her voice. She swallowed, cleared her throat. When there was no answer, she said, "You were awfully quiet at lunch. Did you have a nice swim?"

Ashli shrugged, then lifted her feet off the ground, sending the tire into a dizzying spin that fanned the blond hair straight out behind her. When she came to a stop, Elizabeth tried again.

"It's pretty out here, isn't it?"

Another shrug, a cautious step closer.

"Sweetie, I wish you'd talk to me—"

Sullen blue eyes zinged to Elizabeth's face. "I'm not your sweetie."

Elizabeth looked at the ground, then back at Ashli. A streak of sunlight caught her in the eye, making her squint. "Ashli…"

The child rammed the toes of her purple sneakers into the dry soil, stopping dead the tire's sway. "You and Daddy had sex, didn't you?"

She forgot to breathe, for a second. "Do…you know what that means?"

Ashli shot her a look that could have dissolved steel. "It's how a man and a woman make babies. So, did you?"

A hundred explanations, rationalizations, dashed through her head. Stuff about when a man and woman love each other. About grown-ups having needs. That this was something she was too young too understand. However, the only thing that seemed to make sense—if anything did—was a simple, "Yes."

Another glare, then Ashli dug the balls of her feet into the ground, creating a dust cloud around her calves as she twisted herself up again.

"I…care a great deal for your father, honey," she tried. "And you—"

"You don't care about me," the child hurled back over her shoulder. "You don't even know me." Before Elizabeth could answer, Ashli let herself go in a dizzying spin as blurred as Elizabeth's thoughts.

"But I want to get to know you, Ashli." Elizabeth hated how desperate she sounded. "Remember how much fun we had when we went shopping?"

"That was different."

"Why?"

"Because you were my friend then."

"And why can't I be your friend now?"

"Because you broke your promise."

Something snapped. Elizabeth strode over to the swing and clamped her hand on it, stopping it from twirling again. She looked up at a blotch of sky visible through the pines as if hoping the right words would fall down at her feet. They didn't.

Elizabeth leaned against her hand, fisted around the rope, and realized she was on her own. "I know I made a promise to you," she said softly to the top of the blond head, "and I'm very angry with myself for breaking it. But there are times when things happen that grown-ups don't plan, or just aren't ready to discuss with children. You may not like that, and I don't blame you, but that's the way life is. But, honey, no one ever meant to pull one over on you—you've got to believe that."

Ashli jumped off the swing, tried to run away; Elizabeth caught her by the hand.

"You're hurting me!"

"Then stop fighting so hard, for goodness' sake," Elizabeth retorted, loosening her grip but not letting go.

"You can't be my mother! Mama's coming back, I know it! If she sees you and Daddy together, she'll get mad and go away again...."

Elizabeth literally bit her tongue to keep from telling her about Dianne. That was her father's prerogative. Instead she said, quietly, "Why don't you want your daddy to be happy again?" Ashli jerked her head away so Elizabeth could only see her profile. Then, as an afterthought, she added, "Why don't *you* want to be happy again?"

"I will be happy," the little girl said, refusing to look at her, "if you go away."

In her most outrageous dreams, Elizabeth would never have expected an eight-year-old's words could sting so much. Or make her feel so inept.

Eyes stinging, Elizabeth let go of the child's wrist and strode back to the cabin.

Guy woke with a start when Micah rolled into him. Still in a stupor, he thought he heard voices outside. Angry voices.

He slid off the bed, carefully, so the boys wouldn't wake up, hitting the porch just as Elizabeth stormed past him, the full skirt of her sundress slapping his legs as she passed. Confused, he glanced out to the yard to see Ashli take off into the woods.

"Elizabeth!" he called back into the cabin. "What—?"

Shaking, she jabbed a finger toward the door. "I'm tired of taking the heat for her mother's not coming back! So either you tell her about Dianne, right now, or I'm gone!"

This was not the time to tell Elizabeth she was overreacting. He was down the steps and through the yard practically before she'd finished speaking, stumbling through leaf mold and broken branches to find Ashli not fifty feet from the house. She'd collapsed onto a fallen tree trunk, her tiny torso crumpled over her knees as she sobbed.

"Baby, baby...what's going on?" He sank down onto the log, scooped her onto his lap.

"Why'd she have to come?" she wailed into his chest. "We don't need her around. We can take care of each other until Mama comes back. We can—"

"Ashli..." He wished like hell there was an easier way to say this. That he could do as Elizabeth asked and simply tell his daughter her mother was coming back. But he didn't dare. No matter how angry it made Elizabeth, he didn't dare take that chance.

"Honey, I've told you. Mama's not ever going to live with us again. You...might see her someday, or go visit her, but she can't come back to live with us."

"Why not?"

"Because we're not married anymore," he said with as much patience as he could manage, thoroughly weary of the emotional water-treading.

"Don't you love Mama anymore?"

And with each reiteration came a fresh surge of pain. For his daughter, for what he thought he'd had. For his own frustration, after all this time, at not understanding what had happened. "No, baby, I don't."

"Because you love Elizabeth?"

He caught his breath. If he didn't understand what happened the first time, what made him think he knew what he was doing now? After a moment's hesitation, he said, "My feelings changed for Mama long before I even met Elizabeth."

"You can't!" the child screamed, startling him. She jumped up, backing away from him. "You can't just change your mind about who you love!"

"But grown-ups do sometimes," he said, trying to keep his voice, his thoughts, in check. Ashli was still just a baby. "It's not very nice, and it hurts, but it happens." With a sigh, he added, "It's just one of those things about being a human being, honey."

"Then how," she said on a sob, "do I know you won't stop loving *me?*"

"Ashli! Oh, sweetie, no—" He virtually flew to her, catching her in his arms. "Baby, no, no, no—you've got this all mixed up." Wiping her hair away from her wet face, he said, "I'll never, ever, stop loving *you,* no matter what."

He cradled her to his chest, continuing to stroke the silky hair while the child wept. "Is that what this is all about? Because your mother and I don't live together anymore, you're afraid I'll stop loving you? Honey—" he kissed her head, over and over "—that's not possible. Parents don't stop loving their children."

"But Mommy stopped loving me and Jake and Micah," came the tiny voice from underneath his chin. "And it was all my fault. I made her stop loving us, because I wasn't a good girl, so she went away."

For a full five seconds, he couldn't catch his breath.

"Ashli, honey?" Guy held her away from him, willing his heart to beat, searching the tear-stained face. "What on *earth* are you talking about?"

"She said I didn't help her enough around the house or

with the boys. After Micah came, she would cry and cry and say we were all too much, that she was so tired, that she just wanted to go away. That you weren't around enough because you were working all the time. But I tried to help her, Daddy, I did…'' She scrubbed at her cheeks with the heel of one hand. ''And I thought everything was okay, 'cause one day when she was feeling better, she promised me she wouldn't leave, that she loved me and wouldn't leave. Then she got real sad again, and I couldn't make her happy anymore. No matter how good I was, I guess it wasn't enough to make her stay.''

Oh, dear God—how many nights after Dianne had left had he lain awake, haunted by that very thought—that he hadn't been able to make his wife happy, to save his marriage, to keep his daughter from getting hurt?

And with that, doubt blossomed into dread as he thought of Elizabeth, and her inexperience. What right did he have to drag her into this?

He hugged Ashli to him more tightly, trying to squeeze away the pain, the misgiving. The fear. For them both. ''Baby, why didn't you ever tell me this before?''

But she couldn't hear him over her sobs. ''How come grown-ups can lie and it's okay, but it's not okay for kids?'' she managed to ask between the tears, her tangled thoughts and worries apparently becoming more snarled the more she tried to explain. ''Why did Mama leave, when she promised she wouldn't?''

Why indeed? Guy simply held his child and let her cry, waiting until her sobs settled down enough for her to hear him. The baby blues, his mother had said. Postpartum depression, in other words. One of his colleagues in the Chicago office had gone through it with his wife, a severe case that scared the daylights out of the man for weeks.

But…was that it? And even if that had been the case, even to the point of her taking off, why with another man, to another country? And why hadn't she come back, or at least gotten in touch with her children? Who deserved the blame here?

Certainly not a six-year-old girl.

"I doubt Mama left because she didn't love you." Was *that* a lie? Maybe. But maybe not. He'd never know for sure, probably. And neither would Ashli. Whether what he was about to say was *right,* or even the truth, he didn't know. Wasn't as if he had a whole helleva lot of options, in any case. "You know how cranky you get when you don't feel well?" He smiled. "Or how cranky *I* get when I have a headache?"

She nodded.

"Well, from what you're saying, I think Mama wasn't feeling well. In fact, I think she was feeling so bad she didn't even really know what she was doing when she left."

Ashli looked up at him, still sniffling. "You mean she was kind of…sick?" She swatted at her bangs.

"Well, yes, I guess you could call it that." He caught the fear in his daughter's eyes and tried to smile. "But what Mama was going through was much, much, *much* worse than a headache. She was scared and confused and unhappy, and didn't know what was happening inside her. That's why she really left, not because of anything you did. You've got to understand that, baby—you didn't make Mama leave." No sooner had the words left his mouth, however, than he realized the question most likely to pop out of his daughter's—"But why did she *stay* away?"

That's not what he got.

"Is Elizabeth sick, too?"

His eyes shot to the child's streaked, splotchy face. What on earth…? "Of course not. What makes you say that?"

"She doesn't think I see it, but I do, the look she gets on her face when the boys won't shut up or when they're running around her apartment. Like she's real nervous or scared or something. Most of the time, it doesn't last real long or anything, but sometimes, she looks just like Mama used to.…"

"Ashli, no," he heard to his right. He twisted himself around; Elizabeth stood maybe six feet away, hugging her elbows, her face a study in horror. After a second, she sidestepped a mound of ferns and came close, squatting down in front of them, glancing hopefully up at Guy when Ashli shrank further into his arms.

But if she was looking to him for encouragement, she'd come to the wrong place.

Confusion flickered for a second in her eyes before she turned to Ashli. "Honey," she said, licking her lips, "I'm really, really new at this, and I'm going to make mistakes. But no matter what weird look you might see on my face, I'm still not your mother—"

The child grabbed the hem of her T-shirt and wiped her eyes, then slid off Guy's lap. "So stop pretending you are," she shouted, then took off toward the cabin.

As Guy started to go after her, he felt Elizabeth's fingers graze his arm, as if trying to stop him. But he couldn't bear to see the hurt and bewilderment—still, and again—in those beautiful green eyes.

The last thing he needed was to look into a mirror.

Chapter 13

Ashli had downed a cup of warm milk in shaky silence, then fallen asleep on the sofa, emotionally and physically exhausted. The boys were still mercifully asleep as well, although in their case, clear air and water play were the culprits.

Elizabeth sank onto the porch steps, collapsing against the railing like an understuffed rag doll. Ashli's last words still ringing in her ears, she snorted into the palm of her hand, staring at the tire swing where this afternoon's little fiasco had all started.

So maybe they did see fear in her eyes. Wasn't as if she could deny it; it was there. But she was damned if she was going to believe—or let them believe—that what was going on in her head bore any similarity to what must have gone on in Dianne's.

Oh, brother. And what had she herself said, just last night? If Dianne had screwed up, what was to prevent her doing the same thing?

Dianne, Dianne, Dianne—good *God,* she detested the woman and she'd never even met her. Oddly enough, though, her distaste had nothing to do with either her being Guy's ex or her actions. What galled Elizabeth was that, in spite of Dianne Sanford's not being in the picture for more than eighteen months, her presence was as palpable as if she were on this trip right along with them.

And just think. If she could wreak this much havoc when she *wasn't* around, what demons would be let loose once she returned?

Elizabeth shut her eyes, chiding herself for feeling so…bitchy. Unreasonable.

Justified.

Her lower back renewed its complaints; she tried massaging it herself, to no avail. She heard the porch floorboards creak under Guy's weight.

"Here," he said softly, sitting beside her and replacing her ineffectual rubbing with strong, rhythmic strokes that made her sigh. "That's something I *am* good at." There was no teasing, no smile, in the words. The afternoon had taken its toll on him, too.

"Oooh, yes…there," she said with a soft groan. "I don't know why my back should hurt. I didn't pull anything that I know of."

"Gee, you don't think you might have built up a little tension in the past twenty-four hours, do you?" He brushed a kiss against her shoulder, but it didn't linger. "Maybe you should go take a nap, too. You didn't exactly get a lot of sleep last night."

Last night. It seemed like weeks ago. "That's okay," she said carefully. "It was worth it."

"I wonder," was his reply, and she clamped shut her eyes against the regret in his voice. He shifted a little to get to her shoulders. "Things haven't exactly gone well."

She had to laugh even though there was absolutely nothing funny about any of this. "Trial by fire, remember?"

"And…what's the verdict?"

His fingers were bringing as much apprehension as relief. "I'm still here, aren't I?"

"Doesn't count. I drove."

She twisted around to catch a sadness in his eyes that put

her on instant alert. "Okay, you want it spelled out? Despite what just happened, do I still want to be with you? Yes. Do I still want to work this out? Yes—"

He gently turned her back around, pushing her head forward. Kneading the sides of her neck, he said quietly, "Be honest, sweetheart." His palms came to rest against her bare shoulders. "If nothing else, be honest."

She sagged back against him. "I never pretended this wouldn't be a challenge."

He wrapped his arms around her and kissed her hair, but his silence said far more than she wanted to hear.

"Daddy?" Micah's voice floated out from the cabin. "Where Daddy go?"

Guy got to his feet. "I'd better go get him—"

"I'll come, too," Elizabeth said, dusting off her bottom as she rose.

"Never mind," Guy said, almost sharply. "There's no need." Then, as he reached the door, he added, "I think…maybe we should just go back home after Ashli wakes up."

Stunned, Elizabeth simply watched him disappear inside the house.

When Ashli didn't wake up until after seven, Guy suggested waiting until morning to return. "Fine," had been Elizabeth's tight-lipped response.

Which, as it happened, was the only word she'd said to him since their earlier conversation on the porch. But her pot-banging symphony as she prepared dinner said plenty. Not to mention her refusal to smile for him, or even look at him, through the entire meal. Not even Micah's antics relieved the tension.

Now the boys were outside, chasing fireflies in the dusk, while Ashli resumed her communion with the swing. He'd cleared the table, feeling like a sloth in comparison to Elizabeth's sudden burst of hyperactivity. Apparently, when she got mad, she cleaned.

"Okay. Let's have it," he said, snagging her wrist as she energetically wiped crumbs off the kitchen table.

She yanked her hand away from him. "I have no idea what you're talking about," she replied, striding to the sink. The night had cooled down; she'd changed to jeans and a light-weight oversize cotton sweater which flapped around her hips as she moved. She wrestled with the dishpan for a moment, trying to get it out from beneath the sink.

Guy tried to take it from her. "Here…you cooked. I'll do the dishes—"

"I've already got them." The plastic pan smacked into the sink. "Unless you think I'm no good at this, either?"

He leaned up against the counter beside her. "Is this about going home?"

She turned on the water, pretending she couldn't hear him. He reached across her and turned it off. "Elizabeth—"

"Yes, Guy!" Now she scorched him with glittering green fire. "Yes, this is about going home. It's about breaking the pact we made with each other, to stick this out until the whole weekend was up! It's about giving up on me, about not even giving me a *chance* to work this out with Ashli. *That's* what this is all about." She knocked his hand away from the faucet and twisted it on again full force, creating a mountain of suds in the dishpan.

"I just thought—"

"No, Guy, you didn't think," she said over the running water, then shut it off. Her hand still on the faucet, she said, "You reacted." She looked at him, then away. "I'm not Dianne. I'm not sick. Scared, yes. I've admitted that. But I'm not going to run away."

"How can you be sure you won't?"

"How can *you* be sure I won't, you mean?"

Bingo. He leaned both hands against the counter and hung his head, shaking it.

"Yeah. That's what I thought." Elizabeth plucked a wet dish out of the suds, rinsed it off. "Well, if you're interested, I can answer that question." She set the plate in the drainer, attacked the next one. "It's called *trust.* Short word, not difficult to spell or say." That plate clanked against the previous one. "But apparently, difficult to *do*."

"Sweetheart—"

"For crying out loud, Guy—how the hell are we supposed to deal with Ashli's problems before you've dealt with *yours?*"

Her words shot anything he might have said right out of his head.

"You didn't even give me a chance," she muttered again, swishing out a glass with the sponge. She rinsed it, set it in the drainer, then wiped her hands on the dish towel. "Here." She slapped the towel into his chest. "You dry. In fact, you can do it all, just like you have been doing. Obviously, I'm not needed or wanted around here, so you're on your own. I'm going to bed."

He hadn't felt this guilty—or responsible—for something since he broke his mother's favorite lamp when he was nine years old.

After an hour of tossing and sighing, Elizabeth got out of bed and sat in the bentwood rocker in the corner of the bedroom, rocking so hard her feet left the floor each time the chair tilted back. She knew she'd hurt Guy. She'd meant to. Maybe the shock of hearing the truth from *somebody* would open up the whole ugly mess once and for all, get it out in the open. Just as she'd suspected all along, it was *his* pain, *his* fears they were confronting, much more than Ashli's. Not that she didn't believe or understand what the child had to handle and overcome. But it was crystal clear that nobody was getting anywhere until Guy got his act together.

Nor did she doubt for a minute how much he cared for her. But as long as Dianne held this...*power* over all of them, the relationship was doomed to failure, clubbed to death by ghosts from the past.

With a sigh, she wondered just when Dianne would return. Maybe then things would finally straighten themselves out? Of course, there was the other possibility, that things might straighten themselves out too much....

Geez. Add one more worry to the pile, why doncha?

The thin crack of light underneath the door went out: Guy had apparently gone to bed, too. Irrationally, knowing there was no light in the rest of the cabin suddenly made her feel trapped. She needed to get out, to get some air.

No more than a few feet lay between the bedroom and the cabin's front door; the sleeper sofa sat way on the other side of the main room. If she was real quiet, she could probably sneak out without disturbing anyone.

She waited nearly fifteen minutes, according to the fluorescent dial on her travel alarm, then slipped her cotton chenille robe over her shortie pajamas, wiggled into her espadrilles. Slowly, she opened the bedroom door, relieved it didn't squeak, quickly crossed to the front door and let herself out.

For a minute, she just stood on the porch, looking up at patchy, swiftly moving clouds playing peekaboo with the moon. One moment, the clearing around the cabin was flooded with an almost phosphorescent silver light, only to be plunged into blackness the next. A breeze had come up, too, sensuous and invigorating, hinting of rain. Elizabeth hugged herself, her nipples tightening in the sudden coolness. Like the fickle moonlight, brilliant memories of last night alternated with worries and doubts and longing, choking her heart. She glanced up at the sky; the clouds had dissipated, for the moment. At least enough to take a short walk without a flashlight.

She moved silently down the stairs, away from the house, toward the lake.

A minute later, she stood at the edge of the pier, trying to determine how far down the water was. Oh, what the hell—she slipped off her shoes and clumsily lowered herself onto the edge, cautiously dipping one foot down, only to gasp at the sharpness of the cold, black water. After a moment, though, enjoying the wetness licking at her ankles, she plunged her other foot in as well.

Shutting her eyes, she breathed deeply—once, twice, then again—until at least a few of the heebie-jeebies took a hike. The air smelled so sweet and real, scented with pine and forest soil and lake water; for just a moment, she felt removed from everything that lay so heavily on her heart. She leaned against the pile and kicked one foot, sending an arc of glittering onyx droplets back out into the night An owl hooted, as if in disapproval, making her jump and giggle simultaneously. In defiance, she kicked again, harder, sure she could almost isolate each sparkling drop as it seemed to halt, suspended, before spattering back into the water.

She thought she'd imagined the tremor in the wooden planks underneath her, until she felt it again. She lurched around; Guy stood a few feet away, his hands in his robe pockets. The moonlight had silvered him as well, like some extraterrestrial being.

She turned back to the lake, frowning. "What are you doing here?"

"Making sure you didn't end up as fish food."

"I'm insomniacal, Guy. Not suicidal."

"Who said anything about suicide?" she heard behind her, closer than before. "*Blind* was what worried me."

A soft grunt was her only reply as he squatted beside her. "You okay?" he asked in that aggravatingly mellow voice.

"I've been better."

He looked out over the lake for a moment, then back at her. In spite of her best efforts, in spite of its being the middle of the night, she couldn't avoid those eyes. "Would saying 'I'm sorry' help?"

She pulled in a long, slow breath and let it out again in an even longer, slower sigh. "It…might."

"How about…I was a jerk?"

"I like that one better."

The weather-beaten planks groaned as Guy lowered himself beside her; she heard a soft plunking splash as his feet settled into the water. "Ooh…" he winced. "Cold."

She snickered. "Wuss."

"Now who's being cruel?"

"Nah. Just perverse enough to find other's sufferings amusing."

Guy shook his head, gazing out over the water. "Doesn't swim, fish or like dogs. And a sadist to boot. I must be out of my gourd."

"Yeah, well," she said after one of the world's longer pauses. "Guess that makes two of us."

He twisted to her, pulling one foot out of the water and leaning against the pile on his side of the pier. "Does this mean you're not mad at me anymore?"

"Oh, buddy," she said, shaking her head. "You've got a looong way to go before you're off *that* hook."

He held his hand out to her. She stared at it for several seconds, then took it. Instantly, she knew either she'd just done something very right or very wrong, but damned if she could figure out which it was.

"And what," he said with that smile of his, "can I do to speed up progress in that department?" He had pulled her hand onto his thigh, stroking the inside of her palm with his thumb while he talked. That must have been the one erogenous zone he'd missed last night, she realized as her head began to buzz.

"How about apologizing?" she murmured.

"Thought I had."

"Uh-uh," she said, swallowing hard. "None of this generic Gee-baby-I'm-sorry stuff. I want an itemized accounting."

A low chuckle rumbled from his throat as he sidled closer to her, hung one arm over her shoulder. "Where would you like me to start?"

"What? Oh!" He was nuzzling the nerve-rich skin just behind her earlobe, sending little crackles of need shooting to her toenails. "Right there is good," she murmured on a sigh and his low laugh nearly sent her right into the lake.

He stood up, bringing her to her feet as well, slipping warm, strong arms underneath her robe, tugging her close. "Can't stay out here," he murmured in her ear, flicking his tongue over its outer rim. "Can't hear the kids."

"No," she agreed, somehow.

"Besides," he whispered, sprinkling kisses down her neck, while his hands—hard and smooth and gentle—roamed underneath her pajama top, "I apologize much better lying down."

With a groan, her head fell back. So, naturally, he dipped to taste one nipple through the soft cotton of her top. "As it happens," she replied, spiking her fingers through his hair as his spellbinding mouth worked its way back up her neck, "I accept them much better that way, too."

Hand in hand, they tiptoed into the cabin, Elizabeth's heart sputtering inside her chest. Guy held his finger to his lips, then pointed to the loft. Nodding, Elizabeth paused, too, listening.

Silence.

Then he yanked her through the bedroom door, shut it, and tumbled down with her across the bed, joining their mouths in a frantic kiss of anticipation. She clung to him, savoring his deep, unabashedly hungry kisses as she felt him unbutton her pajama top. The newness of it all was so deliciously erotic, this simple act of being undressed, of being desired so much that the fingers doing the undressing shook. He spread the open top, revealing her breasts, and all she could think was how natural and good and right it felt to lie exposed to this man. She wanted to watch him, wanted to see as well as feel what he was doing to her, but the sweet, sharp pleasure he stoked soon made her shut her eyes to all but the sensation of being loved. With each caress, she gasped in wonder as tiny, needle-hot flames of desire melted her, moistened her, quickly burning away all thoughts except the most primitive one of an aching need for release.

He paused for a moment, smiling at her, tenderly stroking her hair off her face. "Why do you feel so good?" In the silvery light, his smile was more than a little wicked.

"Hmm..." She pushed his robe off his shoulder. "Not half as good as something tells me I'm going to feel in a few minutes."

He chuckled softly, then encouraged her to lift her hips so he could slip off the pajama bottoms. Seconds later, persuasive, practiced fingers almost immediately proved her prediction true. The surprise climax shimmered through her, leaving her more startled than satisfied.

"What on earth was that all about?" she gasped through a haze of confusion, her arms looped around his neck.

He laughed and shifted her so she lay on top of him, pressing her against his arousal. "Call it an hors d'eouvre," he said, nipping at her chin, tracing her upper arms with his fingertips as if she were something delicate. Cherished. And yet, she could tell from his breathing, from his thudding heartbeat underneath her breasts, what his little "sampling" had cost him. Deliberately, she pressed against his hardness, sucking in a breath as her own heat once again flared.

"Now, this is my idea of seeing how well we hold up in a cramped space," he said, winnowing his fingers through her hair.

"Speaking of holding up..." She pushed herself back, returned the favor, efficiently, playfully, undressing him. She contemplated him as he lay on his back before her, now the vulnerable one, and smiled.

Oh, yeah...serious payback time.

She had no idea what she was doing or even what he'd like, but she wasn't about to let a minor detail like ignorance stop her. One eyebrow raised, he rested his head on one arm, letting her have her way, and his trust in her ability to give him pleasure sent a ripple of satisfaction through her. She smiled more broadly when he closed his eyes to her ministrations as she had done his earlier, as she first let her novice fingers explore and tease, then her mouth, relying on his soft murmurs of approval to guide her. At last, unashamed, she kissed what two days before she'd never even seen.

"Oh, no you don't—" He tumbled her back onto the bed, dusting her belly, her thighs, her feet with lightning-hot kisses before cradling her to him. His tongue flicked over one achingly tight nipple; she shut her eyes on a sigh, almost unable to absorb the electrifying sensation. His lips closed over the peak, suckling, taking, so hard and sweet and hot. She arched to him, cried to him, lost to everything but the need to *feel*.

His mouth left her breast, the breeze from the open window wicking the dampness from her nipple, making her shiver, making him laugh. She was one enormous erogenous zone, again so ripe for climax she could hardly catch her breath. She was no longer sure if she loved him or hated him as he so expertly played his cat-and-mouse game, taking her just close enough to the edge to see over it, then pulling her back, over and over again until she thought she'd die from pleasure and frustration both.

No! Not yet! She willed herself to calm down, wondering if that was even possible. For a minute, though, she managed to lie still, trembling but quiescent, marveling at the sensation pulsing, building, spiraling in her body.

For *just* a minute.

He hesitated one last time, smiling at her, and she touched his face with questioning fingers. "Time for the main course?" she whispered.

"With all the trimmings, honey."

Then they were a tangle of limbs and laughter on the quick-silver-streaked bed, as if desperately needing to cement their love before circumstances clawed it—and them—apart. Guy now demanded the best she had to give, his kisses bruising, insatiable, possessive, and she gave it, frantically, eagerly, wiggling against him and under him, giving instinct its head.

Then he was on top of her, his heat and weight so welcome, so perfect. His arousal teased her, seeking entry into that which wanted nothing more than to receive. She raised her head to lick his chest, loving the rasp of chest hair against her tongue. She kissed, sucked, licked his nipples as he had done hers, and was rewarded with a deep chuckle of approval in her ear. Then:

"Damn! I didn't bring—"

"Tote bag. Dresser. Right pocket. *Hurry.*"

"Stay right where you are," he croaked, jumping up from the bed.

"No problem," she muttered, shivering. But before the goose bumps had settled down, he was back, he was with her.

He was deeply, completely inside her.

She accepted him with a sharp sigh of fulfillment and joy, instantly overcome by a need so fierce she almost slugged him when he began the slow, cautious thrusts of the night before. "No!" Clamping her legs around his waist, she jerked him to her as she simultaneously hoisted her pelvis to take him deeper.

"Are you sure—?"

"Shut *up!*" she cried, riding on a knife's edge, digging her heels into his back, yanking him to her again. He caught on, plunging into her again, again, again, as she exulted in the on-slaught of lavalike heat building so fast—so fast!—until, in a split second of blinding white light, she heard in her head the single word *Now!* and exploded with a climax so powerful she screamed with it, laughed with it, clutching her lover to her and finding joy in his cries of simultaneous release in her ear. Her own body spasmed in a series of aftershocks as she felt him shudder inside her, around her, on top of her and she realized, even before she began the slow, quivering descent back to earth, that having to give this up would be a damn shame.

Would he ever be able to make love to this woman and not feel regret?

She had been absolutely right last night: sex didn't fix or change anything. Just put things on hold for the moment, maybe, but that was all. Shame, too, because sex like this should be worth more than just an avoidance maneuver.

He held her, still pinned underneath him, limp and sweaty, her heart racing with his as her delicate, pretty breasts pushed into his chest. He kissed her, twice, then lifted off her, imme-diately gathering her into his arms. She wrapped her leg around his thigh, possessively.

"I don't dare stay," he said.

He felt her nod against him. "Yeah. I figured." She shifted to stroke his lips with her fingertips. "Short class tonight, huh?"

"We kinda covered the material more quickly than I'd thought we would."

"Mmm." Then she snuggled against his chest, letting her hand stray down his ribs, then over his hip, his belly…

Incredible.

"Not even for you, witch woman, could I make a comeback that quickly."

She scrutinized him for a moment, then rolled onto her back. Putting space between them. "Pity. I could get really used to this."

"Yeah," he said, trying to ignore the twinge of fear in his heart. "Me, too."

* * *

Guy caught one look at Elizabeth when she shuffled out of the bedroom the next morning, the old patchwork quilt pulled haphazardly over her shoulders, and nearly spilled the milk he was pouring over Micah's cereal. She hadn't even combed her hair, which made her look, he thought with an inward smile, not unlike Einstein.

She looked quickly around. For Ashli, he presumed.

"In the living room," he said.

"And...?"

"And I told her we were staying. She rolled her eyes and sighed a lot, but that was about it."

Elizabeth gave a sharp little sigh of her own and settled gingerly into one of the kitchen chairs, squinting a bit in the glare of the overhead light. The rain had begun in earnest about an hour earlier, and already it promised to be one of those days when you stuck to everything you touched. Elizabeth looked thrilled as all get-out, too. He put a cup of coffee into her outstretched hand, for which he received a wan smile in return.

"What is it?" he asked over Micah's jabbering.

She jumped a little, brows knit in annoyance. "Oh, um, nothing. But I need to go into town after breakfast to pick up a few things. Can I use the car?"

The woman looked like death warmed over, yet she wanted to go into town. Uh-huh. He'd been down this road before. "How bad are they?"

She sipped her coffee, frowned. "What?"

"The cramps."

Even her nose turned red. "I'll be fine," she said in a squeak of a voice.

"I take it this was unexpected."

Her knuckles went white where she clutched the blanket to her chest. "I, um, forget to check the calendar."

He grinned. "You telling me the inimitable Elizabeth Louden *screwed up?*"

She glared at him.

"Well, I'll go to the store for you," he said easily, wiping up a lumpy lake of cereal and milk where Jake had been sitting.

"Oh...no, Guy. I couldn't ask you..."

"To do something I've done dozens of times before?" he finished with a grin. "All I ask is that you just write down *exactly* what you need. I'm certainly secure enough to go buy the stuff, but don't ask me to make a decision about it."

That got a small laugh, followed by a long sigh as she looked past him through the kitchen window. "What awful weather. What are the kids going to do all day?"

"A *Sanford* is always prepared," he said, wiping off the baby's face. "There are tons of puzzles and games up in the loft. And—" he saved the best for last "—there's a TV in the bedroom closet."

Her brows flew up. "A TV? In a rustic mountain retreat?"

"Ah…if you recall, my dear, I said rustic, but not primitive. Only a fool would risk being cooped up with a batch of kids in a small cabin without electronic stimulation. Want some breakfast?"

She grimaced and shook her head. "Not on your life."

"Wanna crawl back into bed?"

Another head shake. "I hate being isolated like that." Her mouth stretched into a wry grin. "I'd rather hole up here on the couch and let everyone share my misery with me, if you don't mind."

"Fine with me. When do you need…?"

"I'm okay until midafternoon," she quickly supplied, her cheeks coloring again.

"Good. That way, I can get Micah and Jake down for their naps and won't have to drag them with me through this downpour." He stepped over to the window and shook his head. "More like trial by flood, if you ask me."

Out of the corner of his eye, he saw her take another sip her coffee, huddle more closely underneath the quilt, and try to laugh.

By the time Guy left to go into town, the cramps had settled into more of an uncomfortable annoyance than anything else. The boys were asleep, Ashli had been silently occupied all morning with a five-hundred-piece puzzle of the Disneyland castle, and Guy assured Elizabeth he'd be back within an hour at most.

The minute the door closed behind him, apprehension gripped Elizabeth's heart. Here she was, in charge of three children—one of whom had yet to speak to her that day—out in the boonies, with no phone, no car and no resources to fall back on save the untested ones in her own brain.

She was being paranoid, she told herself. And silly. She settled back against the four pillows Guy had piled behind her back on the sofa, rearranged the quilt over her knees and tried to doze off. Might have succeeded, too, had it not been for the crash from the bedroom.

After nearly killing herself getting untangled from the quilt, Elizabeth sprang up from the sofa and flew into the bedroom, her wool socks snagging on the wooden floor as she ran. She found Micah happily plopped on the braided scatter rug by the bed, the contents of her tote bag scattered hither and yon in a five-foot radius. Jake had awakened as well, sitting up on the bed as he rubbed one eye and yawned. So much for "They *always* sleep for at least two hours."

Elizabeth quickly gathered up the tote bag's innards before Ashli came in and, as only she could, figured out what some of them were. Unfortunately, this did not meet with Micah's approval. He let out a series of ear-ringing screeches, culminating in a crimson-faced howl as he pitched himself backward.

"Micah! No, baby!" Elizabeth dropped everything in a futile effort to catch him before he whacked the back of his head against the floor. She winced at the dull crack as head hit flimsily padded wood, winced again at the even louder screams which resulted. Figuring the baby wasn't going to go any farther than he already had, she hurriedly restuffed the tote bag and set it back up on the dresser, then tried to pull the wailing child into her arms.

No dice.

"He doesn't want you to hold him." This from Ashli, standing in the doorway with her hands on her hips. Great. *Now* she talks.

"But what if he's hurt...?"

"He does this all the time. Daddy just ignores him."

Elizabeth warily eyed the oldest, then the youngest child. "You sure?"

"That's what Daddy does," she repeated, then said, "By the way, did you know Jake's got the milk out and is trying to pour himself a glass?"

Her attention snapped to where the four-year-old had been sitting on the bed, catatonic, not thirty seconds before. Geez, Louise, he was fast. Leaving Micah still sobbing on the floor, Elizabeth sprinted to the kitchen—just in time to witness the glass hit the floor, spraying milk and shattered glass in a thousand directions.

She swore, loudly, then dashed across the floor and swept Jake out of the mess, forgetting she was in her stockinged feet herself. No glass got through, she was pretty sure, but now her socks were saturated with cold milk. Then Einstein, ever the opportunist, meandered into the room.

Ohmigod—glass in a dog's gut would not be a good thing.

"Einstein, *no!*"

With a yawn, he sat down, giving her a "well, gee, you didn't have to go nuts on me" look.

Elizabeth carried Jake to the living room and deposited him on the sofa, turned on the TV and prayed there was something on besides *Jenny Jones* or soaps. *Power Rangers!* There was a God!

"Ashli, *please* keep an eye on Jake for a few minutes while I get that mess cleaned up, okay, sweetie?"

Pleasepleasepleasepleaseplease…

The little girl glanced at the program, made a face, but—bless her!—sat.

It wasn't until several minutes later, after Elizabeth had the kitchen clean and safe once again, that she remembered the baby. The very *quiet* baby. Scurrying past the other two kids in the living room—who were beginning to argue with each other—she went back into the bedroom.

And groaned.

It was everywhere. Her best Dior lipstick, now the medium of choice for a two-year-old's artistic expression. The walls.

The floor. The dresser. The sheets. And, last but not least, the artist himself.

"P'itty," Micah said, lifting the completely empty tube to her with a huge, satisfied grin on his war-painted face.

Elizabeth folded to her knees in front of him, removing the tube from his pink-tinged hands. He had even scooped out the insides with those adorable little fingers. As she kneeled in front of him, wondering where to start, the bickering in the next room escalated into all-out war.

"Is there a phone I could use?" Guy asked the gum-chewing clerk in the time-warped convenience store as he paid for his purchases. He hadn't missed the lifted eyebrows at the assortment of feminine hygiene products: they didn't have anything on Elizabeth's list, so he decided to err on the side of overkill.

"Outside," the redhead said, dropping the last box into what looked like a recycled brown paper bag.

He nodded his thanks, then hunched his denim jacket up around his ears as he headed back out into the wet. Even under the wooden overhang, the dampness penetrated his bones. Chilly enough to make a fire when he got back to the cabin, he decided as he punched in his remote access number for his answering machine, provided the chimney was okay. He chuckled as his phone rang, thinking that, with three children around, he was about to waste a perfectly good romantic fire. Then he remembered why he'd come to the store in the first place and sighed. So much for—

"Mr. Sanford, Henry Wilkens here. Just wanted to let you know, got an offer on your house. Good one, too—guy's being transferred to Chicago next month, needs a place right away. Call me—612-555-8300."

Yes! Images of bills marked "Paid in full" danced through his head. And filthy shag carpeting was soon to be but a distant, unpleasant memory…

"Guy? It's Julie. Dianne's sister? Listen, she just called. She flies out of Milan next Friday, arriving at O'Hare Saturday night."

There was a pause, during which Guy's ears started to ring.

"Guy, hey, listen…Di's real broke up about what she did and she wants to see the kids something fierce. Don't say no, huh? She's not gonna do anything stupid, ya know? Give me a call when you get in, okay? Bye."

He hung up, leaned his forehead against the cold, slimy glass. She was really coming back.

He sucked in a sharp breath, stuffed the bag as best he could underneath his jacket and sprinted to the car. The door slammed shut behind him; he shook water out of his hair, then dragged a wet hand across his face.

The reservations were made. She'd even told Julie.

He pulled out onto the road, driving slowly, his windshield wipers barely able to keep up with the deluge. Enough, already, he thought, not even sure himself whether he meant the rain or the goings on in his life. Between the drenching rain and his thoughts, he never even noticed the board in the middle of the road. Let alone the four-inch nail sticking out of it. Not until the loud *bang!* scared the bejeebers out of him and the car went into a wobbling dance for several seconds until Guy eased it onto the shoulder.

He shut his eyes, too annoyed to even swear. Then, feeling about a hundred years old, he stepped back out into the downpour to fix the flat.

The rain pounding the cabin roof drove right through Elizabeth's skull. She'd managed to get most of the lipstick off the wood, but the wall and sheets were something else again. One thing the ads failed to mention about the formula's staying power was that they weren't just talking about *lips*.

She leaned against the kitchen sink, her wrists moaning from trying to scrub out the stains from the sheets. Her wrists, her head, her back…there was little left happy about the situation. To top it off, the two older kids had been fighting nonstop for most of the past hour. God! They could argue about the *stupidest* things!

She lugged the sodden top sheet out of the water, soaking the front of her cotton sweater as she tried, however ineffectually, to wring it out. Micah sat on the floor beside her with every pot, pan and cooking utensil she could find that he could neither damage himself nor anything else with, the extra racket stretching her patience dangerously thin.

Elizabeth glanced up at the kitchen clock, frowned. How had it gotten that late? Guy should have been back ages ago. She brushed aside the little café curtains and peered outside at the dreck, not amused to see it was raining so hard the back of the yard wasn't visible from the cabin.

Great. Something else to worry about. In the midst of transferring the twisted, heavy sheet to the dishpan, she heard a solid *thonk* followed by shriek of furious pain. She let the sheet drop like a carcass and tramped out into the main room. Raw, burning hands jabbed into hips. "What?"

"He's *such* a baby—"

"Am not!" came the tearful reply as Jake rubbed his arm. "You slugged me!"

"You deserved it, creep," the little girl snapped back, now appealing to Elizabeth. "He kept sticking his tongue out at me!"

"You did it first!"

"Did not—"

"You did!"

"Enough!" Elizabeth roared, her hands pressed to her head. She let them slowly drop, then pointed at each child in turn. "Cut it out," she managed to demand in a low voice, "or…" She stopped. Or what?

She caught the look of triumph in Ashli's eyes. Elizabeth's face flamed with anger, embarrassment, inadequacy.

"Or you can spend the rest of the day in the loft, both of you. No TV."

Ashli rolled her eyes and sighed the sigh of the perpetually put-upon. But she said nothing, and for that at least, Elizabeth was immensely grateful. She gave them her best and-I-*mean*-it glare for several more seconds, then returned to the kitchen…just as the electricity—and consequently the TV— went out.

"Ha-ha, pea-brain," Elizabeth heard from the main room. "Now you can't watch *Rugrats* anyway." She could just imagine the tongue-sticking-out that went with the jibe. She waited, half expecting an explosion, but none came. Instead, Jake came into the kitchen, crestfallen but coping, and asked for some milk.

"Oh...sure, sweetie." Elizabeth poured some into a plastic cup this time, settled both cup and child at the kitchen table, then began a search through the kitchen drawers for candles and matches. Although only midafternoon, the cabin was gloomy from the rain. And cold. Now that Elizabeth wasn't burning up a million calories a minute cleaning up smeared lipstick, she could feel the chill. So the question of the hour was, was dimly recalled Girl Scout training sufficient to start a fire in the woodstove?

Just as Elizabeth struck pay dirt with the candles and matches, she heard Ashli plant herself at the kitchen table across from Jake.

"This really sucks," she said, and Elizabeth's last nerve frayed a little more.

She lit two enormous candles and set them on the back of the stove, where the baby couldn't reach them. "While I agree with your assessment, Ashli, I don't agree with your choice of words." She turned to the little girl. "Please don't say that again."

Incredulous blue eyes zeroed in on her own. "You can't tell me what to say. Only Daddy can do that."

Elizabeth hauled in a long, cautious breath, then replied, "But I'm the resident grown-up at the moment, so what I say goes—"

"You're not my mother."

Micah tugged at Elizabeth's sweater, asking to be picked up, the swell of pleasure she felt at his request battling with her increasing irritation with his older sister. As she obliged the toddler, she said, "We've been over this, honey. I'm not trying to be your mother. But I am in charge. And..." She swallowed, hoping. "And I will not tolerate back talk. So I'm afraid you'll just have to get used to it."

Ashli shot up from her chair, her eyes blazing, her face contorted and red. "Why? Why should I get used to it? It's not as if you're gonna stay or anything…"

"Ashli…" Shifting the baby to her hip, Elizabeth tried to touch Ashli's hair, but the child jerked away. Jake began to cry, which set Micah off, too.

That did it. "Why don't you like me?" she said, unable to check the hot tears. "What have I done to make you so angry with me?"

"What do you care?" the child shot back, tears streaking down her face as well. "All you care about is Daddy and being with him! You don't really want to be with us!"

"That's not true!" Elizabeth parried, frantically stroking the baby's head. Jake had left the table and now threaded his arms around her thighs, sobbing softly. "You just have to give me a chance—"

"Stop pretending to be our mother!" Ashli shrieked. "If I can't have Mama back, I don't want anyone else! I want you to go away! I hate you, I hate you, I *hate* you—"

"Ashli Nicole Sanford!"

Elizabeth's gaze shot to Guy standing in the kitchen doorway, soaked through and dripping all over the wooden floor.

"Apologize to Elizabeth this instant!"

"No!" the child screamed, then ran past her father, her sneakers thudding on the floorboards until silenced by the slam of the bedroom door.

Elizabeth hitched Micah further into her arms and looked helplessly at Guy. She couldn't read the expression in his eyes. But she could guess.

He looked at her for a single, horrible moment, then went to his daughter.

Chapter 14

For the rest of the evening, they all sidestepped each other, literally as well as emotionally. Guy did insist Ashli at least pay lip service to an apology to Elizabeth, who seemed to accept the child's unfelt words in about the same spirit in which they were given. He'd gathered the two hours he'd been away had been hell for Elizabeth but couldn't seem to muster any enthusiasm for consoling her that these things happen and not to worry about it and in a week she'd laugh the whole thing off.

The fight had gone out of her eyes. That's what made the difference. Had she been simply angry, or exhausted, or even more emotional, he would have said, "Okay, this was a bad spot, but we'll keep trying." But her features registered nothing but defeat. Not about the normal stuff, he knew. Despite everything, she couldn't keep the smile out of her voice when she told him about Micah's attempts to usurp Picasso—but Ashli's intractability, not to mention her Jekyll-and-Hyde attitude toward Elizabeth, was something else again.

Their experiment had failed.

It was past eleven before the kids fell asleep. He knocked

on the bedroom door, entered to find Elizabeth packing. Flickering light from a lone kerosene lamp danced eerily across the wall behind it, lending the perfect touch to the already dreary scenario. He rubbed his face, afraid to look at her.

"Let me save you the agony," she said at last. "This just isn't working."

Only her words were placid; her hands trembled as she folded up a sweater and neatly tucked it into the bag. When he didn't answer, she looked up, nodded, then turned back to the dresser drawer. Suddenly, as if timed, they spoke simultaneously:

"If my being around causes that much pain—"

"It just doesn't seem right to put either of you through this—"

More silence. Then:

"Ashli needs help," Elizabeth said quietly, folding, packing her other pair of jeans.

"Yeah. I know. When we get back, I'll look into it." He closed his eyes and sucked in a breath. "Dianne's coming in, end of next week," he said on a rush of exhaled air, bringing Elizabeth's head up.

"How did you find that out?"

"I checked my messages by remote when I was at the store."

"Oh. I see."

"It…just makes things even more…complicated."

She gave a single, sharp nod.

"Elizabeth…?"

Again, she looked up, those soft green eyes revealing nothing. Everything.

"I really do love you, you know."

She snatched her gaze away, her mouth small and angry. "That was the wrong thing to say," she murmured. "Please, Guy—just…go."

Feeling like a complete idiot, he paused, his hand on the doorknob. "We'll leave about nine."

She said nothing.

* * *

Elizabeth pushed the redone plans for Shadywoods back across her dining table. "Very nice." She adjusted her glasses, stared again at her laptop screen.

"Gee," Maureen said. "Don't knock me over with your enthusiasm."

She glanced up, not bothering to smile. "'Fraid you'd have to dig back in a past life for that, Mother. But I'm sure they'll sell like hotcakes, all the homes being nestled in the trees like that. The new architect did a wonderful job."

"Thanks to Guy's input."

Elizabeth snapped her attention back to the screen.

Maureen seated herself, folding her hands in front of her in that school-principal position Elizabeth had always hated. Feared. "Okay, Missy. It's been a week—you planning on working from home for the rest of your life?"

"Why not? It's quiet, peaceful, phone doesn't ring all the time—"

"Elizabeth—shut up."

Her mouth still open, Elizabeth lifted her eyes to her mother's, now smoky with anger as she leaned across the dining table.

"Since when do you run from a challenge?" Maureen held up a hand to fend off Elizabeth's protest. "Not from something that really matters, anyway. How can you just abandon that young man like that, just when he needs you most? You know that ex-wife of his is due back in the States tomorrow?"

Elizabeth blinked back the sting of tears. "Which has nothing to do with me. In case you missed it, Mother, we crashed and burned." She got up from the table and went into her kitchen, pulling the coffee carafe off the stand, hoping her mother wouldn't notice her palsied hand. "Coffee?"

"Don't change the subject. I'm not one of your clients, young lady." But she joined her daughter in the kitchen anyway, fetching a cup and saucer from the cabinet. She took the carafe from Elizabeth's hand, pouring as she said, "Tell me you don't love him."

Elizabeth took back the carafe, filled her own cup. Stalling. "I never said I didn't."

"And how was the sex?" her mother asked calmly.

Somehow, Elizabeth managed to get the container back on the pad. "What makes you so sure—?"

"Elizabeth. Please."

She took a sip of coffee. "Let's just say the thought of not having it again is not making me a happy camper."

Maureen grinned, which blew the top off Elizabeth's tenuous composure. "Dammit, Mother! Okay, fine—I feel like crud, all right? I'm miserable, my heart is broken, and I haven't been able to eat or sleep for the past week. Will that do?"

"For starters," Maureen allowed, then squinted at her daughter. "And this is a good thing?"

"Of course it's not good! Why on earth do you think I'm here and not at the office? I'm about to go stir crazy in this bloody apartment." She swept out of the kitchen and clattered her cup on the table, then crammed her folded arms into her ribs. "I feel like a child who's been banished to my room for eternity."

"So come back to work. Give Cora someone else to pick on."

Elizabeth allowed a weary laugh, then shook her head. "I can't."

Her head inclined to one side, Maureen asked, "You miss the children?"

Bull's-eye. "Do me a favor, Mother."

"What, dear?"

"Butt out."

Maureen slowly downed her last sip of coffee, then carefully placed the cup and saucer on the counter. "Sixteen years ago, I let a certain little girl influence my decision about whether or not I should remarry." She looked at her daughter, nearly expressionless save for the not-so-mild regret shadowing the amber eyes. "I sacrificed my own happiness for yours," she said simply. "Took me quite a while before I realized how stupid that was. Do you remember?"

Elizabeth let out a sharp breath. "All too clearly." She

turned to her mother. "I had no right to do that to you. I don't know what I was so afraid of—"

"You were twelve. The problem wasn't your objections. It was my reaction to them." She sighed. "I didn't trust myself enough to fight for what I knew was right. Dave was a good man, and he adored you. Given time, you would have come around. But..." Her shoulders hitched briefly. "But I thought I was doing the right thing. At the time."

Elizabeth walked into the living room, pinged the edge of a Baccarat bowl with one fingernail. "Is there a statute of limitations on apologies?"

"Yes," came the unequivocal reply. "And you missed it by more years than you want to know. Besides, *you* didn't make me do anything, Elizabeth. Maybe I let you influence me, but I ultimately made the decision."

Elizabeth faced her mother, hugging herself. "So you're saying—"

"—It's up to you. Yes, I am."

"And I should just ignore the fact that Ashli hates me?"

"You really think she does?"

A glance out the living room window, a shrug. "It just seems wrong for us to stay together if it upsets his daughter that much—" She sank into the sofa just as the first tears came, barely reacting when she felt her mother sit beside her.

"She's an eight-year-old *child,* honey," Maureen said gently, rubbing Elizabeth's back. "She's just mixed up and afraid. I doubt whether she knows herself what the truth is. But you can't just give up on what you and Guy have."

"*I* didn't give it up!" Elizabeth cried, smoothing away tears with her fingertips. "It was a mutual revelation, that we'd all be miserable. We agreed it wasn't working...."

"What's not working is your being apart. Sweetheart—the man is a wreck. Not even Cora can get a rise out of him—"

"Mother, please—don't do this."

A second or two passed, then Maureen sprang up from the sofa and walked briskly to the window. "What is it with young people these days?" she said, seemingly to herself, then turned to Elizabeth, twisting her black pearl necklace around one finger. "What they say about anything worth having is worth fighting for is true, you know."

"But I did fight, Mother. I did try—"

"Not hard enough!" Maureen stared at her daughter for several seconds, then crossed back into the dining room in a flash of silvery raw silk, yanking her pocketbook and the plans off the table. "All I have to say is, I sure as hell wouldn't give any kid this much control over my life. Not anymore. You want to make amends for what happened sixteen years ago? Then don't make the same mistake I did! For God's sake, Elizabeth—tell that overdeveloped brain of yours to go take a hike and listen to your *heart!*"

A second later, the door slammed behind her.

Elizabeth sat stone-still for several seconds, staring at her crystal collection. So pristine and perfect and emotionless. Pure beauty with no soul. Was this all she'd achieved in her life? Her gaze zipped around her condo—a dustless, mussless, lifeless shell. Why, it was as if no one even *lived* here!

The rage bubbled up from nowhere, from a pit of emptiness she'd been nourishing with pointless rationalizations for the past week. With a howl of anguish, she rocketed from the sofa, reaching the étagère in three strides. In one eerily graceful motion, she grabbed a vase and hurled it against the far wall, collapsing into sobs as it struck and shattered into a million needle-sharp bits all over her just-vacuumed carpet.

"Come here, squirt," Guy said quietly to Micah, sliding the baby forward on the bed so he could get him socked and shod. The baby observed his father's subdued expression in that wise way babies have, uncharacteristically quiet himself. When Guy finished, he gathered the little boy in his arms and hugged him as if it were the last hug he would ever give anybody.

"Daddy, Jake won't stop giving the dog cookies."

"Then why don't you stop giving *Jake* cookies, Ashli?" Guy said on a sigh as he stood, the toddler still clinging to his neck. "Okay—everyone gone potty?"

The boys—only—were spending the weekend at his parents'. Ashli, who'd been on trepidaciously good behavior all week, would stay with him. Alone. First, because he didn't want distractions when he—finally—told her about Dianne's return. And second, because—now that he'd had a week to mull things over—he realized he had a bone the size of a tyrannosaurus femur to pick with his daughter.

The ducks glided in a feathered convoy across the pond the instant they spotted Elizabeth approaching the bank. A few of the bolder ones scrambled up to snatch pieces of bread right from her hands, giving rise to a laughter of sorts in her throat.

It had taken nearly two hours to get all the glass out of the rug. Having to hand remove all the infinitesimal shards, she decided, was fitting penance for her impetuousness. And her obstinacy. She supposed resisting her mother's arguments was just one of those mother-daughter things. But, after an afternoon spent picking up glass and mopping up her own tears, she had to admit the woman had a point.

It all stemmed from her father's death, so long ago. He'd been her best buddy, the parent who'd do the crazy stuff with her while her mother would sit back and watch, smiling indulgently. His sudden passing—the heart disease had been undetectable, the doctors said—had ripped her apart. She felt betrayed, although she never figured out exactly by *what.* And then to be plunged into financial hardship on top of the grief…

Appalled at life's capriciousness, Elizabeth determined early on to never again be its victim. Hence her orderliness, her myopic determination to succeed, her obsession with financial security, her resistance to forging a real relationship with a man.

Her *inability* to forge a real relationship with a man.

Fear, and nothing else, had kept her at arm's length from romantic involvement. Fear of losing control, of feeling trapped, of letting emotions make decisions for her that would only lead to heartbreak and loss. She'd seen it happen to her mother; she saw no reason to go through that herself. Nor could she, as a child, bear to see her mother suffer a second time.

She tossed a handful of bread out onto the water for the

more reticent fowl, then flopped down on the grass, her arm shielding her eyes. She'd been a real brat about Dave Ballard. She'd cut off her own nose to spite her face, too, if memory served. Dave was not only nice, and kind, and clearly besotted with her mother, but he'd been fairly well off, too. Had her mother married Dave, things would have been very different. But Elizabeth, still tender from the loss of her father, could only see potential for more pain—what if Dave died, too? What if the marriage didn't work out for some reason? What was the point of some fleeting moment of happiness when it was just going to end unhappily, anyway?

So she pitched fits and cried buckets of tears and may have even threatened to kill herself. So her mother called off the wedding, citing Elizabeth's fragile mental state. And Dave Ballard eventually married someone else.

That her mother had ever forgiven her at all was in and of itself astounding. Did Elizabeth have it in her to love a child that much?

Talk about your no-brainer.

Glowering at nothing, Elizabeth rolled over onto her stomach, resting her chin on her hands. *Had* she given up too easily? Or was she being pragmatic, logical, choosing the course of action that would cause the least pain to the least number of people?

That last thought brought her up short. There were lots of people hurting here, including the boys. They'd both wept bitterly when she got out of the car on Monday afternoon, and it broke her heart that she couldn't say, "But I'll see you tonight, okay?"

And was Ashli really happy about the turn of events? Elizabeth might not know much about little girls, but she remembered what it was like to be one well enough to recognize a sense of triumph over having gotten one's way. Ashli's features bore no trace of smugness. Only confusion, and pain.

With a groan, Elizabeth flopped again onto her back—she was beginning to feel like a landed fish—squinting in the sunlight. Oh, God—there was no life without taking chances, was there? None worth living, at least. Yes, she'd known more fear and anxiety and heartache this past few weeks than she had—than she'd allowed herself—since she was a little girl.

She also never known such joy. And the thought of deliberately denying herself that joy—even if it meant occasional doses of pain and fear as well—was suddenly incomprehensible.

The KFC was a stalling tactic, but Guy was desperate.

He'd finally run out of excuses. And time. Julie had confirmed it: Dianne's plane was due in this evening, she wanted to come see the kids on Sunday.

Although both Guy and Ashli had made noises about how much fun it would be to have a picnic out by the lake, neither seemed to be exactly having a rip-roaring good time. Ashli nibbled halfheartedly at a drumstick for a minute or two, then abandoned it on her paper plate. Guy, too, couldn't get food past the thick, heavy knot of dread and anger and pain lodged in his stomach. Maybe Ashli was only eight, and, sure, he was as fiercely protective of his daughter as the next parent, but sacrificing his own shot at happiness for her sake…right or wrong, resentment sizzled in his veins. Before he could even begin to deal with that, however, he had to tell her about her mother.

Elizabeth would have his hide if she knew he'd waited this long.

"Guess what?" He stumbled right into a pair of questioning eyes. "I have a surprise for you. Mama's coming to see you."

He watched the news register, bit by bit. First two wisps of light-brown eyebrows lifted, followed by a spark of surprise, then realization, flickering to life in the brilliant blue eyes. Finally, the mouth came into play, the lips spreading into an enormous grin. "Really? When? Are you sure? Daddy, when?"

"In a couple of days, maybe. I'm not sure."

Thin arms strangled him. "I knew it! I knew it! Mama's coming back!"

"Ashli." Guy pulled her off his neck, held her at arm's

length. "She's coming to *visit*. Not to stay. You've got to understand that. This isn't permanent."

The face fell, but only slightly, and not for long. "But I'll get to see her? And the boys? Are you bringing them back to see her?"

"Yes—"

But she hadn't heard him, since she was now dancing around him and singing, "Mama's coming ba-ack, Mama's coming ba-ack," having the good sense to stop before Guy exploded. Then she fell to her knees in front of him again, leveling him with a far too trenchant gaze. Chipped pink fingernails swept back a hank of filmy blond hair. "You said she wouldn't, Daddy. But she is."

"I *said*," he corrected, "I didn't *think* she'd ever come back."

Ashli gave a no-matter shrug, then grinned so widely her eyes nearly vanished. She pushed herself back onto her lavender-shorts-clad bottom and tucked into the fried chicken as if she hadn't seen food in a month. Guy watched her, wishing he could at least envy her her happiness. But his own rotten mood was hardly going to be assuaged by the thought of his ex-wife's imminent return.

Well. Ashli's getting what she wants. Now it was Daddy's turn.

He crossed his legs, laced his hands in his lap. "We have to talk, baby."

The chicken leg demolished, she'd started in on a biscuit. "About what?"

"Elizabeth."

Her brow furrowed as the biscuit found its way back to her plate. "Why? I thought you broke up?" She lifted a grease-and-crumb splotched face to him; automatically, Guy picked up a napkin and wiped her mouth.

"Which I didn't want to do." He shifted his position, speaking cautiously, feeling his way. "And I think you know how unhappy that made me."

Silence.

She seemed so small, and vulnerable. He'd always had a

soft spot for her anyway, one that was plumb going to rot out if he wasn't careful. And damned if the child didn't know exactly which buttons to push. Or to use. The quavering lower lip, for example.

"What really bothers me, though, is how much you *wanted* us to break up."

She dipped her head, plucking at a clump of clover beside her ankle, but said nothing.

"It's true, isn't it?"

After a moment, she nodded.

"Why?"

She shrugged.

"I don't understand. You and Elizabeth were getting along like gangbusters before…up until a week ago. So…what's the deal? What happened?"

When Ashli didn't answer, he continued. "I love you, baby. You know that. But I love Elizabeth, too, and I wanted her to part of our lives. And so do the boys—"

"I know," the child interrupted unexpectedly, squinting out over the lake as she brought her knees up under her chin. "Jake won't leave me alone, keeps asking me where Elizabeth is, like all the time."

Guy canted his head at her, waiting.

She idly picked at a loose scab on her knee, then said, "I just figured it would be easier…" She swallowed the rest of her sentence, then said on a shuddering sigh, "She lied to me, just like Mama did. She promised to tell me if you asked her to be your girlfriend, but she didn't. Mama said she loved me, and she didn't."

Maddeningly, she stopped. But she'd given him enough pieces to at least take a stab at the what the puzzle might be once completed. "So…you think because Elizabeth broke one promise—even though she didn't mean to break it, and even though she apologized—she might break others? Is that it?"

"Sorta."

Guy felt like an archaeologist, scraping away sand one grain at a time. "And…?"

"And…I figured it wouldn't hurt as much if she left now. Before she decided she didn't like being my mama, either."

Guy concentrated on breathing for a few seconds, then said, "So, you decided to act like a little snot so she'd feel like a failure, in order to keep from getting hurt yourself down the road. Is that what you're saying?"

Tears trickled down her cheeks, now, as she nodded.

"Ashli. Ashli, look at me!" She pivoted her face only as much as necessary to make eye contact. "You know, Elizabeth thinks *she's* to blame for what happened. That, as much as she wanted to, as hard as she was willing to try, that she just couldn't get through to you. So she gave up. Gave up because she cares about you so much, she couldn't bear the thought of seeing you miserable." At that, she quickly looked away, before he could see whatever impact his words might have had.

But he had seen it. Seen it and realized in an instant that he'd somehow, finally cracked through the child's barrier. He reached for her hand, gently chafing it between his own, as if she had fainted and he was trying to bring her back to consciousness. "Baby, what you did was wrong. And I'm not going to tell you it wasn't, even though I understand why you did it. But because you were afraid of what might happen to *you,* you just made a whole bunch of people very unhappy. And I know that's not what you meant to happen, is it?"

She shook her head so hard her hair stuck to her damp cheeks, and with that, Guy's soft spot rotted a little more. He swept her into his lap, tucking her head underneath his chin. "You've got to believe me, honey—I'd do anything in my power to be sure you don't get hurt like that again. Anything. But you've gotta trust me here."

His own words caught him up short. Why hadn't *he* trusted more, too? Why hadn't he fought harder for the thing he'd just told his daughter meant so much to him?

After a second, he said into her sweet hair, "The worst thing that could happen is that you'd have *two* mamas."

Ashli suddenly wiggled off his lap, crawling back to the open KFC box. She shrugged her shoulder across her nose, sniffed, made a great show of shooing away a fly. "Can we go home now? I wanna go tell Emily about Mama."

Just that easily, she'd dismissed their conversation, leaving absolutely nothing resolved.

She was only a child, Guy reminded himself as he got to his feet and quickly cleaned up their mess. "Yeah. Sure," he squeezed out through the runaway vines of irritation and disappointment choking his heart. Ashli skipped on ahead, already intent on sharing her good news with the little girl who lived next door, while Guy trudged behind, dumping the chicken box in a large trash can at the edge of the park.

Evening-long shadows stretched and bobbed in their path as they walked home, Ashli babbling beside him, apparently oblivious to his silence. Guy nodded and exchanged the requisite "Evenings" with folks out jogging or washing cars, but his brain was otherwise engaged.

Just how thick was the scar tissue around Ashli's wounded heart? Perhaps, to avoid being hurt again, she'd never let Elizabeth get close. So, was it fair to force the issue, if that's what the result would be? God knows, he had no wish to put his daughter through any more stress.

Or the woman he loved so much his heart screamed every time he thought about her. Look how many barriers of her own she'd bulldozed through to let herself get as close to Guy—and his offspring—as she had. But if he did marry again, he'd like to have a *happy* wife this time. A perpetually sullen daughter could put a serious crimp in that plan.

Ashli clanged up the metal stairs ahead of him, fidgeting when she got got the door. "I've gotta *go,* Daddy! Hurry up!"

Guy sprinted up the stairs, unlocked the door. Ashli shoved Einstein aside as she barreled into the apartment and down the hall to the bathroom. Guy sank onto the sofa, letting his head fall back as he automatically reached for the spiky head responsible for the hot breath bathing his knee. "You know something, boy? Be grateful you're a dog. Being human ain't all it's cracked up to be."

"Dad-*dy!* There's no toilet paper! *Again!*"

With a groan, he pulled himself off the sofa. As he passed

the kitchen counter, he noticed the flashing message light on his answering machine. Probably his mother. Or worse yet, one of his blissfully wedded brothers.

Or maybe it was Elizabeth.

He punched the play button.

"Hey, Guy? It's Julie. Listen...you're probably not going to like this..."

"Dad-*deee!*"

"Hold your horses, for crying out loud! I'm coming, I'm coming!"

"Never mind...I'll use a tissue—"

"...but I just heard from Dianne. Rudolfo apparently caught her before she got on the plane, and they made up. So she changed her mind...she's not coming back...."

Chapter 15

"Daddy? Who's on the phone?"

He stabbed the Stop button and spun around, his heart beating so hard it hurt. His head felt as if a flock of birds had just been spooked inside; he could hardly hear his own words for the whirring, beating wings. "It was your Aunt Julie, sweetheart—"

Ashli beamed. "Is Mama back already? Is she coming to see me?"

Was this going to hurt any less ten minutes from now? Tomorrow? Ever? "Honey…" Oh, *hell.* "Something…came up. She's…she can't make it."

The child darted back, stepping on the dog sprawled across the floor. Over his yelp of surprise, she cried, "It's not true! You're just saying that so I won't have to see her! Why don't you want me to see Mama?"

"What?"

"I don't believe you!" she shrieked. "Why are you saying this?"

"Because it's *true!*" Guy yelled back in frustration and

stunned surprise. He knew this would be rough, but it never occurred to him she wouldn't believe him.

Now whimpering in reaction to his anger, she'd backed herself into the corner of the sofa, hugging her knees to her chest. He lowered his voice. "Oh, Lord, baby, believe me, I wish this wasn't happening." He took a deep breath, then said, "But it is. You can listen to the tape if you want to."

She shook her head but not as emphatically.

His phone rang again; he ignored it, grateful the volume was turned down. Whoever it was, whatever it was, could wait. Indefinitely.

He lowered himself onto the edge of the sofa in front of his daughter, wishing some magic words would pop into his head. He reached out, intending to stroke her hair. "I'm so sorry, honey."

But she shrank back. "It's not fair," she sobbed, over and over and over, huddled in her little corner, staring at nothing, until she suddenly jumped up and screamed, "This really *sucks!*" and bolted from the room.

Guy caught her before she was halfway down the hall, gathering her into his lap as he slid, back to wall, down onto the floor. For several seconds, she fought him like a wildcat, then curled her arms around his neck and crushed her twiglike body into his—crushing, too, his last breath of compassion for Dianne. A compassion he might have still felt, had she opened up to him to begin with; had she tried to fix things before their divorce; had she even managed to haul her carcass back to the States *this* time.

Had she given a bloody damn about her children.

He cupped Ashli's head in his hand, rubbing his cheek over her hair, squelching a primal urge to roar in grief and fury for what this woman had done to her children.

To him.

For eighteen hellish months, guilt had silently gnawed at his heart, whispering that, somehow, his marriage had failed because of something *he'd* done—or not done. Now he knew, irreversibly, that wasn't true. He shuddered, sobbed his release, and in a supernova flash of disintegration, rage incinerated the last vestige of doubt, the fear of failing a second time…leaving in its place a fierce determination to win back the woman who'd understood all along what he couldn't even see.

It wasn't until Elizabeth heard Guy's answering machine click on that she remembered her mother had said he was taking the boys to his folks' house tonight. Maybe they hadn't come back yet, or he'd taken Ashli to dinner or something. No reason for him to be sitting by the phone, just because she'd decided to call him.

And say what, exactly? "Hey—I miss you so much I'm about to lose my mind, and I wanna try again, but I'm scared and flawed and yes, human, and I haven't the foggiest idea if I've got what it takes to make us all happy?"

Oh, yeah. That'd work.

She prowled her living room, hands on hips, occasionally wagging her hands in a vain attempt to shuck off some of the tension. *Did* she have what it took to trust that she and Guy, together, could lick whatever this was with his daugh—?

She came to a dead stop, slapping her forehead with the palm of her hand.

Together, twit-brain. No one expected her to make this work *all by herself.*

Laughing, Elizabeth ran to the phone, swearing when she got the machine again. The nerve of him, not to be around when she was in major groveling mode.

Buzzing like a high-voltage wire, she stalked into the kitchen and threw a package of popcorn into the microwave, picking dead leaves off her African violets on the windowsill while she waited for it to pop. She opened a cupboard door, hauled out a stack of dishes, clattering them to the counter below.

She had ten hours before she could reasonably show up on his doorstep. In that time, she could get one helluva lot of cupboards cleaned out.

Had anyone asked, Guy could have told them exactly when the first bird started to sing the next morning: 5:36. He supposed he'd dozed off in the recliner for an hour or so, only be awakened by disturbing dreams around four. Like a robot, he took a shower, threw on a pair of shorts and a T-shirt, brainlessly watched a few minutes of some local early-riser newscast.

Einstein smacked an insistent paw on his knee. Oh, right. Ashli would probably stay asleep long enough for him to run the dog down to the curb…but if she did wake, she'd freak if he wasn't there. Better to let her know what he was doing. So he tiptoed down the hall, avoiding the creaking floorboard in front of the bathroom, and slowly pushed open her door. The draft from the gaping, screenless window blew dust into his eyes…and across an empty bed.

"Ashli!" he whispered, fear exploding in his gut. Then, on the next breath, as if invoking her name could summon her presence, her aid, her support: "Elizabeth!"

She had circles under her eyes rivaling manhole covers, she reeked of Eau de Spic and Span, and she was wearing a ponytail, for the love of Mike. But she was deathly afraid if she waited any longer, she'd chicken out. Good thing she hadn't had any coffee yet; she was already so wired she could hardly push Guy's buzzer.

Einstein's whuffles at the bottom of the door was the only response. Maybe they still weren't home…? She leaned out over the metal railing on the landing—no, his car was there. And the front windows were wide-open—

"Elizabeth!"

She started, grabbing the railing for support. Guy stood at the foot of the stairs, looking far worse than she did. He hadn't even gotten as far as the ponytail. Or a shave.

"Guy…" She clumped down the stairs toward him, apprehension rising like bile in her throat. "What's wrong—?"

"Ashli's gone!" He grasped her arm, his words tumbling over each other. "Dianne changed her mind—she's not coming back—and Ashli went ballistic when I told her. Took me hours to calm her down last night, but I thought we were over the worst of it. I had no idea she'd do something like this—''

His head snapped from one side of the street to the other, scanning the block he'd probably searched a dozen times already. "I've been looking for her for more than an hour—where could she have gone? She's just a baby—''

"Guy! Hey…hey…get a grip, honey—'' Elizabeth lifted her palm to his stubbled cheek. "Come on, now, take a breath before you hyperventilate—''

"Take a *breath!* That's not your daughter out there!'' She reeled from his sudden, misdirected anger. "She's *my* baby…*mine!*'' He jabbed at the air with his fist. "And you're telling me to take a *breath—?*''

"Damn straight, since I can't lug you up all these stairs if you faint!''

"This is no time for cracking jokes, Elizabeth—''

"Which is what I do when I'm scared, you bozo, in case you haven't noticed. I'm the control nut, remember? Staying calm is part of my job description. Besides, two panicked parents is one too many, and you got dibs.''

He stopped ranting for a second, both hands suspended out to his sides. "Did you say…parents? With an *S?*''

"Yeah. How 'bout that?''

"And you're really worried about her?'' he whispered.

She took a wide swing at his arm, except he handily ducked it, sending her spinning right into the rhododendren bush by the house. "Oh, geez, honey—'' Guy hauled her out of the bush. "You okay?''

"No, I'm not,'' she sputtered, plucking leaf bits off her bottom. Then she lit into him again, wildly gesticulating like the wronged wife in a sixties Italian movie. "What? You think you've got some divine right to be the only one to care what happens to your daughter, just because she's carrying your genes? *Of course* I'm worried! If I wasn't prone to worrying about these kids, I wouldn't be here to begin with, wouldn't be about to make an idiot of myself telling you that I love *you,* which means—heaven help me!—I love *all* of you. Ashli and Jake and Micah and even Einstein, long as I'm upwind of him—oommph...!''

This kiss was brief, noteworthy and knocked the breath clean out of her.

"Are we on the same side now?" she asked, panting.

Guy engulfed her in his arms, rested his chin on the top of her head. "That would be my guess."

"Good." She pried herself out of his grasp, grabbed his hand, and dragged him up the stairs. "Then I think we have more important things to do than to stand around necking all morning."

After Elizabeth handed him a cup of coffee—which actually tasted like something a sane person would drink—he called the police, nearly climbing through the phone when some lead-in-his-shorts cop started this schpiel about how kids run away and it had only been a couple hours and had they checked all the neighbors?

"Look, officer, maybe you didn't hear me. My daughter is *eight*. And extremely upset. We've only lived here for a month, she knows all of three families in the neighborhood— whose houses I've obviously already checked—and there's a damn *lake* within walking distance of the house." Which was only a few feet deep and Ashli had known how to swim since she was four, but that was beside the point. "Now, as I doubt you guys aren't exactly breaking up drug rings at the end of Main Street, I could use a little help here."

They promised to send someone right over. He hung up, turned to Elizabeth. For some odd reason, he was glad she was wearing her glasses.

"Is it really you?" he said at last, his hand still resting on the receiver.

"You're asking this *after* you kissed me? How flattering."

He walked over to her, gently tugged her ponytail. "You came back."

"Like a damn homing pigeon."

In a heartbeat, they were in each other's arms. Guy squeezed shut his eyes, absorbing her warmth, her scent, her *here*-ness. How could he have even considered a life without her in it? "You were right. I…did need to straighten out some things in my head about Dianne."

She skimmed her hand over his back. "I take it you have."

"Yep. My daughter, though…" Fresh panic surged through his bloodstream, chilling his skin.

"I'm sure she hasn't gone far, Guy," she said gently, reading his thoughts. "Statistics show most kids who run away never get farther than a few blocks."

He passed a hand over his eyes and let out a rueful, exhausted half laugh. "If books were banned, you'd be at a total loss, wouldn't you?"

"Not really." She snuggled closer, offering comfort, strength. Herself. "I've already read everything published through last year."

He smiled, but fear wiped any comeback he might have made.

"We'll find her, honey," he heard muffled against his chest, followed by the sound of tires crunching gravel and the indecipherable crackle of a police radio.

Guy knew, a year from now, he'd have no recollection what the police officer looked like. His only impressions were tall, gangly, thin and nice in that impersonal way people have who've had seminars on how to deal with the public.

"She take anything with her?" the officer asked after the preliminaries had been dispensed with, including Guy's assurance that his daughter had had the fear of God drummed into her about getting into strangers' cars, so the likelihood of her having tried to hitchhike somewhere was pretty slim.

"I don't…" Guy thought, then led the way back to the kids' room. "I don't think so, but now that you ask, I don't really know." He indicated the open window, the screen pulled out and left lying across Jake's bed. "I don't think she would have carried much, seeing as she jumped out the window."

The officer's brows slid up. "From the second story?"

"The garage roof is below the bedroom windows. And there's an ivy-covered trellis that reaches from the yard to the top of the garage."

The man nodded, wrote this down, as Guy noticed Elizabeth idly poking at this or that in the room.

"Where did she keep the crystal heart I gave her?" she suddenly asked.

"What?" It took a minute for the question to register, then his gaze flew to the top of the chest of drawers where he remembered last seeing it. Ashli had put it there, not only to keep it out of reach of her little brothers, but to catch the morning light so it would throw a spray of rainbows across her wall.

It wasn't there.

For some reason, realizing she'd taken *something* spurred him to check if anything else was missing. And indeed, she'd taken her backpack, into which, as far as Guy could determine, she had packed one of her new nightgowns, her toothbrush, the heart, and the twenty-dollar bill her grandparents had given her for her birthday.

"Well, it's a pretty safe bet she hasn't gone far," the officer said, slipping his pad into his back pocket. "Nine times out of ten, when kids run away like this? They don't get farther than a coupla blocks."

"Uh...yes. So I've heard," Guy said.

He walked the officer to the door, accepted the man's assurance they'd have his little girl back to him in no time, then turned around to find Elizabeth with Einstein's collar and leash in hand, the beast himself seated in front of her with hopeful anticipation written all over his scruffy face.

"You think this thing might have a little bloodhound in him?"

Einstein looked from one to the other, his wiry brows bouncing up and down like a seesaw.

"Guess this is as good a time as any to find out," Guy said, taking the collar and leash from Elizabeth and snapping it around the dog's neck. "C'mon, boy. Let's go find your baby."

Oh, yeah, Elizabeth was scared, all right, although not about finding Ashli. Her gut told her they'd find her soon, and safe.

But what then? Considering how things had gone so far, Elizabeth wouldn't be surprised if the child spat venom at her.

Guy'd go nuts, she knew, unless he could take an active role in looking for his daughter—they'd left a neighbor in the house, in case Ashli came back, with Elizabeth's cell phone number to call if she did. Never mind that they were covering the same territory the police were, not to mention a half-dozen kindly neighbors who'd joined in the search. And each one, it seemed, told about a Melanie or a Bobby or a Ricky who'd pulled the same stunt as a child, each of whom had been safely reunited with his or her family, though not before taking five years from said family's collective life.

At first, the anecdotes might have been helping. But as each half hour passed, each block they searched, each time one of the neighbors said he'd checked the lake or the park or the parking lot behind the minimall and come up empty, Guy's anxiety grew.

"What I can't for the life of me figure out is when she did it. And how I didn't hear her. I mean, I heard her go to the bathroom about five, and I was awake again not forty-five minutes later." Elizabeth saw no point in reminding Guy she'd heard him give this account to the policeman earlier. "Where *could* she be? And *this* bag of fur—" he tugged at the dog's leash "—is totally useless."

Plodding along, enjoying the stroll, the dog swished his tail a time or two in response. They'd even given him one of Ashli's dirty socks to smell, but, thinking it was a toy, he only tried to snatch it out of their hands.

"It's okay, honey," she said, entwining her fingers with his and leaning her head against his arm as they walked. "She's around somewhere. She's just hiding, that's all."

"And are these the words of the designated calm person in the group?" was his edgy response.

She tugged at his hand until he looked at her. "No," she said. "These are the words of someone who did the same thing when I was a kid. When I was twelve, and I thought Mother was going to get married, and I didn't want her to. I ran away, to one of the barns on the Malone Farm—the Shadywoods site? I wasn't a fool, Guy. I had no intention of doing anything that might put me in danger. They found me a few hours later, perfectly fi— Oh my God! Guy!'' She clutched his arm. ''I know where she is!''

The dog, too, suddenly started whining and yanking at the end of his leash, wagging his preposterous tail, then tugged at the leash again, pulling them away from the lake and down one of the side streets, woofing for all he was worth.

Heading right for the Lakeside house.

Elizabeth caught the curious glances of several neighbors out watering their gardens or mowing their lawns as they sprinted—or gallumphed, as the case might be—past house after house, quickly getting out of breath as she attempted to outpace the dog, whose legs were probably longer than hers.

Einstein pulled them up onto the porch and through the partially open door, where Guy let him off the leash. The dog's overlong toenails clacked against the bare wooden floor as he circled the vestibule twice, made one false start toward the kitchen, then bounded up the stairs, Guy hot on his heels.

Now Elizabeth froze at the bottom of the stairs.

Guy pivoted, his head canted. ''You knew she was here?''

A nervous smile flitted over her mouth. ''You think the dog picked it up from me, or the other way around?''

He held out his hand. ''We're in this together,'' he said softly, ''come hell, high water, or ornery daughters. Come on, sweetheart…it's going to be okay.''

They found Ashli asleep, curled up on the windowseat in ''her'' room, the fragile glass heart hanging from its satin cord in the sunny window, splashing a thousand trembling rainbows across the ancient, faded wallpaper.

Rainbows—symbols of promise. Elizabeth slipped her hand into Guy's and swallowed hard. The child must have felt that every promise made to her since her mother's leaving had been shattered. Trust had become an illusion, and the only reality the one that she herself could control. Foolish child, Elizabeth thought, letting go of Guy's hand and moving toward Ashli. Foolish, beautiful child…so much like her.

The old floorboards squeaked; Ashli's eyes flew open and

she sat up so suddenly she bumped into the heart, knocking it off the lock. With uncanny coordination, Elizabeth reached behind Ashli and caught the heart before it fell, just as Ashli fell into her father's arms, hysterical and apologetic, oblivious to Elizabeth's presence.

But only for a moment.

Fear and mistrust blazed in the watery blue eyes as she clamped her arms more tightly around her father's waist. "What are *you* doing here?"

"Taking a chance," Guy said quietly, and Elizabeth's eyes jolted to his.

It was true. She was putting her butt on the line, big-time, for the first time since she was twelve years old, admitting she couldn't control it all.

No longer wanted to.

The sun-warmed crystal shimmering in her hand, Elizabeth sat on the window seat in front of Ashli, brushing the tears off her cheeks as the child clung to her father. She might well get clobbered for her efforts, but oh, well.

"Ashli, we gotta get something straight here. I just can't go away. See, I love your father, and the boys—" she swept back a tangle of spun-gold hair "—and you, sweetie, too much to leave. No matter how you feel about me, that's not going to change how I feel about *you*. Maybe it'll take you ten, fifteen years of having me around to make you believe this, but I'm not going *anywhere*. So I'm afraid you're just going to have to deal with that, because I'm miserable without you guys, and I don't like being miserable all that much, you know?"

Ashli didn't clobber her. Or pull away or even flinch. Instead, she fell against Elizabeth's chest, locking her thin arms around her ribs, and sobbed her heart out. Love swelled, sweet and full, in Elizabeth's chest as she stroked the child's matted hair. "I'm so sorry, baby," she whispered. "So very, very sorry."

"She lied," Ashli said. "She promised she was coming back to see me."

"I know, sweetie," Elizabeth whispered, rocking her, rocking her, never wanting to let her go. "I know."

Guy knelt in front them; at the do-I-dare-hope? expression in his eyes, she thought her heart would simply fall apart, right there.

"I hate her," Ashli said into Elizabeth's shoulder.

"No, no...don't hate her. Hate uses up too much energy." Not that she wouldn't deck the woman herself if she ever met her.

"And...I don't hate you," said a very small voice. "I never did. But I was just so scared...."

"Shhh, honey, it's okay, I understand." After several moments, during which she and Guy just smiled at each other like a pair of doofuses, she held Ashli back enough to see her face and ventured, "What do you think we should do now?"

That got a sad little shrug and a sniffle or two. Elizabeth fished in her shorts pocket for a tissue, which Ashli took. "Up for a suggestion?" she asked.

A nod.

"Maybe...we should think about concentrating on the present, and the future, and forget about the past. Or at least, forget about the bad stuff. The good stuff, we can keep." She smiled. "Like cleaning out a closet—pitch the junk just taking up space, keep whatever you can still use." At Guy's chuckle, she lifted an eyebrow. "What?"

"Only you would come up with a cleaning metaphor."

"Hey, don't knock it until you've tried it...."

"I clean—"

"No, uh-uh. *I* clean. *You* rearrange the dirt."

Ashli's giggles caught their attention. "Oh, Daddy," she said with a huff. "You forget. I've seen Elizabeth's house."

"Hmm, yes. I see your point. So—would you rather live with her?"

The child's smile faded as she gave Elizabeth a tentative look. "Well...Elizabeth's house smells nice," she said, which got a started laugh from Elizabeth and an "Ain't that the truth?" from Guy. "Like flowers. And she's definitely a better cook than you are."

"Nooo arguments there."

"And she doesn't look like her stomach hurts when she takes me shopping."

Guy shifted on his knee, sliding one hand around Elizabeth's hip, the other one capturing his daughter's hand. "So...what are you saying?"

She nibbled her bottom lip for a moment, then said, "Well...I think you should ask Elizabeth to marry you."

"Ex*cuse* me? Just like that, you changed your mind—?"

Ashli stared at her sneakers, hard, for several seconds. "After Elizabeth and you broke up," she said at last, barely above a whisper, "I realized how dumb I'd been, trying to make her go away. But then I figured it was too late, that I'd messed things up...." Tears trickling down her face once more, she looked from one to the other. "And this time, I knew it was my fault for real. But I didn't know what to do to fix it."

Guy smiled for Elizabeth, then wiped the tears from Ashli's cheek. "Well, there's one good thing about messing things up, which is that you can usually unmess them up by simply admitting you made a mistake. So—" he tugged her to him, planted a noisy kiss on her cheek "—whaddya say we forget the whole thing—"

"Hey—" With a laugh, Elizabeth gave Guy's shoulder a little shove. "I believe your daughter made a suggestion? So whatcha waiting for? An engraved invitation?"

Grinning, Guy cantilevered himself up on one knee, kissed Elizabeth on the lips. "You really in the market for a broken-down single dad with three kids?"

"And a dog," Ashli put in.

"And a dog?"

Elizabeth looked over at Einstein. She could've sworn he winked at her. She faced Guy again. "That's manipulation."

"Tough. I'm the ruthless one, here, remember? Love me—" he kissed her again "—love my kids—" and again "—love my dog."

"Oh, *brother,*" Ashli moaned behind them, making them both turn around. "Are you two gonna be kissing, like *all* the time, now?"

Guy stood and swept his daughter into his arms, causing

the dog to jump clumsily to his feet and start barking, just because. "You better believe it, sweetie-pie. Lots and lots and lots. And extra on Valentine's Day. Isn't that right, honey?" he said to Elizabeth.

But she only half heard him. Her mouth pulled into a wide grin, she was looking out the window over the front yard, right at the Poole-Strong sign...that no longer had a Sold sticker on it. "Hey, honey," she said, waving Guy over. "Look."

He let Ashli down, then walked over to the window. "Well, I'll be hornswoggled." Ashli giggled. "Sale must've fallen through." He looked at Elizabeth. "You wanna call Sybil, or shall I?"

"The way you bid?" Elizabeth said on a laugh. "Forget it!"

He clamped an arm around Elizabeth's waist. "As if I'd let a good thing get away a second time. Besides, I forgot to tell you—I got an offer on the St. Charles house, so no more Mr. Cheap Guy—"

"We're gonna live *here?*" Ashli asked.

"You betcha," Elizabeth said. "Never let it be said that Liz Louden lets an opportunity slip through her fingers."

"*Yes!*" Ashli jumped up and down, clapping her hands, then ran out of the room, presumably to scout out the rest of "her" house.

"*Liz?*"

She laughed at Guy's perplexed expression, shrugged. "Thought I'd try it out for size. Whaddya think?"

"I like it." He chucked her under the chin. "Bold. Sassy. Unpredictable."

"Great. Now I sound like a California wine."

"I could think of worse things to be compared with." His expression turned serious. "Are you sure? About taking all of this on?"

She looped her hands around his neck. "Yes."

"All the noise?"

"Every earsplitting note of it."

"And the messes?"

"*I* clean, remember?"

"So did I, before I had children. You wanna talk exercise in futility…"

"Oh, well," she said, "I recently read where people who live in dirty houses are actually healthier because they develop more immunities to bacteria."

Guy just shook his head. "And your crystal…?"

She sighed, kissed him. "Can go into the attic for a while. And the white sofa will go to my mother, because I'm tired of seeing that blue-flowered number. And her piano comes here, because I want to hear you play, every day, and I want to learn how to play ragtime and I want the children to learn, too. And I hope you're planning on continuing to dig up those bones of yours, because I really don't want to work full-time for a while, especially once I become pregnant, since I really think these kids need a mom who's around a lot more, don't you—?"

"Hold the phone—did you say, *pregnant?*"

"Hey. This is a big house. I figure it needs at least two, three more kids."

"Good God—you're serious!"

"Deadly. Oh, and one more thing—"

He smiled into her eyes, the sun glinting off his earring. "And what's that?"

She lifted up on tiptoe, catching the gold-studded earlobe between her lips, then whispered, "If you ever hope to see me naked again, I suggest you bathe the dog."

Guy dropped her like a hot potato, then slapped his thigh. "Einstein? Come on, boy! Have I got a surprise for you!" He looked up at her, his eyes shining with laughter. "You coming home with us?"

She crossed the room and clasped his hand. "Just try and stop me."

* * * * *

MONTANA
MAVERICKS
Big Sky Brides

Legendary love comes to Whitehorn, Montana,
once more as beloved authors

Christine Rimmer, Jennifer Greene and Cheryl St.John

present three brand-new stories in this exciting anthology!

Meet the Brennan women:

SUZANNA, DIANA and ISABELLE

Strong-willed beauties who find unexpected
love in these irresistible marriage of
covnenience stories.

Don't miss
MONTANA MAVERICKS: BIG SKY BRIDES
On sale in February 2000,
only from Silhouette Books!

Available at your favorite retail outlet.

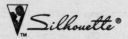

Visit us at www.romance.net

PSMMBSB

If you enjoyed what you just read,
then we've got an offer you can't resist!

Take 2 bestselling love stories FREE!

Plus get a FREE surprise gift!

Clip this page and mail it to Silhouette Reader Service™

IN U.S.A.	IN CANADA
3010 Walden Ave.	P.O. Box 609
P.O. Box 1867	Fort Erie, Ontario
Buffalo, N.Y. 14240-1867	L2A 5X3

YES! Please send me 2 free Silhouette Intimate Moments® novels and my free surprise gift. Then send me 6 brand-new novels every month, which I will receive months before they're available in stores. In the U.S.A., bill me at the bargain price of $3.57 plus 25¢ delivery per book and applicable sales tax, if any*. In Canada, bill me at the bargain price of $3.96 plus 25¢ delivery per book and applicable taxes**. That's the complete price and a savings of over 10% off the cover prices—what a great deal! I understand that accepting the 2 free books and gift places me under no obligation ever to buy any books. I can always return a shipment and cancel at any time. Even if I never buy another book from Silhouette, the 2 free books and gift are mine to keep forever. So why not take us up on our invitation. You'll be glad you did!

245 SEN CNFF
345 SEN CNFG

Name	(PLEASE PRINT)	
Address	Apt.#	
City	State/Prov.	Zip/Postal Code

* Terms and prices subject to change without notice. Sales tax applicable in N.Y.
** Canadian residents will be charged applicable provincial taxes and GST.
  All orders subject to approval. Offer limited to one per household.
  ® are registered trademarks of Harlequin Enterprises Limited.

INMOM99   ©1998 Harlequin Enterprises Limited

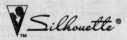

**Start celebrating Silhouette's 20th anniversary
with these 4 special titles by
New York Times bestselling authors**

*Fire and Rain**
by Elizabeth Lowell

King of the Castle
by Heather Graham Pozzessere

*State Secrets**
by Linda Lael Miller

*Paint Me Rainbows**
by Fern Michaels

On sale in December 1999

Plus, a special free book offer inside each title!

Available at your favorite retail outlet
**Also available on audio from Brilliance.*

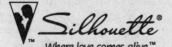

Silhouette®
Where love comes alive™

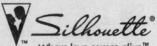